# MYTH
## and
# SEXUALITY

# Books by Jamake Highwater

## Fiction

*Mick Jagger: The Singer Not the Song* (1973)
*Anpao* (1977)
*Journey to the Sky* (1978)
*The Sun, He Dies* (1981)
*The Ghost Horse Cycle: Legend Days* (1984), *The Ceremony of Innocence* (1985), *I Wear the Morning Star* (1986)
*Eyes of Darkness* (1986)

## Poetry

*Moonsong Lullaby* (1985)

## Nonfiction

*Song from the Earth* (1976)
*Ritual of the Wind: Indian Ceremonies and Music* (1976/85)
*Dance: Rituals of Experience* (1978/85)
*The Sweet Grass Lives On: 50 Indian Artists* (1980)
*The Primal Mind* (1981)
*Arts of the Indian Americas* (1983)
*Native Land, Sagas of American Civilizations* (1986)
*Shadow Show: An Autobiographical Insinuation* (1986)
*Myth and Sexuality* (1990)

# MYTH
## and
# SEXUALITY

## JAMAKE HIGHWATER

**NAL BOOKS**

**NEW AMERICAN LIBRARY**

A DIVISION OF PENGUIN BOOKS USA INC., NEW YORK
PUBLISHED IN CANADA BY
PENGUIN BOOKS CANADA LIMITED, MARKHAM, ONTARIO

Published simultaneously in Canada by Penguin Books Canada Limited

*Permission*
Excerpts from INTIMATE MATTERS by John D'Emilio and Estelle Freedman. Copyright © 1988 by John D'Emilio and Estelle Freedman. Reprinted by permission of Harper & Row, Publishers, Inc.

NAL BOOKS TRADEMARK REG. U.S. PAT. OFF. AND FOREIGN COUNTRIES
REGISTERED TRADEMARK—MARCA REGISTRADA
HECHO EN DRESDEN, TN, U.S.A.

SIGNET, SIGNET CLASSIC, MENTOR, ONYX, PLUME, MERIDIAN
and NAL BOOKS are published *in the United States* by
New American Library, a division of Penguin Books USA Inc.,
1633 Broadway, New York, New York 10019,
*in Canada* by Penguin Books Canada Limited,
2801 John Street, Markham, Ontario L3R 1B4

**Library of Congress Cataloging-in-Publication Data**

Highwater, Jamake.
    Myth and sexuality / by Jamake Highwater.
      p.    cm.
    ISBN 0-453-00708-2
    1. Sex—Religious aspects.   2. Sex role—Religious aspects.
    3. Mythology.   I. Title.
    BL65.S4H54   1989
    291.2'2—dc20                     89-38162
                                           CIP

First Printing, February, 1990

1   2   3   4   5   6   7   8   9

PRINTED IN THE UNITED STATES OF AMERICA

IN MEMORY OF JOHN WILLIAMSON

(1948–1988)

*Pero ya duerme sin fin.*
*Ya los musgos y la hierba*
*abren con dedos seguros*
*la flor de su calavera.*

—F. Garcia Lorca

The opposite of a correct statement is a false statement. But the opposite of a profound truth may well be another profound truth.

—Niels Bohr

# Contents

# Acknowledgments

The subject of *Myth and Sexuality* has been a focus of my thinking for many years. Although it was always my hope to write this book, its realization had to be delayed until I completed a long series of preparatory efforts. My writing about the social history of the human body began simply enough with a term paper on Plato's concept of love which I wrote for an introductory course in Western philosophy at the university. My collegiate research acquainted me with several authors whose influential attitudes about sexuality and myth have stayed with me for the rest of my life: Joseph Campbell, Robert Graves, Jane Harrison, James Frazer, Robert Briffault, and J. J. Bachofen. A few years later, in the 1960s, when I lectured and wrote extensively in San Francisco on the use of the body as an organ of expression, I became convinced that dance and theater are rituals that reveal the unique and fundamental mentality of all the societies of history. Nothing betrays more about who we are than the way we dance. Eventually, in 1978, I revised two books I had written during those San Francisco years, and produced a study entitled *Dance: Rituals of Experience*. Work on that project suggested to me that sports are also an intrinsic part of the social history of the human body, resulting, ten years later, in the book *Athletes of the Gods: The Ritual Life of Sports* (to be published in 1991). Finally I turned to this concluding book in an informal cycle of studies of the history of the human body.

Everywhere in this book my debt to the late Joseph Campbell is evident. I grew up under the influence of his books. Eventually I met him and we worked together during the filming of a television series about his works and ideas. To know him was a great delight, but to become his friend was an indescribable honor. Campbell's editor has called that friendship "an exceptional bond," and indeed it was. I was fortunate enough to share many hours of discussion with him. The central subject of *Myth and Sexuality* was a persistent focus of the conversations Campbell and I had over the years. I only regret that this great friend and remarkable teacher cannot share in the results of his many suggestions, encouragement, and enduring inspiration.

Since my theme draws upon the most essential ideas of my lifetime, I cannot possibly give adequate credit to all the influences reflected in *Myth and Sexuality*, but perhaps the selected bibliography at the close of this book will help to highlight some of the major sources of ideas and opinions in my depiction of the way our beliefs about the cosmos are reflected in our conceptions of our bodies, our destinies, and our sexualities.

I am especially grateful to Elaine Pagels for her friendship and many influences in the creation of this book. I am also grateful to my editor, Arnold Dolin, for his professional concern for my work over many years. It has been a special pleasure to be associated with him in the realization of this book.

Jamake Highwater
Hampton, Connecticut, 1989

*Note:* Attribution for all materials quoted in this book may be found in the bibliography under the author's name. If there is more than one book or article listed for a given author, then the date of publication of the work from which a quotation is drawn is listed after the name of the author each time it appears in the text: e.g., (Campbell, 1986).

# ONE

# INTRODUCTION: Sex as Destiny and Destiny as Sex

Sexuality seems to be one of the few implacable facts of life. Theories come and go, but there is certainly no reason to question our basic assumptions about sex. As far as most of us are concerned sex is either natural or unnatural. Good or evil. There is probably more talk and gossip about the sex act than any other subject, yet most of us feel no serious need to discuss the basis of our sexual attitudes. For this reason, sexuality is not looked upon as a matter of cultural attitude, but rather as a matter of physical fact, like geography. As Freud put it, *anatomy is destiny.*

That Freudian mandate persists even today. From the first moment of our lives a mechanistic philosophy dominates the definition of what we are and how we are supposed to behave. At the time we are born our parents and doctors identify us as male or female by the anatomic evidence of our genitals. Genitalia seal our fate, for at once we are initiated into the separate cultural constructs that are related to the rearing of male or female children. As far as most of us are concerned, there isn't the slightest question that this arbitrary reading of our anatomies is exactly what we truly are in mind and spirit. We are convinced that with sex there is no room for ambiguity.

This perception of sexuality is shaped by the belief in an innate, transhistorical, and transcultural "natural man." Such a commitment to the notion of a fixed and eternal human nature permits us to envision all the characters of history as possessing our motives, concerns, and goals, so that Moses and Jesus, Leonardo and Manet, Chaucer and Joyce are identical human beings removed from one another only by the happenstance of time and culture. (Gagnon/Simon) We assume that sexuality meant to all these historic figures exactly what it means to us. We believe that what is normal for us in our particular time and society was also normal in very different times and societies. Thus we presume that psychology is as fixed and eternal as anatomy. Such an insistence upon the transcendency of human psychology prompts us to imagine that there is a single and inflexible truth about sexuality, about normalcy and abnormalcy, about what is proper and improper in the behavior of men and women.

The concept of "natural man" is a creation of the seventeenth century. Among other things, it provides the basis for our belief in "natural" as opposed to "unnatural" sexual behavior. The fixity of such concepts and rules also provides us with a sense of transcendency and purpose. Without it we feel as if we are at sea, lost in a tide of endless possibilities. So strong is our need for certainty and permanency that we do not question the sources of our rules and concepts until they begin to falter and collapse. Then, quite suddenly, we must re-think everything that seemed comfortably resolved. We must begin again the process of defining who we are and what we are becoming.

Given the fact that the best minds of our time have entirely abandoned the seventeenth-century mechanistic world view, why have we retained its antiquated fallacy of "universal man" in matters of sexuality?

## Introduction: Sex as Destiny and Destiny as Sex

As historian of science Thomas Kuhn noted, in the seventeenth century the metaphorical vision of Newtonian mechanics not only determined the mentality of the field eventually to be known as physics, it also influenced most of the epoch's fundamental ideals in biological science, religion, morality, art, and politics. The mechanistic paradigm of Rene Descartes sprang from Newton's metaphor of the cosmos as a great clock running its immutable rounds after being created and set into motion by God, the "Unmoved Mover." That vision has been thoroughly debunked by physical science, yet it remains entrenched in every aspect of our thinking because it has steadily undergone cultural facelifts that disguise the fact that it is an antiquated notion.

For instance, the seventeenth-century politico-economic imperative of Thomas Hobbes pitted the individual against the authority of the state. This contest between "natural instinct" and "civilized restraint" was invented by Hobbes as a picture of the conflict between the state (civilization) and its internal dissidents (instinct). The philosophers of the Romantic Movement did not have much sympathy for Hobbesian philosophy, but they did not abandon it. They simply transformed it into a doctrine suited to their own imperatives, namely, the conflict between exceptional individuals and the repressive cultures in which they live. Eventually the Romantic viewpoint was again recast by post-Romantic thinkers, and particularly by Sigmund Freud, who envisioned the old Hobbesian struggle as a contest of mind (civilization), sexuality (instinct), and parent-child confrontation. The Freudian tradition emphasizes the image of the sexual drive as a biological necessity that attempts to express itself despite the rules devised to control it by culture and civilization. The Freudian view gave impetus to the concept that we are only civilized to the extent that we have been able to suppress our animalistic and sexual instincts. That archaic notion still has immense authority. In fact, Freud's modest transformation of a seventeenth-century ideology is so pervasive that even among psychologists and sociologists who deeply oppose Freudian theory, that Freudian vision of sexuality "as an innate and dangerous instinct" is steadfastly perpetuated. In short, we cannot escape our mooring to the fallacy of the *universal man*, despite the fact that it is clearly a collapsed paradigm of a prior time and place.

At no point is the Western belief in the existence of a natural and universal man more entrenched than in the study of sexuality. Species survival, through reproduction, is made a central aspect of our model of men and women. Thus biology is translated into socio-cultural imperatives. Our behavior, as such, is seen not as a result of free choice but as the necessary response to sexual organs and hormones.

Since the time of its inception, sexual research has been obsessed with anatomy. When we think about sex, nearly our entire attention is given to the mechanical operation of genitalia. Rarely do we turn our attention away from the sex organs themselves to the subtle sources of meaning that are associated with them. Many sociologists see this trend as the result of the masculinization of sexual attitudes: the inclination to focus sexuality entirely in the groin. In the long view, however, sex is not so narrowly focused. Quite the contrary, sex is a vehicle for a variety of feelings and needs. But for most men it is difficult to grasp the possibility of such variety because of the emotional illiteracy which is an implicit aspect of male socialization.

The earliest known usage of the term "sex," in the sixteenth century, was a precise reference to the division of human beings into males and females—to differences in gender. The dominant meaning since the early nineteenth century refers to physical relations between the sexes, "to have sex." The extension of the meaning of these words indicates a shift in the way that "sexuality" (the abstract noun referring to the quality of being "sexual") is understood in our culture.

The social processes through which these changes in definition and focus have taken place are complex reflections of major transformations of the whole scheme of social values in the West. Despite the flexibility of such values we usually assume that "sexuality" is immutable. This view of sex is profoundly embedded in our culture. There is, for instance, an assumption of a sharp distinction between the sexes, a strict difference in behavior, temperament, and interests, even the famous antagonism called "the battle of the sexes." In short, men are men and women are women, and it is not expected that the two will have much in common. There is also a belief that "sex" is an obsessive natural force, a biological imperative focused entirely in the genitals (particularly the male organ) that dominates our decisions and actions. This scheme suggests what sociologist Jeffrey Weeks calls "a pyramidical model of sex . . . a sexual hierarchy stretching downwards from the apparently Nature-endowed correctness of heterosexual genital intercourse to the bizarre manifestations of 'the perverse' hopefully safely buried at the base but unfortunately always erupting in dubious places."

Since the late nineteenth century this view of sex has had the ostensible scientific endorsement of the discipline broadly known as sexology, the so-called science of desire. Though there has been considerable disagreement among leading sexologists such as Krafft-Ebing, Havelock Ellis, Auguste Forel, Magnus Hirschfeld, and Sigmund Freud, on one point they seem to be in accord.

They have all endorsed the naturalistic concept that the key to sex lies somewhere in the recesses of "Nature."

Against the certainties of this tradition I hope to summarize an alternative way of understanding sexuality which has been shaped and discussed by a wide variety of excellent social historians and anthropologists. As Jeffrey Weeks has pointed out, such an alternative viewpoint suggests that sexuality is not a "primordially 'natural' phenomenon but rather a product of social and historical forces . . . a 'fictional unity.' " As such, sexuality is an invention of the human mind.

Sexuality is shaped by social forces. Far from being the most natural force of our lives, it is, in fact, the most susceptible to cultural influences. This viewpoint does not attempt to deny the importance of biology, for the physiology and morphology of the body certainly does provide the preconditions for human sexuality. But biology does not cause the patterns of our sexual lives. It simply conditions and limits what is likely and what is possible.

It is unreasonable to continue to set up an antagonism between sex and society as if they were biologically dissociated elements arising from separate domains of Nature. We must recognize that sex is highly socialized and that each culture designates various practices as appropriate or inappropriate, moral or immoral, healthy or unhealthy. We constantly construct boundaries that have no basis in "Nature." Yet we continue to indulge the fantasy that our sexuality is the most innate and natural aspect of being human, and that sexual conduct between men and women is predestined by biology forevermore by the dictates of our inborn "human nature." As Jeffrey Weeks commented, "The Darwinian revolution in biology, which demonstrated that man was part of the animal world, encouraged the search for the animal in man, and found it in his sex."

Female sexuality, on the other hand, was inevitably an enigma to the males in charge of studying sex. Female sexuality was a "dark continent," in Freud's famous phrase.

We must now speak and ponder about sexuality because we are loosed from our moorings and are indeed at sea. At the end of the twentieth century, relativity governs our lives as surely as it governs the matrix of the cosmos. The philosopher Michel Foucault has pointed out that sexuality is no more and no less than a historical construct. Its meaning and expression are no wider or extensive than its specific social and historical manifestations, and explaining its forms and variations cannot be accomplished without examining and explaining the context in which they were formed. For me, that context is the mythology that underlies and informs the structures and values of societies.

Though I am specifically concerned with the relationship of myth and sexuality in the Western world, nothing provides more incentive to rethink the things we take for granted about ourselves than the contrast between our world view and that of an entirely different culture. The lesson of cultural relativism is that mythology and the sexual symbolism based upon it are highly variable from time to time and from place to place. Freud denied that lesson when he postulated the notion that anatomy is destiny. It is my suggestion in this book that, to the contrary, each society's vision of destiny (its mythology, biases, fashions, and social attitudes) is the basis of its understanding of both the body and sexuality. The history of how we conceive of the human body is therefore the history of the most fundamental value systems of our societies. Our bodies are the cosmos. Our mythological place in the cosmos is inevitably transformed into anatomical metaphors which we take to be facts of life. Looked at from another vantage, we can rechart our vision of the cosmos by studying how we conceive of the body. In each culture and in each era, the conception of the physical body becomes an anthropocentric world model. Sexual modes and roles are derived from these cultural paradigms, from the ways in which sexuality is integrated into the large social narratives which provide our fundamental notions about physical reality. Those paradigms are vividly depicted in our religious, political, social, and scientific myths, for mythology, in its broadest and most affirmative sense, is the means by which each society responds to the fundamental questions about our origins, our lives, and our destinies. It is this amalgam of the vision of the body and the mythological sources of attributed meaning that is the core of our sexuality at any given time. It is that central and mythic vision of sexuality which many scholars believe is largely missing from the mentality of the Western world.

Sex historian Vern L. Bullough provides a striking example of the way dissimilar sexual attitudes arise out of various mythologies and are then socialized into custom: "The base for many [sexual] assumptions often appears in the creation myths, usually involving the earth and the sky. Western culture in general is built on an old assumption that the earth is female, mother earth, and the sky is male, the heavenly father; this deeply engrained mythological assumption has served as the norm for sexual relations with the male on top, the female underneath. Some cultures have considered the earth as male and the sky as female, accepting the woman-superior position as natural, whereas others have looked elsewhere for symbols of maleness and femaleness."

All human beliefs and activities spring from an underlying mythology—those metaphors, informing imageries, and paradigms which deeply influence every aspect of our lives and which determine our attitudes about reality— about the world and about ourselves: good and evil, normalcy and abnormalcy, fact and fiction, justice and injustice, beauty and ugliness, power and powerlessness. This book is concerned with the multitude of ways in which our sexual values and precepts are reflections of those mythologies which are the core and substance of what we vainly call *reality*.

# TWO
# The Mythic Basis of Sexual Values

Because Western ideology insists that sexual activity is wholly instinctual, that it is natural and innate, we are reluctant to recognize that sexuality has a history. Instead, we are convinced that sexuality is impervious to change, and therefore exists outside of time. Research, however, indicates that there have been many major changes in both sexual behavior and the significance we attached to it. Social historians have provided countless examples of such shifts of meaning, making it clear that sexuality does possess a history.

For instance, our Western view of women has been influenced equally by the "evil Eve" myth and by the subsequent reversal of that myth into the story of the "virginal Mary." The long-standing Judeo-Christian (patriarchal) view of woman (as Eve) as an undisciplined and highly sexual creature was thoroughly altered in about the seventeenth century, resulting in the view that women (as Mary) are far less lustful than men. Sociologist Pat Caplan points out that by the last half of the nineteenth century, medical opinion had become an authoritative basis of such public opinion: "Women were usually characterized by medical men as having sexual anaesthesia." This imaginary dormancy of passion made the female into "Sleeping Beauty," while the male, by the standards of the same period, was transformed from the dutiful spouse into a sexual athlete. According to such a premise, the male became the passionate, sexual creature, initiating sexual activity, despite the "natural" resistance to sex of the female. Thus, apparently, sexual aggression was not only natural in the male, but it was also supposed to be beneficial. Without appropriate sexual release, it was believed that the male's health suffered.

By the Victorian Age this attitude about unbridled male sexuality had changed again. The unlimited sexual activity of men was now perceived as harmful. In fact, medical theory of the period considered the loss of sperm to be debilitating. Men were strongly advised to avoid intercourse before important activities, such as sporting events, military maneuvers, and economic or political confrontations. Male masturbation was even more strongly condemned than sex with a partner. It was believed to lead to a great variety of diseases, including insanity.

These random examples of shifts in Western attitudes about sexuality make it clear that sexuality has fundamentally changed from time to time and from place to place. Today it is also clear that such changes take place because sexuality is a culturally constructed phenomenon. Equally apparent is the fact that such sexuality exists as a temporal phenomenon, and that it therefore has a history as distinctive as the history of political ideas.

The study of the human body and how it is perceived at different times and places reveals an important element of cultural symbolism which has strong implications in relation to sexuality. A particularly brilliant scholar who has discussed these implications is Mary Douglas, who shares my premise that the body has to be looked upon as a metaphor for society. In her view, there is a strong correlation between how people see their bodies and how they see their society: "Societies, like other bounded groups, are vulnerable at their intersection with other groups. Thus much attention is paid in many societies to the orifices of the human body, for here matter passes from outside to inside, and vice versa. Societies which deem it important to maintain their separateness will also guard their [cultural boundaries, i.e., margins] against intrusion and pollution . . . and this may be symbolized through taboos on food and sex." (Douglas, 1984)

There are numerous twentieth-century studies indicating that it is, in particular, the bodies of women that serve as social symbols of the important boundary markers between the group and outsiders. The guarded isolation of women often represents "the privacy of the group." Therefore, female chastity is sometimes justified as the means of guarding against the intrusion of "strangers" upon a kinship-based society, in which clear biological lines of descent are of great importance.

All cultures, including our own, are a series of related structures which comprise social forms, values, and cosmology, plus the entire body of knowledge through which every aspect of experience is mediated. This fact is far clearer to us in its manifestation in alien cultures than it is when we view our own society. And for this reason it is important, at least in passing, to explore the social forms, values, and cosmologies of other people. But in every case, this series of related social structures is the basis of mythology as I use the term in this book. Whether we speak of America, Africa, Europe, or Asia, this mythic basis of religious, social, political, and scientific reality manifests itself as actions commonly called rituals. "The rituals enact the form of social relations and in giving these relations visible expression they enable people to know their own society. The rituals work upon the body politic through the symbolic medium of the physical body." (Douglas, 1984) Rituals are the *embodiment* of the whole of a society's knowledge—they are cosmology transformed into physical action; mind transformed into body. Rituals are the bodily expression of mythology. And mythology itself is a highly viable expression of values which assumes many different forms in different places and times: the characteristic narratives of origins which are the most familiar aspects of myth, as well as the less familiar social paradigms which mythologist Joseph Campbell called *the myths we live by:* national epics, political treatises, scientific theories, and such contemporary urban myths as those which dictate fashion, etiquette, and media communication.

It is the special relationship among myth, ritual, and sexuality that interests me—the process by which the rituals of sex carry within them the mythic values of societies.

From the outset it is important that we agree what is meant here by the term "mythology." The noted mythologist David Maclagan explains it best: "Myth, in its deep structure as well as in its superficial content, is about this compound relation between body/mind and word/world. It is metaphoric, not in the sense that it uses what we call 'figures of speech,' mere rhetorical devices, but in the root sense of the word: 'carrying across' the convenient boundaries we establish between sexes, seasons, species and stars. This metaphoric leakage is not consciously contrived, nor is it peculiar to myth; it penetrates, in the act, *everything* we do, all the sense we make—even in the most narrowly specialized branch of science."

In this way, by mythology I do not mean only those tales of creation which answer essential human questions: *Why are we here? Who are we? What is our place in the world, in time and in space?* I also include in the definition of mythology the metaphoric capacity of myth to shape intellectual and social forms of thinking and behavior, to transcend the sacred cosmogonies of religion and to become secular forms that give value to absolutely everything we do in art, science, communications, and every other experience of life. I am therefore using the word mythology much as twentieth-century philosophers use the term paradigm.

As mythologist Barbara C. Sproul observes, myths "involve attitudes toward facts and reality." As such, the questions they raise are most effectively answered by the metaphoric mentality which is at the heart of mythology. Myths constellate our grasp of reality. Whether we adhere to them or not, the myths at the foundation of our societies remain pervasively influential. I believe with Sproul that myths "deal with first causes, the essences of what their cultures perceive reality to be . . . So it is no accident that cultures think their creation myths the most sacred, for these myths are the ground on which all later myths stand. In them members of the group can perceive the main elements of the entire structure of value and meaning . . . But because of the way in which domestic myths are transmitted, people often never learn that they *are* myths; people become submerged in their viewpoints, prisoners of their own traditions. They readily confuse attitudes toward reality (proclamations of value) with reality itself (statements of fact)."

Creation myths have strong religious significance, so we often think of them entirely in terms of sacred cosmogony. But creation myths also determine the shape of secular myths that function as the paradigms of nonreligious thinking in science, politics, and law. Social behavior and even fashion and etiquette are built upon a value structure indistinct from mythology. Our ideas about sexuality do not escape this mythic influence. For instance, the mythic basis of sexual attitudes in many societies is highly dichotomized. This dichotomy is especially strong in the thinking of the West. We are therefore inclined to take for granted that the Asian concept of Yin and Yang confirms our attitudes about the universality of opposite forces in nature, rather than seeing Yin and Yang as the expression of a different paradigm of Taoist tradition. But actually, Yin and Yang cannot be used to exemplify the pragmatic dualism of the West, for they are symbolic representations of the synthesis of opposites that exists at the core of a unitary Asian mentality. In the East, Yin and Yang, light and dark, consciousness and unconsciousness are in an active, dialectical balance. However dramatic their opposition, each opposite depends for its wholeness upon its counterpart.

In contrast, it is characteristic of Western viewpoint to think of sexuality in terms of binary opposites: male and female, heterosexual and homosexual, marital sex and pre- or extramarital sex. "And in every case, one of these pairs is privileged, is seen as the 'normal.' " (Caplan) In many other cultures the dichotomized value system does not advocate or even comprehend what we in the West mean by binary opposites. That fundamental difference in the ways in which we know and understand the world makes it almost impossible for us to see others in any terms except those that we use to define ourselves. Failing to see our own myths as myths, we consider all other myths false. Therefore, nothing challenges our factualized mythology as much as the values of other cultures which contradict those categories of privilege and normalcy which our cosmogony attributes to nature. To suggest any flaw in those things which are at the heart of binary opposites throws us entirely off balance. We cannot comprehend any congruity between what we have defined as "opposites" because our mythology has become the guiding principle not only of religion and moral conduct, but also of science and social behavior. Choices for us are strictly a matter of either/or: male or female, good or evil, light or dark, heterosexual or homosexual, natural or unnatural. We have even forfeited the purely statistical basis of terms like "normal" and "abnormal" in favor of a curious form of biological morality: normal-good and abnormal-evil. This obsession with opposite forces and their connection with morality makes it difficult for us to understand the sexuality of other peoples and other eras. For instance, when we discuss the sexuality of ancient Greece we inevitably rely upon a term of our own: *bisexuality*.

The philosopher Michel Foucault (1985) asks: "Were the Greeks bisexual, then? Yes, if we mean by this that a Greek could, simultaneously or in turn, be enamored of a boy or a girl . . . that it was common for a male to change to a preference for women after 'boy-loving' inclinations in his youth." But if we want to understand the way in which the Greeks themselves understood this ambiguity of desire, we must take into account the fact that they did not recognize two different drives. When we speak of their "bisexuality" we are probably thinking that they allowed themselves a choice between the sexes, whereas, for them, this option was not an expression of a dual, ambivalent, and bisexual desire. As Foucault (1985) puts it, "To their way of thinking, what made it possible to desire a man or a woman was simply the appetite that nature had implanted in man's heart for 'beautiful' human beings, whatever their sex might be."

As we shall see, for the Greeks the body was an idealized conception of beauty made visible. Not only was the entire aesthetics of the Greeks built upon this concept, but so too were their cosmology, morality, science, and politics. Not only did the Greeks think of the body differently from us, but their vision of the body had certain congruities and incongruities with other world cultures, which, though not the focus of this book, can shed a great deal of light on the malleability of conduct which we in the Western world take to be forever fixed by nature.

For instance, in Mombasa the relationship between gender identity and sexuality is closer to that of the Greeks than it is to the premise of Anglo-Americans. Gender is assigned solely on the basis of biological sex, not sexual behavior. Therefore, in Mombasa lesbians remain women and dress as women. In nearby Oman (despite its many historical connections with Mombasa), there is just the opposite view of sexuality. A male homosexual is looked upon as a transsexual, and may change his gender and effectively become a woman. Here, it is the sexual act and not the sexual organs that determine gender. Therefore, among the people of Oman, behavior and not anatomy is the basis of the conceptualization of gender identity.

What we want, and what we do, in any society, is to a very great extent what we are made to want and what we are allowed to do. Emerson verbalized this symbiosis of the individual, society, and sexuality when he said that the whole of nature is a metaphor of the human mind.

Mythology is built upon just such a nature-metaphor. Usually that metaphor is turned into truth, becoming a devout picture of a single reality. Sexuality, like science and politics, is also seen in cosmological terms. We deduce with equal certainty that the morality of sexual behavior, the truth of scientific facts, and the righteousness of political values are valid reflections of cosmic reality. It follows that we are right and everybody else is wrong. Our most pertinacious assumptions are those which remain unconscious and uncritical. Those are the attitudes I hope to explore, and the best way to challenge fossilized assumptions is to subject them to the shock of contrast with an entirely alien tradition. For even so fundamental a matter as the epic story of the origin of the world has as many forms and variations as there are different peoples on earth.

Myths often speak of the creation of nature as a form of procreation. Barbara C. Sproul has made some important observations in this regard. In such a scheme, she writes, a father god and a mother goddess produce as offspring all the forces and creatures of the cosmos. This Yin/Yang principle is significant even when only one deity is envisioned at the center of creation. "When the power of being is characterized overtly as feminine, an earth mother goddess gives birth spontaneously and independently, without need of a mate." If the sole deity is male, either he externalizes himself as a female partner and produces creatures with "her," or he retains within himself aspects of the feminine "other," and from that mythic amalgam creates new life.

In various cultures, the birth of the cosmos is envisioned in wildly different forms, thus providing a wide spectrum of metaphoric social values. Some creative deities sacrifice part of themselves, cutting off a portion of their bodies and fashioning it into the world. Others give birth to the world by vomiting or excreting it. In such cases, human physiology is dramatized as deriving from deity and therefore possessing great cosmological power. For instance, in the Aranda genesis of Australia, the great ancestor gave birth to people by sweating them through his armpit.

For some societies vomit, excrement, and sweat are less powerful procreative substances than sexual fluids, such as sperm. Though many societies have had fabulous notions about the relationship of semen and ovum in procreation, sperm has usually been understood as important, if not essential, to reproduction. Therefore, divine masturbation is often a significant mythic basis of the creation in many cultures. The Egyptian god Neb-er-tcher is said to contain all opposites: male and female, words and ideas, body and mind. These aspects interact as the god masturbates into his clenched hand and places the semen into his mouth where it fertilizes his cosmic womb. Then he spits it forth as creation. All the myths that use such sexual activity as the basis of creation emphasize the fertility and abundance of the power that imparts upon deities their symbolic stature as absolute beings in whom creation is not only a possibility but a necessity. Sexual abundance becomes associated with creation. This is precisely what many primordial myths celebrate when they speak of the extraordinary fecundity of the earth Mother Goddess or, even more graphically, when the Australian Aborigines lavishly depict their Djanggawul gods with immense genitalia.

There are countless variations on this theme. In cultures with a sacrificial attitude about the human body, blood from the male genital may substitute for sperm as a generative fluid. According to pre-Columbian Mexican cosmogony, the Toltec deity Quetzalcoatl drew blood from his penis with a cactus spine, and with that blood he anointed the ground bones of a prior race of humankind, from which sprang the Toltec people.

The point I'm making here deserves repetition. The way the body has been envisioned and evaluated by various eras and cultures is a history of the sexual messages transmitted by social myths and the customs based upon such myths. The act of sex flows into the mythic imagination and, consequently, the mythology of a people largely determines its attitudes about sexuality. Once these procreative aspects of genesis are accepted as a significant part of the framework of theology, sexual attitudes are reinforced by law and philosophy and, eventually, also by science, social fashion, and mass communication—all of which focus upon the prohibition or sanction of specific forms of sexual conduct. Genesis may be the starting point for this process, but mythology in its largest sense is not simply a religious convention of the past, but a repertory of socializing concepts that persist as active metaphors of our own century. Now and in the past, the means by which mythic concepts become the basis of sexual values is often veiled by the metaphoric language and imagery that is at the heart of mythology. Perhaps this point can be clarified by a few relatively transparent examples of how sexuality and religious and secular mythologies are fused into some of our fundamental attitudes about sex and gender.

According to Vern Bullough, the crossing of sex roles is common among the Balinese. One of their most honored religious figures is Syng Hyang Toenggal (the "Solitary" or Tijinitja), who, according to Balinese cosmology, represents a deity combining both husband and wife before the era when the gods were envisioned as being separated by sex into males and females. The cross-dressing associated with the ritual celebration of Syng Hyang Toenggal obviously represents transvestite conduct, which implies the religious sanction of crossing sex roles and, perhaps, of homosexual activity among the Balinese.

Unlike most cultures in the West, the Egyptians, as I have already mentioned, believed that the proper position for sexual intercourse was with the female on top, a position that coincided with a reversal of the positions of the gods in Egyptian cosmology. In Egypt the earth was a male deity and the sky was female. Consequently, the earth god Geb is usually depicted as lying beneath his spouse Nut, the sky goddess.

Another custom among the Egyptians was the marriage of brothers and sisters, an incestuous arrangement often depicted in the myths of various cultures but rarely socialized as custom. The godly status of Egyptian royalty, however, motivated the imitation of the gods, thus socializing incest as a royal privilege. The role models for this behavior are clear. The goddess Isis had married her brother the god Osiris, and the goddess Nephthys was the wife of her godly brother Seth. How common these incestuous marriages were is a controversial matter, particularly since the term "sister" was often used in ancient Egypt to mean wife and lover. But there is no doubt that in Greek times, during the reign of the Ptolemys, it became the rule for pharaohs to marry their sisters. "In the Greek-Egyptian city of Arsinoe, it has been estimated that two-thirds of the marriages recorded during the second century A.D. were between brothers and sisters." (Bullough)

Jews, like most of the peoples of the Middle East, were devoted to a male-oriented religion and a social orientation that placed men in a superior position to women. The degree of the socialization of male dominance may be seen in the Judaic association of masculinity and the phallus. In fact, a castrated male was denied entrance to the temple. "He that is wounded in the stones, or hath his privy member cut off, shall not enter into the congregation of the Lord." (Deuteronomy, 23:1) And a castrated animal was not an acceptable offering upon the altar.

Masculinity was revered, while the low status of women offered them little protection from men. Hebrew soldiers ravished the women captured in war. The sons of Jacob killed Shechem for raping their sister Dinah, but Jacob condemned them because he believed that the assault of a female member of one's family was not sufficient cause for violent retribution. An eye for an eye but not a life for a rape. What had perhaps begun as a religion built upon an all-powerful male deity had become the basis for a social mythology that decreed the proper forms of conduct in regard to women.

At the center of the Judeo-Christian female-negative and sex-negative mentality is the mythic origin of women. The early pages of Genesis give two accounts of the creation of woman. In Talmudic lore Lilith was the wife of Adam before Eve. Like Adam, Lilith was created from the dust (*adamah*) of the earth. She had been one of the wives of Sammael (or Satan), but, being wild and passionate, she left her spouse and joined Adam in Eden. Lilith, however, rejected the subordinate role of women and refused to be subservient and submissive to Adam on the ground that since both had issued from the dust, they were equal. They quarreled and Lilith left Paradise for the regions of the air. Adam prayed that Lilith would be returned to him, and the Lord sent three angels in her pursuit. He ordered them to command Lilith to return to Eden, and if she refused to obey, then one hundred of her offspring would die each day. Lilith resisted all efforts to return her to Eden, and vowed vengeance against children for the destruction of her own offspring. In medieval rabbinical literature Lilith is described as a spirit who roams about at night seducing men and killing children, especially the newly born. For her unsubmissive spirit, the first woman of Genesis was condemned as a monster and as the mother of all demons.

The reputation of the second woman created by the Lord is only slightly better than that of Lilith. Eve was made from one of Adam's ribs. She was made of man for man and for this reason she is regarded as the subordinate and the weaker of the two sexes. She is also looked upon as the agent through whom sin came into the world, a temptress who persuaded Adam to eat the forbidden fruit. Because of her sin she was fated by the Lord to bear children in misery and pain. Philo, an Alexandrian Jew born in the last quarter of the first century B.C., argued that the original sin of Eve was the result of sexual desire, the desire for bodily pleasure, and that such pleasure was the "beginnings of wrongs and violation of the law." Philo believed that, for the sake of sex, humankind had forfeited a life of immortality and bliss for one of mortality and wretchedness. Femaleness, for Philo, represented sense perception, the created world, while maleness represented the rational soul. Progress meant giving up the female gender—the material, passive, corporeal, and sense perceptible, for the male—active, rational, and incorporeal. The association of Eve with sexual desire was not a Judaic concept, and Philo had little direct influence on the Jews of his day, but he had considerable impact on Christianity, which formalized the association between Eve and sexuality. Augustine, for instance, held that Eve felt shamed by her desire, causing her to cover Adam's and her nakedness by sewing fig leaves together to conceal their genitals. Lust was born with the expulsion from Eden. If sex existed before the expulsion, it had existed innocently and without appetite. Eve, the temptress, became the symbol of female subordination and the overindulgence of women in lustful thoughts and actions. As we shall see, eventually the female was absolved of sin through an association with the virginity of Mary, mother of Jesus Christ. But attitudes about women have changed very little in regard to the pervasive and powerful attitudes derived from Judeo-Christian mythology. Women are still regarded as inferior creatures torn between the innocence of Mary and the lustful willfulness of Eve.

Though Judaic mythology has many examples of sex-negative ideology, sex really did not get its dreadful reputation in the West until various Near Eastern cults impacted upon Christian dogma. In Hellenic times, there were numerous sources of this sexual negativity, but one of the most powerful was an Orphic religion that had great influence on several major theological thinkers. Though the Orphic mysteries were never incorporated into the state religion of classical Greece, Orphism had strong influence on the Pythagoreans and the Platonists, as well as on many later Greek philosophers. From these Hellenic sources, a fanatic dualism entered Christianity. So deeply rooted is this mythology, that even disbelievers are strongly influenced by the principles of that vision of the sacredness of soul and the profanity of body.

The cardinal belief of the Orphic religion was the effort to attain immortality through a life of purity and through rituals of purification. Central to this doctrine of purity was the belief that the soul was undergoing punishment for ancient sins and that the body was a prison in which the soul had been incarcerated. According to Orphic teachings, in the beginning there had been night. Eventually a silver egg containing Eros ("Love") formed in the nothingness and grew until it burst and separated into two elements: heaven (Uranus) and earth (Gaia). Uranus and Gaia copulated and gave birth to Cronos and all the other gigantic Titans. Cronos became the father of Rhea, Demeter, Hades, Poseidon, and Zeus. Zeus sought to dominate the cosmos, and so he swallowed up his father, Cronos, thus encompassing all creation, from which he created our present world. Then Zeus copulated with Persephone, who gave birth to Dionysus, to whom Zeus gave dominion over the newly created world. Before Dionysus could take control, he was destroyed by the jealous Titans. When Zeus discovered what they had done, he burned the Titans to ashes with his thunderbolts. From these ashes, Zeus fashioned humankind, an act usually interpreted to mean that his new creation contains something of the sacred and something of the profane. This myth was the basis of the Orphic belief that human beings possess a twofold nature, in conflict with itself: godlike goodness and the evil which is the legacy of the Titans. The result of this mythic mentality is fundamental to our own values: To achieve divinity, we must cherish the divine in us and purge away the evil.

From this brief survey of religious mythologies, it seems undeniable that our corporeality and sexuality are implacable aspects of the mythic basis of Judeo-Christian evil. We may be fully aware of this fact of theological history, and we may also be thoroughly aware of the profound shifts in moral values which have been championed by most of the major thinkers of the Jewish and Christian world, but nonetheless many of the most sophisticated and powerful people of the West still doggedly base their day-to-day attitudes and moral judgments upon a morality that grew out of a now obsolescent mythology. The mythology has been beheaded but the dogma based upon that mythology has survived as an expression of faith disguised as common sense.

We realize that societies are deeply influenced by this decapitated dogma—by a morality without an operative, rational head. Yet many powerful people are apparently guided by a dogma which they take to be common-sensical truth: politicians who create public policy, people in health care who determine the destinies of those who suffer from disease, educators who build the sexual mentality of future generations, and members of the media who shape the sensibilities of millions of people. Many of us consciously and unconsciously build our social and political values upon biblical conceits in which we have no particular investment of faith. We may not recognize that our justification for morality has a mythic basis, and we may therefore act upon such beliefs as if they were elements of an absolute, revealed truth. It is not surprising, therefore, to discover that an influential television newscaster delivered the following statement to students at a college commencement ceremony:

"Enjoy sex whenever and with whomever you wish, but wear a condom. No. The answer is no. Not because it isn't cool or smart or because you might end up . . . dying in an AIDS ward, but no, because it's wrong. Because we have spent 5,000 years as a race of rational human beings trying to drag ourselves out of the primeval slime by searching for truth and moral absolutes . . . In its purest form, truth is not a polite tap on the shoulder. It is a howling reproach. What Moses brought down from Mount Sinai were not the Ten Suggestions."

A close look at this invective brings home the exceptional impact that mythologies still have on sexuality. The "primeval slime" that the newscaster talks about is sex from the view of a "sex-negative" religious culture. The "reproach" he mentions is a greatly troubled moralism which is not supported by late twentieth-century anthropological, sexual, or philosophical opinion. And the "truth and moral absolutes" he salutes are the effluence of a Western mythology which is contradicted and countermanded at every turn by our own thinkers as well as by countless other mythologies which have been produced by multitudes of highly ethical peoples who have labored over their own moral reality with a concern and an intelligence equal to ours for far more than 5,000 years.

Through the study of the history of sexuality as a manifestation of a people's most fundamental mythic vision of themselves, we are led to question not just the literal truth of our own religious cosmogony, but also to discover a need to reassess the countless scientific and social values, standards, and codes of behavior which inevitably arise from mythology and which have become extensions of that mythology in the form of social conventions in the modern world of "commodification," industry, and science. To recognize that our mind-set is the product of such a mythology makes it possible to understand that we may have options beyond those ancient strictures that have overgrown our lives. We cannot discover what we are becoming until we can see who we have been. We cannot discover the values emanating from a new mythology until we recognize the possibility that the truth of mythology is not fixed and singular but pluralistic and malleable.

My premise is that the body is constantly transformed by the flux of a mythic mentality. There are many possible approaches to the story of these transformations, and the story I wish to explore is by no means inclusive. It follows just one of many threads that make up the history of myth and sexuality.

In its basic outline, this story begins at a time so remote that we can no longer hear the voices of those who were the keepers of the myths about a life-giving Mother Goddess. We can know this ancient community only dimly through its remarkably provocative artifacts that tempt us to reconstruct a matrocentric world utterly different from today's masculinized societies. Cast over the egalitarian image of Neolithic Europe is the shadow of an invasion by the male-dominated religious mythologies that changed the life-giving body of woman into a "male womb" in which men believed themselves capable of sowing the seeds of life and producing their own progeny. Then, with the eventual influence of a triumphant Christian mythology, even the generative body of males was transformed into an embodiment of sin. The paradigms which gave shape to these transformations of the body are familiar to us as religious mythologies. But mythic mentality also assumed uncharacteristic shapes. For instance, the "cosmic machine" was envisioned by the Church in Rome as a grand stellar design made by God and set in orderly motion by His hand. The sacred was gradually secularized, and by the seventeenth century, the Great Machine of God became the basis of the highly influential mechanistic philosophy of Rene Descartes. Later, during the Industrial Revolution, that Christian cosmology, which envisioned God as the draftsman and designer of the cosmic mechanism, facilitated the transformation of the body into a machine. Workers became indistinct from the machines of industry. Eventually, this mechanistic attitude had far-reaching physiological implications. Sexology was invented in an age obsessed with "scientific" observation. As we shall see, sexology attempted to calibrate every aspect of the mechanism of sex, and though these elaborate efforts were disguised as "the science of desire," they nonetheless became an expression of both the prevailing mythology and science of the time. Science was the new religion, with its own complex myths. And physicians largely replaced ministers as the arbitrators of normalcy and decency.

The story of the influence of mythology on our ideas about the body continued along these secular lines. Early in the twentieth century, the introduction of a social mythology built upon the capitalistic belief in self-gratification gradually gave rise to a form of consumerism in which the body was both a machine and a commodity. Eventually this commodification of the body was sexualized, and every conceivable kind of product was offered to the public as a means to achieve personal attractiveness and pleasure. Such influences on our ideas about sexuality were no less mythic in origin than the earlier influences of religious mythologies. In fact, many social observers believe that the myths of consumerism not only resulted in the eroticizing of advertising, entertainment, and communications, but also transformed every other aspect of morality and sexual behavior. There is also evidence that the old myth of male dominance remained at the core of these vast changes in sexual attitudes. In the view of many sociologists, it was men who invented a pornographic commodity in which violence was sexualized. As such, sadomasochism became a prominent element of masculine eroticism.

It is this succession of sacred and secular myths which provides the historical outline which I intend to explore in order to grasp the relationships of myth and sexuality.

# THREE
# The Body as Woman

First came Nothingness. It existed without time or space. For Nothingness knew neither birth nor destruction. It was perfection, existing before existence. A perfect impossibility . . . being together something and nothing.

From this unthinkable void came Gaia, the great mystery of being, the source of all things. She took shape suddenly, coming out of Nothingness, dancing ever more quickly until she became a whirlwind of light.

This is the way the world began.

It is a story of creation that comes from a time that greatly predates the Olympic world of male deities and their subordinate goddesses. Gaia existed in her wholeness for an eternity before she gave birth to the Greek gods who banished her. She signifies earth and the powers of earth. "Her sanctuary is the omphalos—the navel of the earth and the tomb of the daimon-serpent Tython." (Harrison, 1903)

From her body Gaia made the land and the sea. She moved and her spine arched outward, forming the high mountains. In the mysterious hollows of her flesh she made valleys and caves where her voice still lingers. She sighed and thus the rain was made, pouring down upon tidal pools where Gaia gave life to infinitesimal creatures that blindly wriggled through the fertile mud. Green sprouts pressed outward from the pores of her mantle. Flowers grew upon her many breasts. From her body came all the life that would ever be, so rich was her fertility. She was ever creating something from out of her mysterious being. One day Gaia made six women and six men and placed them gently upon her massive body. There they thrived and multiplied.

But these creatures were not happy. Despite the abundance Gaia spread before them, they groaned with fear and discontent. When they saw the flowers die in winter, they came to understand death. They cried out against their mortality. And they were afraid. They detested the mysteries of the unknown, so they became utterly obsessed with dreadful things to come. They could not take joy in the present because they greatly feared the future. So great was their fearfulness that Gaia took pity on them and sent among them an oracle from which they could learn the nature of coming events. In the hills at the place called Delphi, Gaia sent up vapors from the innermost center of her being. The fumes arose from a cleft in the rocks, surrounding the priestess of Gaia with the whispers of the future. The priestess fell into a trance, and thus she could understand the messages rising from the dark interior of Gaia's body. For countless generations mortals traveled long distances to consult the oracle of Delphi.

Gaia was the source of life and death, of nourishment and knowledge. The sustainer of all being. The wide-breasted mother of all mortals. At Delphi the ritual began with the words: "First in my prayer before all other gods, I call on Earth, primeval prophetess." But gradually this supreme power of the Earth Spirit and Great Mother was usurped by the new gods of Olympia. Gaia's name vanished from Delphi, and that famous center of divination became the domain of the rational, sunlit male deity Apollo. The mysterious pneuma which issued from Earth's heartbeat was no longer heard by Gaia's priestess. Although the Homeric *Hymn to Gaia* had heralded her as "the oldest of divinities," her power was eclipsed by the young gods who became the beacons of classical Greece.

Charlene Spretnak has provided an excellent insight into this process: "For thousands of years before the classical myths took form and then were written down by Hesiod and Homer in the seventh century B.C., a rich oral tradition of mythmaking had existed. Strains of the earlier tradition are evident in the later myths, which reflect the cultural amalgamation of three waves of barbarian invaders, the Ionians, the Achaeans, and finally the Dorians, who moved into Greece from 2500 to 1000 B.C. These invaders brought with them a patriarchal social order and their thunderbolt God, Zeus."

Anthropologist Jane Ellen Harrison (1903) was one of the first scholars to note that beneath the surface of Homeric myths of the Olympic gods lies a stratum at once more primordial and more permanent. After years of research and scholarship, Harrison rediscovered a pre-Hellenic mythology dominated by a matricentric earth spirit. She concluded that the concept of a male supreme deity is a relatively recent invention, dating from the appearance of Zeus in about 2500 B.C., followed in about 1800 B.C. by the emergence of the first patriarch of the Old Testament, Abraham. Archaeological research supports Harrison's contention that women were the primary focus of religion. Votive statues of "goddesses" are dated as early as 25,000 B.C. According to many scholars, the upstart patriarchal priests coopted the ancient symbols and rituals of the Earth Spirit and inverted their sexual meaning, eclipsing the power of the female, trivializing and villainizing it, and subordinating it to a masculine religious hierarchy.

Prior to the decline of the goddess there was a different world view. Its traces can be found in pre-Hellenic Greece, pre-Christian Europe, India, and Asia. The Great Mother Gaia had many forms. One of her oldest manifestations was Ishtar of Babylon. Gaia was an archetype known by many other names: Ataentsic of the Iroquois Indians; Awonawilona of the Zuni Indians; the Algonquin Nokomis; the Mexican Ilamatecuhtli; Mama Quilla and Pachamama of the Incas; the goddess Astarte of the Canaanites and Phoenicians; Cybele of Phrygia; Isis of Egypt; Anahita of Persia; Annis of the Celts; the Greek goddesses Rhea, Demeter, Themis, Artemis; the Roman Tellus Mater (or Terra) as well as Tellus, Ceres, and Maia; the Nordic goddesses Nerthus, Erce, and Freyja, as well as the Sanscrit Prithivi, and the Virgin Mary of medieval Europe. The histories of these female deities have been extensively researched, making it clear that they were the focus of an exceptionally powerful and world-wide reverence for the feminine principle. We shall only touch upon their fascinating histories. What really interests us here is the primordial aspects of sacredness that surrounded the generative power of women. For it is with that primal mythology that the first conception of sexuality seems to have had its origins.

For many people, history is slanderous. It is the story of victors—not victims. It strongly influences our attitudes about people who have been politically vanquished. It also shapes our perception of those who have been sexually disenfranchised. Social critics have faced the prejudicial framework of sexual history by deconstructing it and recovering the ancient sources of legends that were rewritten by males to serve their own patriarchal interests. This revision of history has been a task filled with contradiction, for in attempting to reverse the masculinization of the past, we are always inclined to accept as a rule of "truth" the masculine premise that the sexes are involved in an eternal antagonism which is an implacable aspect of "human nature." For most experts, that assumption is incorrect. Cross-cultural studies do not support such a dualistic vision of human sexuality. The subjugation of women does not occur in all societies, especially those which are not built upon the division of the sexes. In other cultures, the tension between men and women escalates in proportion to the breadth of the mythic chasm which is socially constructed between the sexes. Our sexual predicament is, therefore, not a matter of fact, but an expression of cultural constructs.

Mary Douglas (1970) makes this point when she notes that the Mbuti pygmies of Africa give little importance to the separation of male from female spheres. "Men and women share in tasks of erecting huts and even in hunting." Such informality about the division of labor by sex is a reflection of the pygmies' religious informalities and their general lack of concern for "sin." In contrast, the Hadza hunters in Tanzania are divided by a social category so dominating and all-inclusive that males and females seem to belong virtually to different species. "Wherever Hadza are, and whatever they do, they are always controlled by the division between the sexes. This division is between two hostile classes, each of which is capable of organizing itself for defence or virulent attack against the other. This extraordinarily intense consciousness of sexual difference is the only permanent level of organization the Hadza ever achieve." (Douglas, 1970)

The masculinized mentality of the West insists that the division of the sexes is a "natural phenomenon" and an abiding condition of "human nature." Anthropological and biological evidence does not support such a premise. During this century it has become an essential aim of sexual politicians to rediscover the basis for a scholarly redemption of women. That cause has required heroes— often scholars who have been resurrected from oblivion. Such a neglected hero is the nineteenth-century Swiss historian Johann Jakob Bachofen. In his own time, Bachofen was quite famous for his theory of social development, which maintained that the primary period of human history was matriarchal. He noticed, for instance, that the position of women in Homeric legend was much more dignified and authoritative than it was in historical Athens, where the negative attitude toward women apparently emerged in Western consciousness. The women of the *Odyssey*, though both good and evil, are not subservient to Zeus. Nausicaa, Circe, Calypso, and Penelope are dimensional beings with power and conviction.

By pointing out such positive attitudes in the depiction of women in mythology, Bachofen implemented the late Romantic vision of women which deeply influenced several major scholars and artists of Bachofen's day: the Germans Friedrich Nietzsche, Jakob Burckhardt, Rainer Maria Rilke, and Hugo von Hofmannsthal, and the American Lewis Henry Morgan. Bachofen's theory of a matriarchal society out of which modern patriarchal cultures evolved was widely accepted among sociologists until the beginning of the twentieth century. Today the attitude about Bachofen has in general changed. His theory is almost universally discredited. His critics point out that there is no historical evidence that a matriarchy has ever existed. For them that "fact" is the end of the debate. But such a dismissal of matriarchy is a bit facile. Bachofen himself made a strong distinction between what he called *ideas* and what he called *facts*. He pointed out that scholars are always inclined to ignore "ideas" in their stampede to get at the "facts."

"What cannot have happened was nonetheless thought." He insisted that what is thought and felt and imagined by the people of a society (factual or not) is essential to our understanding of the nature of that society. If our notion of "history" ignores the inner life of a people, we end up with all the "facts" but we are likely to miss the point.

Why is this? Because there is far more to history than a succession of external events. "Any culture is a series of related structures which comprise social forms, values, cosmology, the whole of knowledge and through which all experience is mediated. The rituals enact the form of social relations and in giving these relations visible expression they enable people to know their own society. The rituals work upon the body politic through the symbolic medium of the physical body." (Douglas, 1984)

It is just such a *vision* of human societies which deeply influences the research of scholars who reject the sufficiency of facts. They believe that there is a great deal to be learned from the interpretation of the elusive and mythic imprints of ancient peoples who left no trace of factual history. The mythologist Joseph Campbell was such a scholar. He looked *inward* upon the iconography of Neolithic people in order to discover the "history of their inner life." Campbell had far less interest in external facts than he had in the vantage provided by myth, icon, and ritual. As a result of his research, he was able to recreate a time forever lost in history but fully alive in the river of memory called mythology. "There can be no doubt," he wrote in 1964, "that in the very earliest ages of human history the magical force and wonder of the female was no less a marvel than the universe itself; and this gave to women a prodigious power, which it has been one of the chief concerns of the masculine part of the population to break, control, and employ to its own ends."

The origins of this legacy, according to Campbell, were neither in India, as many scholars still suppose, nor in China, but in the Near East—the Levant—where recent archaeological explorations have uncovered an unbroken continuity of mother goddess worship going back to approximately 7500 B.C. At about this period, in the high mountain valleys of Asia Minor, agriculture and stock-breeding were developed. Most anthropologists now believe that it was women who first discovered the art of planting seeds and cultivating crops. Associated with this innovative venture by women were the herding of animals as well as the invention of herbal medicine and the first household crafts. The first spun cloth, baskets, and pottery were undertaken by women. The first congregations at marketplaces were the undertakings of women, who bartered surplus goods and produce and thus invented a primary form of commerce and economic activity.

It is generally agreed that the responsibility of women to grow the crops that sustained their extended families resulted in a distinctive mentality: a oneness with the soil and, by extension, with nature as a whole. Such a sensibility encourages a homogeneous attitude about the world, rather than the decisive dualism which eventually overtook the masculinized Western mind. During Neolithic times, it seems that consciousness was not splintered into irreconcilable opposites: heaven and earth, matter and spirit. In a maternal world the earth is the all-giving "Primal Uroborus," as Jungian historian Eric Neumann calls it. But this Mother Earth was not just a female construct of the familiar dualism of males. Mother Earth was mysteriously whole, self-perpetuating, combining both male and female attributes.

Erich Fromm speculates on the social meaning of such

a mentality, basing his thinking on archaeological evidence. Among hundreds of skeletons in just one Neolithic city of Anatolia (Catal Huyuk) there is not a single indication of violent death. The skeletal remains of at least 800 years of continuous habitation at Catal Huyuk strongly suggests the social and religious dominance of women. Apparently women were buried with greater honor than men, and such female burials greatly outnumbered those of men.

"The data that speak in favor of the view that Neolithic society was relatively egalitarian, without hierarchy, exploitation, or marked aggression, are suggestive," Fromm writes. "The fact, however, that these Neolithic villages in Anatolia had a matriarchal (matricentric) structure, adds a great deal more evidence to the hypothesis that Neolithic society, at least in Anatolia, was an essentially unaggressive and peaceful society. The reason for this lies in the spirit of affirmation of life and lack of destructiveness which J. J. Bachofen believed was an essential trait of all matriarchal societies."

These observations have lent a basis to speculation about human sexuality in Neolithic times. Such a scenario has been suggested by social scientists Ann and Robert Francoeur: "Human sexuality was viewed in an unsegmented way, and placed in the same context as animal sexuality. It was a primal sexual consciousness with a polymorphic character that blended sensuality and sexuality into one. Controls over sexual behavior emerged naturally from the tribal community. Typically, in matrilinear societies, there were no double moral standards to guide the social or sexual behavior of men and women. Because property was communal, people were not concerned about paternity or legitimacy of heirs. Family lines were traced through the mother, the source of all life."

It is likely that Neolithic people had no concept of the relationship between sexual intercourse and pregnancy. That dissociation persists among many of today's primal peoples. And, although there is no reason to assume that the mentality of twentieth-century tribal societies has any direct relationship to Neolithic cultures, it is nonetheless useful to note that many primal groups in our own time have an unspecific conception of the relationship between sex and pregnancy. For instance, the Pueblo Indians of America's Southwest believe maidens can be fertilized by a heavy summer shower. Among the Aborigines of Australia's Queensland, the thunder god is thought to create infants from swamp mud and then insert them into their mother's womb. This at least suggests the possibility that such dissociation of sex and conception existed among some Neolithic peoples.

Such a dissociation of the act of sex and procreation generates the polymorphic character of matricentric societies that blends sensuality and sexuality into one. In such a nonpatriarchal concept, the body of the female is not the property of her husband, often bought for a considerable sum from her father. Nor is it her virginity that brings such a high price. The virginal bride is not "given away" in a ritual that underlies the concept that a woman is not her own mistress but the property of her father "who transfers her *as property* to her husband." (Harding, 1971)

Just as it is true that everything symbolizes the body, so it is equally true that the body symbolizes everything else. Virginity is such a symbol, denoting either the self-possession of a woman in a matricentric society or her bondage to her husband as "unused and unsoiled goods" in a patriarchal system. The symbols are constructs of societies, and therefore their meanings shift and change dramatically from one place to another and from one time to another. In most cultures the notion of virginity is a masculine precept. It is very unlikely that that precept had any sway in a matrifocal Neolithic culture, where a woman whom we would now call a "virgin" was probably looked upon simply as an unattached female—and not a female without sexual experience. There is a long tradition to support such a notion. Robert Briffault, the pioneer in matriarchal research, noted that "the word virgin denotes 'unwed,' and connotes the very reverse of what the term has come to imply. The virgin Ishtar is also frequently addressed as 'The Prostitute.' She wears the 'posin,' or veil, which, as among the Jews, was the mark of both 'virgins' and prostitutes. The hierodules, or sacred prostitutes of Ishtar's temples, were also called 'the holy virgins' . . . Children born out of wedlock were called 'parthenioi,' or 'virgin-born.' "

It should be clear that when we use the term virgin in connection with the ancient goddesses, it has a meaning utterly different from the one we now assume. Under our Western system the young, unmarried female belongs to her father, but in earlier days she was her own mistress until she married. Her right to dispose of her own person until she marries is part of the primal concept of liberty. There is much evidence of such liberty. "This liberty of action involves the right to refuse intimacies as well as to accept them. A girl belongs to *herself* while she is virgin—unwed—and may not be compelled either to maintain chastity or to yield to an unwanted embrace." (Harding)

As a virgin she belongs to herself alone. She is "one-in-herself." Thus the female's virginity no longer represents a tribal boundary threatened by invasion and pollution. It is transformed by a precept of primal liberty into the rule of a woman over the estate of her own body.

In our century, the painter Gauguin was astonished by this attitude toward virginity when he discovered it among young Tahitian women, whom he described in his book *Noa Noa*. He recounts that many native women readily gave themselves to strangers who were attractive to them, without the slightest sense of "losing their virginity." To Gauguin's masculine way of looking at things, this seemed to be an unlikely way for women to behave. But what he failed to grasp is that such a Tahitian woman did not *give* herself to a man; she gave herself over to her own sexual appetite, so that even after a sexual act was completed she remained one-in-herself. "She was not dependent on the man, she did not cling to him or demand that the relationship should be permanent. She was still her own mistress, a virgin in the ancient, original meaning of the word." (Harding)

This view of female sexuality is a resonance of an ancient mythology, such as the story of Gaia with which we began this discussion. At the center of that mythology is the primordial Mother Goddess. Classicist Gunther Zuntz has provided an important overview of this female-focused mentality: "To be gripped by the realization of deity in woman, the spring and harbor of life, mankind did not have to wait for the invention of agriculture. Everywhere, from Spain to Siberia, so many Paleolithic documents of this devotion have emerged, and with traits so specific recurring in Neolithic relics, as to forbid the facile inference that this change, however epochal, in man's living habits could by itself account for what is loosely called 'the cult of the Mother Goddess' . . . What evidence there is—and it is not a little—points to concerns more comprehensive and profound. This is the oldest godhead perceived by mankind."

The whole of Neolithic Europe, judging from surviving artifacts and myths, was swayed by a homogeneous religious idea, based upon the worship of a Mother Goddess known by many different names. But whatever her name, she was the supreme center of the societies and sexual concepts built around her influence. At that time, the notion of fatherhood had not been introduced into religious thought. There were no supreme gods in ancient Europe, no law-givers, no patriarchs. Instead, the Great Mother stood above all other deities, immortal and omnipotent. She was associated with the moon (which diminished and regenerated), with bulls (whose horns grew rapidly in a form recapitulating the shape of the crescent moon), and with serpents (which renew themselves by shedding their skins)—all symbols of continuous growth, creation, and change. Feminist Merlin Stone sees these mythic elements as the focus of a time when, as she puts it, god was a woman: "From the settings in which her likenesses are found we know that she was worshiped variously as the guardian of childbirth, the source of wisdom, the dispenser of healing, the Lady of the Beasts, the fount of prophecy, the spirit who presided over death. But preeminently she was the symbol of fertility, the guarantor of crops, animals, and humans. In this role she was the Great Mother, the Earth Mother, whose magical powers assured the food supply and the continuance of the human race."

In most mythologies, the Great Mother eventually reproduces, but that reproduction is always parthenogenetic in prepatriarchal mythologies. The fertility goddess Demeter did not, as Hesiod would have it in his history of Olympian mythology, *Theogony*, spring from the union of a male deity, Cronos, and a goddess named Rhea. Demeter was a manifestation of the self-perpetuating Great Mother. Like Gaia, she was self-born. For when the Great Mother reproduced, her children were hers alone. If her child was a daughter, she shared her mother's supernatural powers. If the child was a son, he became his mother's consort and held a subordinate role to her. For instance, Gaia's son and lover was Uranus. He emerged as a powerful deity only after the masculine revision of Hellenic mythology during the Olympian era, when he was envisioned as the father of Gaia's children, who became the first dynasty of historic Greek gods. These offspring were the "old" gods, including the twelve Titans as well as the three Cyclops and three giants with one hundred hands called the Hecatoncheires. In patriarchal Greek mythology the children of the "frighteningly powerful" Great Mother were characteristically envisioned as monstrosities. But certain aspects of their original matriarchal significance inevitably survived their masculinization. For instance, because he was overwhelmed by their ugliness, Uranus is said to have cast his children into the depths of Tartaros, a place of punishment. Gaia solicited the assistance of the youngest of her Titan offspring, Cronos, to accomplish her children's liberation.

> My son,
> If you do my bidding, we shall revenge
> Your father's crime. For it was he
> Who invented shameful acts.
> —Hesiod, *Theogony*

When next Uranus came to make love to Gaia, Cronos sprang from his hiding place and, using a sickle his mother had fashioned for his task, cut off his father's genitals. The falling drops of blood were received by the Earth, who conceived and gave birth to the Erinyes, the giants, and the tree nymphs.

> From his hiding place
> his son reached toward his father
> and grasped him in his left hand,

while holding in his right an enormous sickle.
He swung it sharply,
and cut off the members of his own father.
And he threw them behind him
    where they splattered the earth with
    blood.
And that blood was taken in by Gaia, the
    Earth,
    from which she brought forth the power-
    ful Furies
and the tall Giants shining in their armour
and holding spears in their hands.
               —Hesiod, *Theogony*

From the foam of the sea where the genitals of Uranus had been thrown, the goddess Aphrodite was born. As for the castrated Uranus, he no longer lay around the Earth, longing for love. He stayed in his remote heavens, far from Earth, relegated to the distant sky where he became the symbol of abstraction and disengagement.

Thus the son of Gaia, with his mother's urging, brought a new order of deities into being. Cronos, with his sister-wife, the Titan Rhea, founded the second dynasty of the gods, which presided over the Golden Age of perfection.

The irrepressible potency of the metaphor of women is not unique to the Greeks. Everywhere on earth there is the residue of a time when the generative powers of women were the basis of sacredness. The first fully formed religious image to take shape in the human mind, some thirty thousand years ago, may well have been the likeness of the Great Mother. "The principal object of Minoan worship in Crete, emerging as an individualized figure just before 2000 B.C., was a Mother Goddess akin to Cybele the Great Mother of Asia Minor; and from Mycenae there is a representation of a goddess approached by worshippers bringing flowers and ears of corn, and a group of ivory statuettes that have been interpreted as representing Demeter, [her daughter] Persephone, and the infant Plutos [king of the underworld] . . . for the Earth was apparently believed to guard the dead." (Grant)

In the ruins of the Indus plains many terracotta statuettes of naked or nearly naked women have been unearthed. There are few experts who do not agree that these are icons of an Earth Spirit—a Mother Goddess. There are so many of these images that they were probably kept in every home of the walled cities of the Indus valley. In the Aryan Vedic literature there is no great Mother Goddess. She appears to have gone underground among the survivors of the Indus plains culture. Then she reappeared after a thousand years, when she became a pervasive power in the Orient. Under names such as Great Goddess, Mother, Daughter of the Mountains (Parvati), Inaccessible (Durga), Black (Kali), she remains one of the great deities of modern India. (Parrinder)

The cities of the Indus plain were devastated in the second millennium B.C. The goddess vanished with the culture in which she was glorified. Not for a thousand years would Indus culture regain its stature. And when it did revive, it was doubtlessly influenced by Yoga concepts and a belief in rebirth that survived from ancient times. A new god named Shiva usurped the place of the Mother Goddess. It is a transition similar to the one in which the classical Greek god Zeus assumed the role of the Earth Spirit Gaia. Unknown in the ancient Vedic hymns, Shiva is first mentioned as an attribute of the Vedic god Rudra in the Shvetashvatara Upanishad (ca. 6th century B.C.). Several centuries later, in the great epic Mahabharata, Shiva becomes one of the major gods of India. Yet it is the Mother Goddess, wife of Shiva, who is the most important. She was the Shakti or potency of her consort, most active when he was passive. And she was of vast importance in the scheme of later Tantra creeds. (Parrinder)

No matter the power of Shiva, always the Mother Goddess affirmed herself through him. Her primordial spirit was too powerful to be banished by a masculine deity. She is constantly insinuated. For instance, Shiva and his consort are sometimes represented as a single androgynous human figure, as in the famous male-female sculpture in the Elephanta caves near Bombay. For many Hindus, Shiva and his consort are not opposites but interchangeable beings who are sacred precisely because of the tensions of masculine and feminine spirits.

Despite their low state in modern India, in heroic times the epics presented a reverent image of women. For instance, it is told in the Mahabharata that the sage Agastya formed a superb woman from parts of different creatures. Then he had her born to a great king who was pining for a child. Her name was Lopamudra. As she matured into a woman her beauty increased. The clever Agastya married his creation and, to conceal her beauty, he bid her discard her fine robes and put on the humblest of rags. As time passed she reached maturity, and after her first menstruation, she put aside her rags and purified herself in a sacred bath. Then Agastya summoned her to his bed. Lopamudra asked the sage not only to take her for the sake of children but also to give her as much pleasure as he found in her. The conception of their children, she told him, must be a thing of sensual beauty. He must lie with her on an elegant bed. He must ornament her with jewels, and approach her in garlands and finery. Clearly, the Lopamudra of legend was not chattel as Indian women of later days would become. To the contrary, she was depicted as noble and dignified and free, desiring sexual union as avidly as her husband.

In many parts of Africa god is regarded as female. For instance, in the Niger delta the chief divinity is a mother with many breasts. She is the tutelary spirit of the city of Ibadan in Nigeria. Eighty years ago a European resident of the town reported that when the chiefs were asked what emblem they would like to figure on medals with which they were to be honored, they unanimously selected the image of this goddess. Today there is still an annual festival for the goddess, held at the time when the land is driest and there is much need for rain. Ibadan is no longer a country town. The festival is held on tarred streets and in the shade of great stores and buildings. The festive day is announced in the newspaper. But still the priest of the goddess goes to her shrine wearing his hair in braids like a woman and covering his head with a woman's turban.

And among the Igbo of Africa the Earth Goddess, Ala, is the supreme being. In neighboring Dahomey (now called Benin) the chief of the gods is the androgynous being called Mawu-Lisa—two gods in the form of one. They are closely related to a more ancient and androgynous deity which gave birth to the dual creator and then disappeared. Mawu is the female principle (Moon), associated with fertility, motherhood, and gentleness. Lisa is masculine (Sun), associated with power, war, and violence. Together they provide the rhythm of day and night and, by presenting their two natures alternately to men and to women, the divine pair express complementary elements in Dahomey life.

Among the patriarchal Hebrews, the prime religious struggle was against female deities of fertility. "Solomon's wives turned away his heart, notably towards Ashtoreth or Ishtar the goddess of Sidon, and apparently a temple for this goddess was at Jerusalem until it was defiled three centuries later by Josiah." (Parrinder) The monotheistic Hebrews detested the Goddess as an expression of paganism. When Jeremiah was carried off to Egypt he was outraged to find Jewish women there worshipping Ishtar, the Queen of Heaven. Yet the Jewish repudiation of the worship of a Mother Goddess neglected elements of their own religious history. The worship of a goddess has been documented in papyri from Elephantine, an island in the Nile in Upper Egypt, opposite Aswan. "These writings which belonged to a Jewish military colony, founded at an uncertain date, mention the worship of Yahweh but also of other gods of whom one, Anathyahbu, bore the name of the male deity Anath combined with Yahu, and this suggests that she was regarded as the spouse of Yahweh," the supreme and sole patriarchal God of Jewish monotheism. (Parrinder)

The influence of the Mother Goddess also played upon the earliest Christian veneration of Mary, not as much in lands where the patriarchal Hebrew tradition was followed, but in Asia Minor where the main divinity had long been the Great Mother of antiquity. (Grant)

The worship of all these localized forms of the Great Mother may have evolved from observations in ancient times of seemingly miraculous functions of the female's body. As Charlene Spretnak notes, "Woman's body bled painlessly in rhythm with the moon, and her body miraculously *made* people, then provided food for the young by making milk . . . A further mystery to our ancestors was the fact that woman could draw from her body both women and men."

Anthropologists have observed that males respond to these "female mysteries" with a combination of awe and envy. In many primal societies, the socializing process inclined men periodically to withdraw from the company of women, roving freely through the territory and forming the all-male bands of scavengers which eventually evolved into hunting and warring societies. The influence of the same socialization induced women to remain close to the homeland. In such a setting they became the inventors of some of the major disciplines of civilization. Through plant-gathering and the observation of seasonal rhythms, vegetative death and regeneration, as well as their observation of the synchronism of menstrual and lunar cycles, women understood the primal periodicities of nature. Out of this awareness they greatly influenced (and perhaps singlehandedly discovered) the sexual basis for the first great synthesis of religion, astrology, and science. Most importantly, women became acutely aware of their sexual distinction from other female animals. They recognized that estrus, or heat, plays no role in their lives. The noted sociologist of sex John H. Gagnon tells us that "unlike any other primates, human female sexual interest is not regulated by the hormonal inputs of the estrual cycle. Among monkeys, sexual receptivity is governed quite directly by the hormones—however, human females choose to have sex on the basis of social and psychological factors. They act sexually out of an open genetic program." (Gagnon, 1977) Human males are not sexually unique. They do not possess a sexual distinction from other primates and mammals as remarkable as that of the human female, who is quite unlike any other creature on earth. Out of the female body human sexuality originated. And from the vantage of their sexual uniqueness women were able to envision many of the essential elements that produce the specialness of human consciousness, culture, and civilization.

Through the knowledge of their own bodies women realized that the estrus of beasts restricts mating to one or two days in the month and to one or two unions for each pregnancy. But because human females do not experience estrus, a continuous sexual life is possible for them. This is a remarkable distinction of the human female. For her, sexual intercourse is not simply a means of reproduction, but an aspect of culture. As long as the mysteries of women retained their supremacy over the domination of masculine authority, women were at the center of this sexualization of culture. And the earliest mythologies support and vivify their cultural impact. It was women who humanized animal sexuality. The revolution in human sexuality that made us human resulted from evolutionary changes that occurred in the female body. As long as female sexuality remained a central impetus of the human community, women retained their role as the prime spiritual movers of humankind. The Great Mother was the dominant, worldwide myth supporting these primordial paradigms.

In these most ancient of myths about the powers of women, we are faced with an extraordinary possibility. The unique sexuality of female homo sapiens was a fundamental force in the forging of human consciousness. In this regard philosopher William Irwin Thompson makes several important observations: Human beings have a self-consciousness which emphasizes sexuality, perhaps because the origins of human consciousness are somehow related to the origins of human sexuality. Humans are far more libidinous than beasts. They do not follow biological necessities; to the contrary, they have conceptualized sexuality. And it therefore makes no sense to assume that sexual passion is the archaic heritage of our animal nature. Contrary to popular opinion, it is our passionate sexuality that is the most human and the least animalistic element of our character. Female sexuality was the model of human sexualization and the initiator of the hominization of primates. For these reasons, Thompson concludes that "she is the creature who, with a unity of mind and body, moves from the estrus cycle to the menstrual cycle

. . . The religion of the chimpanzees is animistic; the religion of humans is sexual, but out of the association of sexuality with the forces of nature, human females were to create our first religion, a religion of menstruation, childbirth mysteries, and the phases of the moon."

The reign of the Mother Goddess passed into oblivion long ago, but during her countless years of dominance she provided the foundations upon which human communities continue to exist. Despite centuries of denial and the rise of patriarchal values that contradict her influences, the impact of the Mother Goddess remains central to our mythic visions of ourselves and our world. In the words of religious historian Mircea Eliade, "every primordial image is the bearer of a message of direct relevance to the condition of humanity; for the image unveils aspects of ultimate reality that are otherwise inaccessible" —forms of knowledge that are unknowable in any but mythical metaphors. Robert Graves was so convinced of the power of the Earth Mother that he designated that power to be the prime source of poetry, insisting that the language and metaphors of the poet are bound up with the female principle rather than with the rational Apollonian patriarchal mentality by which, in Graves' view, the greatest mythology was masculinized, contaminated, and trivialized.

We are what we think we are. "Each civilization, whether it is religious or scientific, is merely an externalization of consciousness. It is, therefore, very important for our politics of knowledge and our knowledge of politics to appreciate the common foundation of myth and science." (Thompson) Werner Heisenberg made the same point when he said that we cannot have any such thing as "a science of nature"; we can only have a science of humankind's knowledge of nature.

In summary, an aspect of our humanized vision of nature is discovered in the primordial power of the female spirit, which provided the first and foremost basis for the mystification of nature. This exceptional impact of feminine mentality upon our knowledge of the world has revolutionized human history. It even seems possible that human consciousness itself was at least in part a primordial response to the unique character of female sexuality. There is also historical evidence that female mentality provided the impulse behind inventions such as agriculture, crafts, and bartering that were essential to the process of human socialization that gave rise to culture and civilization. There is also reason to believe that the sexual physiology of women and their generative capacity were the impetus behind the first mythologies devised by humankind. Such myths, in turn, gave way to worldwide rituals and ideals that shaped our first religious forms and, very possibly, influenced our first social systems. Finally, it seems that the origin of human sexuality developed out of the female condition which departs from estrus, unlike all other mammals, and thereby came into possession of a self-determination unique to homo sapiens.

Given this centrality of women in the evolution of human sexuality, human consciousness, and human culture, we must examine the circumstances which brought females down from a position of universal power to a condition of subjugation and powerlessness.

# FOUR
# The Body as Man

First came Gaia, who is the Earth. Life sprang from her mouth. Of all her children, Uranus, the starry heaven, first emerged from her body, without father or consort. Then again Earth brought forth from herself the hills where the nymphs dance and the sea where the waves swell. Then Earth lay down with her divine son, Heaven, and from their union came the first dynasty of the gods: the children called the Titans: Oceanus, Hyperion, Iapetus, Themis, Memory, Phoebe, Tethys, the one-eyed Cyclops, Rhea and her brother and husband Cronos—the youngest and most treacherous of Earth's offspring, who castrated his father and usurped his place in heaven.

This tale of treachery among the Greek gods is a considerable transformation of the same story as it relates to the Mother Goddess. It is based upon the *Theogony*, an epic usually attributed to Hesiod, although its authorship is disputed. Whoever the author may have been, the *Theogony* represents a masculinized corpus of mythology not unlike the works attributed to Homer, the culmination of a long succession of oral traditions which were probably rendered in their present epic form in the later eighth century B.C. These tales compose the fantastic male mythology which gave shape and substance to the Western world.

According to this ancient epic, Cronos and his Titanic sister-wife Rhea founded the second dynasty of the deities, the Olympic gods who ruled over a time of perfection called the Golden Age. One of the offspring of Cronos and Rhea was the most ambitious of the gods. His name was Zeus. Cronos was eventually overthrown by the same treachery by which he had overthrown his own father. He attempted to evade a prophecy that he would be dethroned by a son greater than himself by swallowing each of his children at birth. After five of his progeny had perished, his wife, the again-pregnant Mother Goddess Rhea, escaped to the island of Crete where she gave birth to Zeus. When Rhea returned to her husband, she gave him a stone wrapped in swaddling clothes, and he swallowed it in the belief that it was his son.

When Zeus grew to maturity, he emerged from hiding and overcame his father, forcing him to vomit up his five siblings (Poseidon, Hades, Demeter, Hestia, and Hera) as well as the stone, which became known as *Omphalos*, "the navel stone of the earth." This mysterious stone, which had helped to save the life of the child of the Mother Goddess, was eventually placed in the sacred place of women known as Delphi, where the sun god Apollo would one day fight a crucial battle against the primordial powers of the Earth Goddess. For now, however, there was still harmony among the gods and goddesses. Women retained their ancient place as the givers of life and sustenance. But it was during this mythic time that the relationship of women to the formative elements of society began to shift drastically as the deity of an invading patriarchal people swept over the ancient world.

This warlike god, so familiar to us in Greek mythology, was not native to the Hellenic world but was brought in to Greece by these invaders. He was then named Zeus and integrated into Greek myth as if he had always been a central deity. Zeus was insinuated by his devotees into the pantheon of the most powerful of women, Gaia and Rhea. With this drastic revision of the oldest myths of the Aegean, Gaia and Rhea were now reduced to the status of consorts, consenting to a situation that was anathema to their matricentric world. Zeus was allowed to rule over all the gods—his luminous Olympian siblings as well as his dark and earthy ancestors, the Titans. And so it was that Zeus's Silver Age came into existence, giving shape and substance to most of the fundamental attitudes of the West that we now accept as reality.

The war between the ancient matricentric and new patricentric mentality was fought out in the world of myth. In heaven the new gods had wrenched power away from women. But on the earth itself there was no creature in whom the spirit of the gods resided. When the Titan Prometheus was born he became the first being in the form of a man, and he came down to earth. He was a child of the Mother Goddess, so he possessed a secret unknown to Zeus. He knew that the seed of heaven lay sleeping in the earth, under the mantle of Gaia. So he took some clay into his hands and moistened it with river water, kneading it until it was shaped into the image of the gods. The goddess Athene was fascinated when she discovered what this son of the Titans had made, and so she breathed the divine breath of life into the earth-wrought figure, and it rose up and became mankind.

The gods in heaven took notice of these newly created males and agreed to be their protectors as long as they paid them homage. And so, in the ancient place called Mecone, mortals and immortals sat together upon an appointed day to determine the duties and rights of men. To protect them from being overburdened by the demands of the gods, Prometheus came forth as their counsel. And he was wise and reasonable, until his devotion to the Mother Goddess overcame him and he became obsessed with the notion of playing a trick upon the great Zeus. This prank was a harmless joke, but the supreme god would not endure such an offense. To punish Prometheus for his knavery, he withheld the gift of fire from the mortals that Prometheus had fashioned from clay. But Prometheus could not abide the punishment. He rose toward the sun and ignited a torch from the heavens and gave it to men. Again Zeus thundered with anger. When he saw the campfires of mortals glowing on the distant earth, the supreme god of Olympus ordered the fire god, Hephaestus, to forge a figure in the shape of a beautiful young woman. The fabrication of this new human being clearly represented the ultimate destruction of the power of females. Hesiod made no secret about the extent of this deformation of women: "And wonder took hold of the deathless gods and mortal men when they saw that which was sheer guile, not to be withstood by men. For from her is the deadly race and tribe of women who live amongst mortal men to their great trouble."

How should we read this strategic turn of mythic events? From the viewpoint of the new Greek pantheon the message is clear: Zeus punished man by creating an evil thing called woman as the price of fire. It is in this way that the heroic Olympian gods deformed and demoted the power of the Great Goddess. As for Prometheus, for his complicity in perpetuating the reign of the Mother Goddess and for protecting the Earth's clay-wrought human children, Zeus had him bound to a rock, where each day an eagle tore wounds in his belly and devoured his liver, which grew again each night.

Now Zeus ruled the heavens and earth. But there was no peace between the new gods and the primordial goddesses. Ultimately the antagonism of two opposing world views became the basis of strife between the new gods of Mount Olympus and the old, titanic gods of Mount Othrys. This monumental war was the most important moment in the Doric mythology of the Greeks, which eventually subdued the Mother Goddess and gave birth to the Western world view. Its metaphors are so forceful that we cannot fail to read into them the utter collapse of a matricentric realm that had dominated world communities for countless millennia.

Zeus and the Olympians battled the Titans for ten years. With the unexpected allegiance of Gaia and her monstrous children, the Cyclops and Hecatoncheires, the Titans were eventually defeated and sent to Tartarus, the lower depths of the underworld. Once victorious, Zeus treacherously dismissed Gaia, and his control of heaven and earth was secure.

With this betrayal of Gaia and the supremacy of Zeus came the final submergence of the rule of the Mother Goddess. The symbols of this defeat are fortified by two mythic events. As already noted, for giving men the gift of fire Zeus bound Prometheus to a rock, and he also punished the creatures of Prometheus by creating women. "For woman was the greatest of evils, just as Eve too was the root of all evil." (Grant) In Hesiod's *Works and Days*, that sour view of women is elaborated by a further tale of the first woman. Here she is called Pandora, the all-giver—perhaps because she was originally an earth goddess. According to Hesiod, when Hephaestus created Pandora "into her heart he put lies and false words and treachery . . . so she might be a sorrow to the men of the earth."

The transformation of a pre-Hellenic earth goddess into such a destructive demon as Pandora provides a fascinating insight into the workings of the patriarchal

Greek mind. According to the famous myth about this first woman, all possible torments and evils, all wickedness and sorrow were contained in a box. Despite warnings not to touch the box, Pandora opened it, unleashing endless disaster upon men. Like Eve after her, it was Pandora's beguiling sexuality that allowed her to bring about the Fall. Thus Hesiod reflected the Greek attitude toward women when he wrote: "Do not allow a sweet-tongued woman to beguile you with the fascination of her body." As we shall see, this negative Greek concept of Pandora would become an essential aspect of the vision of women as the *instrumenta diaboli* which the early Christian church recapitulated until it became such a fundamental attitude in the West that it even shaped the way that artists looked upon women. For instance, the sixteenth-century painter Jean Cousin the Elder of Sens entitled his portrait of the banished Eve "Eva Prima Pandora." Thus, the power of women had been villainized. As Semonides of Samos reported in the seventh century B.C., women are "the worst single thing Zeus made for us."

For the rational and patriarchal Greeks, this unreasonable detestation of the power and, indeed, the biology of women was persistently contradicted by a lingering pre-Hellenic heritage which revered the fertility of females as a mystical and superhuman force of chaotic nature. It is this paradox of "male order" and "female chaos" that is persistently repeated and reshaped in Greek mentality and that eventually provided one of the central tensions of the Western mind. So strong was this contradiction of attitudes toward women that even the complete patriarchal revision of classical Greek cosmology and mythology could not entirely eradicate the mysteries of women from the Hellenic world. Thus in a Homeric hymn, otherwise obsessed with masculine aggression, the poet speaks of the universal Mother—eldest of all things. "All creatures that dwell in the sea, all things that fly or that creep upon the ground, all such beings are thine."

In short, the Greeks worshipped the universal fecundity of the Great Mother at the same time that they reviled women. This love-hate attitude about women—the awe of their creative powers and the fear of their influence upon the young—gave enormous energy to the Greeks' dogged efforts to dethrone females from their pre-Hellenic domestic leadership and religious authority. It is a slander so persistent, but also so subtle, that it provides much of the impetus and tension in the celebrated literature of the Greeks. In drama and in epic poetry, time and again the spirit of women is belittled or ignored. This endlessly repeated metaphor of the decline, disgrace, and fall of women has a transparency that reveals the tension of the masculine Greek mind. As we shall see, some of the supreme tragic elements of Attic drama emerge from tales of the defeat of exceptionally strong and willful women. This patriarchal usurping of primordial, matricentric myth represents nothing less than a mythological conspiracy.

This long psycho-mythic struggle against the telluric mother/nature powers is described in a succession of myths of such heroes as Bellerophon, Heracles, Theseus and Perseus, Oedipus and Orestes, as well as Apollo at Delphi. The prototype of this battle between feminine and masculine principles, goddess and god, disorder and order, nature and the city (*polis*) is the famous confrontation between the whirlwind serpent-monster Typhoeus (or Typhon) and Zeus.

According to this tale, Zeus could not be supreme until he had overcome the chaotic nature force which the Titans represented, vanquishing their power of disorder so that enlightenment should prevail. To do this Zeus had to defeat the serpent, the youngest child of the Earth Goddess Gaia and Tartarus. That child was named Typhoeus, and he was a dreadful creature, with a feathered body and great wings. The classical account of Zeus's victory over Typhoeus dramatically describes a metaphorical contest between chaos and order. To read this myth in terms of our discussion of the Greek attitude about women, it is necessary to realize that to the Hellenic mind Zeus was envisioned as the enemy of chaos. He is depicted as a hero who defends the gods against savage upheaval, which is identified with women and their "monstrous" offspring. Thus we are told that the immense body of Typhoeus was half person and half snake. (The serpent, that sheds its skin, is associated with the regenerative powers of women.) He was so enormous that his head touched the stars and his arms extended from sunrise to sunset. According to Hesiod's account, from his shoulders rose one hundred serpent heads, all flashing their fiery tongues while flames flashed from their eyes. The description of Typhoeus as a grotesque expresses a universal bias often used to depict an enemy. But it is not his hideousness that is the reason for the urgency of the defeat of Typhoeus. What is most fearsome is the monster's potential for political power. As Hesiod explained: "This monster would have become the master of the world had not Zeus defeated him in combat."

Joseph Campbell (1964) retells the tale with his characteristic vigor: "Beneath the feet of the father of the gods Olympus shook as the monster Typhoeus moved, the earth groaned; and from the lightning of his bolt, as well as from the eyes and breath of his antagonist, fire was bursting over the dark sea. The ocean boiled; towering waves beat upon all promontories of the coast; the ground quaked; Hades, lord of the dead, trembled; and even Zeus himself, for a time, was unstrung. But when he had summoned again his strength, gripping his terrific weapon, the great hero sprang from his mountain and, hurling the bolt, set fire to all those flashing, bellowing, roaring, baying, hissing heads. The monster crashed to earth, and the Earth Goddess Gaia groaned beneath her child. The corpse burst into flames. And then the mighty king of the gods, Zeus, prodigious in storming wrath, heaved the victim into gaping Tartarus—whence to this day there pour forth from his titan form all those winds that blow terribly across seas and bring to mortal men distress, scatter shipping, drown sailors, and ruin the beloved works of dwellers on the land with storm and dust."

It was this victory which secured the reign of the patriarchal gods of Mount Olympus over the earlier Titan broods of the Great Mother Goddess.

The tale of Zeus and Typhoeus also anticipates the account of another contest. This time, however, the confrontation is between the sun god Apollo and the she-serpent Python (or Typhon). It draws its prototype from the confrontation of Zeus and Typhoeus on Mount Etna, but Apollo's victory was won at Delphi, at the foot of Mount Parnassus.

Today we associate Delphi and its famous oracle with the splendor of Apollo, but long before Delphi was Apollo's it was Gaia's. The Greek playwright Aeschylus suggests that the transition of power from Gaia to Apollo was a peaceful revolution, but, as Carl Olsen notes in his essay on the goddess, "Hesiod and the Homeric hymn to Apollo present a more violent struggle. Python was slain by Apollo to make possible his usurpation of the oracle . . . The establishment of the Olympian order was a revolution . . . Within the hierarchy thereafter ruled by Zeus (especially in Homer's accounts) the goddesses clearly become subordinated divinities. Aphrodite, who in Hesiod is recognized to be generations older than Zeus, is in the

*Odyssey* represented as the daughter of Zeus and Diana. Even Athene, whose stature is less diminished, is made into a goddess entirely dependent on male power, proud to be motherless, Zeus's parthenogenetic creation. The goddesses are not only subordinated to the gods, they are defined as being in their very essence related to men, each in a very particular way: Hera is wife, Athene is father's daughter, Aphrodite is the responsive beloved, Artemis is she who shuns men. Thus they are represented from the perspective of male psychology." This turning point in the domination of masculine attitude among the Greeks is manifested in the archetypical myth of the victory of Zeus over Typhoeus which makes symbolically possible the transference of the oracle of Delphi from Gaia to Apollo.

Located on the Greek mainland, Delphi was ruled by a serpent and a prophetic priestess who served Gaia. The she-snake, Python, dwelled in the *omphalos*, the navel-stone shrine named, as you recall, after the stone that Rhea gave Cronos and which he devoured in the belief that it was his infant son Zeus. The shrine at Delphi was said to be built underground in the shape of a beehive. Apparently, the name "Delphi" derives from "Delphyne," a reference to the great snake often associated with the Mother Goddess in the mythology of the Mediterranean. As militant feminist Monica Sjoo points out, at Malta the goddess was known as Delphyne, since her form was partially that of a serpent, and the name comes from an ancient word, *delphys*, meaning "womb." The female domination at shrines such as the one at Delphi clearly was of the most ancient origin. By comparison, Apollo, the patriarchal sun god of the Greeks, was something of a mythological upstart. His origin is uncertain, although it is believed that he came to the Doric Greeks from Asia by way of Asia Minor. At first he may have been a god of herdsmen. Eventually he became the central symbol of the Hellenic idealization of Greek spirit. But Apollo could not rule at Delphi until he had slain the sacred serpent (Python), just as Zeus before him had to kill Typhoeus in order to triumph over the Earth Goddess.

The significance of this narrative is of great importance to our reading of the myths that shaped the Greek mind. "Whether we think of the victories of Zeus and Apollo, Theseus, Perseus, Jason, and the rest, over the dragons of the Golden Age, or turn to that of Yahweh over Leviathan, the lesson is equally of a self-moving power greater than the force of any earthbound serpent destiny. All stand (to use Jane Harrison's phrase) 'first and foremost as a protest against the worship of Earth and the daimones of the fertility of Earth.' " (Campbell, 1964)

It is said that Python was created by Hera out of anger for Zeus, who had by himself given birth to Athene. So Hera parthenogenetically created the she-serpent Python from the slime of the primordial deluge which had occurred during the Iron Age of Greek mythological history. This flood had swept a great river of mud against Mount Parnassus, and here at the foot of the mountain, where the shrine of Delphi is located, Python was born. She nested near the flower-filled spring of the shrine. According to some Greek writers, this she-serpent was a plague to humankind, having kept the secret of fertility to herself, which is a fault often attributed to women by men who are threatened by the female's generative powers.

It is uncertain just how Python died, but in most versions of the myth, she was mortally wounded by Apollo with his sun-arrows, which, of course, are symbols of "male" enlightenment and order. Then he took over the oracular shrine at Delphi. Yet, true to the Greek love-hate of women, even after the Earth Mother, the original deity of the oracle, was overwhelmed by the Greek sun god, only women were allowed to prophesy there.

Despite a variety of versions of the confrontation of Apollo and Python, it is clear that the story represents the ritualization of an essential Greek concept: Women are the embodiment of untamed nature, and nature represents chaos and disorder. Men, on the other hand, embody the values of enlightenment and order. Thus the sun god Apollo defeats the moon serpent and vanquishes nature so that reason may prevail. For the Greeks, such a transference of power was profoundly important. It paved the symbolic way to civilization and the *polis*. For them the word *agrios* ("savage") designated that barbarous and bestial realm outside civilization.

This vision of the ferociousness of women as embodiments of dark powers, of irrationality, of the chaotic and savage forces of nature (as Nature itself) is constantly repeated as a fact of life in the literature of the Greeks. Subsequently, it became so fundamental an element in our own Western consciousness that we usually read the works of Homer, Hesiod, Aeschylus, Sophocles, and Euripides without noticing that they brilliantly recount history as a vast slander against women.

Here is a typical example of this literary tradition. The trilogy called *Oresteia* by Aeschylus deals with the bloody succession of crimes and their retribution in the royal house of Atreus. The action commences before the beginning of the first play, *Agamemnon*, when Atreus kept his brother Thyestes from the throne of Argos. In *Agamemnon* Thyestes's son Aegisthus and the wife of Agamemnon, Clytemnestra, murder king Agamemnon and seize his throne. In the second play, *Choephoroe*, the son of Agamemnon avenges his father's murder by slaying his mother Clytemnestra and her lover Aegisthus. In the final play of the trilogy, *Eumenides*, the blood

vengeance ends when a newly instituted court acquits
the son of his crime.

This is the mere outline of the tragedies. At least, that was
the outline we used to be taught in school. But recent
scholars have taken a closer look at the text and discovered elements that were previously overlooked or ignored. The trilogy deals with a hereditary curse. Pelops's
two sons Thyestes and Atreus murder their stepbrother
and flee to Mycenae where they attain power and afflu-
ence. A blood feud inflames their animosity and they
become deadly enemies. Then Thyestes seduces Atreus'
wife. Pretending to be reconciled with Thyestes, Atreus
kills his brother's sons and feeds them to their father—a
deed so terrible that the sun hides its face in torment.
From these terrible events, the two branches of the house
of Atreus inherited the enmity and curse that are the
basis of the trilogy of Aeschylus.

Agamemnon has joined the siege of Troy in order to
regain the abducted Helen. But, as Aeschylus proclaims,
Helen was an evil temptress, and it was an indignity that
young men were slaughtered in a war for an evil woman's
sake. Thus the Pandora motif of the dreadful female who
causes misfortune is one of the major undercurrents
of those myths dramatized by Aeschylus. This attitude
toward women prevails throughout the plays, for the playwright wrote lines for the chorus that consistently express
loyalty to Agamemnon, condemning the waywardness of
the beautiful Helen and lamenting the cost of the war in
the blood of young men. But the chorus also elaborates
on the horror of the sacrifice of Iphigenia, the first-born
child of Agamemnon and Clytemnestra. It seems that the
Greek navy could not further its campaign against Troy
because of ill winds. Agamemnon and his brother Menelaus
are told by the prophet Calchas that to have favorable
winds Agamemnon must sacrifice his own daughter

Iphigenia. He lures her to his camp and sacrifices her on the altar of Artemis merely to satisfy his political ambitions, for without her death the army under his command could not sail to Troy. Eventually Agamemnon returns to Mycenae, and with him he brings his Trojan concubine Cassandra, ordering his wife Clytemnestra to provide her with lavish hospitality. Clytemnestra does nothing to betray her rage. She receives him as a conquering hero, with a pretense of cordiality. She beguiles him and flatters his pride as she leads him to his bath. Once he is naked and submerged in the hot water, she entangles him in a net and axes him to death. Cassandra, who senses her doom, willingly enters the palace knowing that she is fated to die with Agamemnon.

Aegisthus appears and gloats over these events, and the chorus is enraged. When her cowardly lover retreats from the angry crowd, the powerful Clytemnestra steps forward and overwhelms the people with her passionate renunciation of Agamemnon. She insists that she was the victim of fate and the instrument of a blood curse that is ruled by the eternal law of retribution. She insists that she had the right to kill the man who dared to sacrifice her daughter.

"Did he not do a terrible crime against this house? For the thing he did he needed to die or fate would have cried out against its undoing. From his seed this child sprang. She was the flower I bore, my long-wept Iphigenia. His death was a worthy deed for a dreadful sin. Proud man! Will he boast in hell of what he did? It does not matter, for the score is settled at last. He has paid, as he sinned, with death."

Clearly, in Clytemnestra we still hear the voice of the Mother Goddess, outraged by the male vanity that sacrificed the life of her child in order to win political favor. But the Doric Greeks could not permit Clytemnestra's triumph. She would have to be brought down, even if it required a fundamental transformation of the creeds that had governed societies for millennia. So the blood curse is not yet finished. Clytemnestra and her lover Aegisthus are eventually murdered with the same ax the queen used to kill her husband. Clytemnestra's daughter, the masculinized Electra, crazed with grief for her beloved father's fate, induced her brother, Orestes, to slay their own mother, a crime so great in the realm of the goddesses that its implications still resound in our psyches. Maddened by his horrendous crime, Orestes flees, pursued by the Furies, whose mission it is to slay those who murder their parents. Ultimately, Orestes is tried by a court assembled by Athene, with twelve Athenian males as his judges. It is in this court that the essential creed of the goddesses is replaced by a new patriarchal mentality. The sun god Apollo, who defeated the earth-empowered serpent Python, now speaks in behalf of the murderer of his mother, Orestes, asserting, against the arguments of the Erinyes, that it is the father, not the mother, who is a child's true parent.

"The mother is not the parent of the child, only the nurse of what she had born. The parent is the father, who commits his seed to her."

The implication of the patricentric mentality signaled by this proclamation is so inescapable that we cannot fail to see in it the total depreciation of the generative powers of women and the consequent demotion of their cultural and political status.

The Athenian court acquits Orestes. As classical Greek scholar Michael Grant notes, this decision is not "just a blow [in behalf of] the rather unattractive Greek cause of male supremacy; it has a deeper national significance as well. Orestes is vindicated by an appeal to patriotic feeling. For the court which is given the glory of ending the vendetta is the court of the Areopagus, the Athenian Hill of Ares, going back to the days of the ancient monarchy." What Aeschylus is really saying here is that the court's authority is a mirror of the laws of heaven. Thus the climax of the *Oresteia* demonstrates the decline of the laws of the earth-bound matriarchal system which had been taken over by a newer form of social organization brought into Greece by the patriarchal people who spoke an Indo-European language. The drama's cultural and sexual implications are clear: The enraged Furies, deprived of their revenge for the murder of a mother by her son, exclaim: "These new gods have violated the laws of ancient days and torn them from our hands!"

It is the sacrifice of Iphigenia and the acquittal of Orestes that have become the focus of much of the debate about the meaning of both the myth and the drama of Aeschylus. In her revisionist tales of goddesses and heroines, Patricia Monaghan tells us that "this complicated cycle of killings and revenge murders express, some interpreters claim, the social upheaval in the Greek city-states when the era of mother right ended and the patriarchal family was established as the base of society. Under a matriarchal system, Clytemnestra acted intelligibly, if brutally, meting out death to her child's killer. Under the new patriarchal system, Clytemnestra's children acted correctly by destroying their father's murderer. Those who favor this interpretation of the myth cite the end of Aeschylus' *Oresteia*: Clytemnestra's son, pursued by the matriarchal [Furies], is absolved of his mother's murder by the supporters of the patriarchy."

The same dramatic issues found in the *Oresteia* are at the center of another Greek tragedy: the *Antigone* of Sophocles. A brief retelling of the plot will assist our interpretation.

Antigone and Ismene are the daughters of the incestuous king of Thebes, Oedipus, who has been vanquished from his domain. Thebes is besieged as the result of the rivalry of the two sons of the king, each of whom wishes to have sole rule in place of their deposed father. The two men slay one another in single combat. Now, in the opening scene of the tragedy, Antigone tells her sister that their uncle King Creon has decreed that only one of the brothers, Eteocles, who was defending Thebes, may receive the rites of burial; while the corpse of Polyneices must be left to the birds of prey on the plain where he fell. Creon further decrees that the penalty is death for anyone who attempts to bury Polyneices. This expression of civic authority sets up the tension which will bring Antigone to a tragic destiny.

Antigone pits herself against this powerful edict, refusing to obey an order which she believes to be both impious and ruthless. Antigone is determined to return her brother's body to the embrace of the earth. Her lover, the son of Creon, begs her not to disobey the law, but Antigone will not be dissuaded from what she believes. She risks death to cover the corpse. When she is captured, she defends herself with passionate brilliance, but Creon condemns her to be buried alive. Now the blind prophet Tiresias comes forward with a terrible warning for the king. "All the altars of the city are defiled with the mire of dogs and birds that have torn at the flesh of that fallen son of king Oedipus. So great is this offense against the earth that the gods will not hear us. The song of the birds no longer contains a message, for the fowl of the air have gorged themselves upon the dead man's blood."

Creon is unmoved by the prophet's warning. "Know that you shall not trade on my resolve," he stubbornly insists.

Tiresias declares: "Then know you, and know it well, that before many more races of the sun's swift chariot, a child of your own shall become a corpse among corpses. This terrible fate is yours because you have thrust children of the daylight into the shadows. You have sent the living to the grave while the dead remain unburied, unhonored, all unhallowed."

In fear, Creon decides to be swayed by the prophet, and he sets out for the plain to bury Polyneices and to set Antigone free. But the fateful mistake cannot be undone. After burning the remains of Polyneices, Creon discovers that Antigone is dead by her own hand. Her lover, Haemon, embraces her corpse and will not come away with his father Creon. "The boy's eyes were filled with rage as he looked at his father. He spat in his face and drew his sword, but Creon escaped the flashing blade. In rage at his failure to slay his father, the unhappy boy shouted and fell upon his weapon."

When she hears these words from a messenger, Creon's wife, Eurydice, turns silently into the palace and stabs herself.

"Creon: Unwittingly I am killer of both son and wife. No help is there for me. I am nothing. I have no life. Lead me away."

Here the play ends.

*Antigone* lends itself to wide interpretation. Hegel saw the dramatic conflict as one between woman defending the family and man supporting the state. Michael Grant claims that "the theme is collision between individuals and their political rulers—between private conscience and public authority." Polish critic and theater historian Jan Kott believes that "her loyalty to the dead has alienated her from the community of the living. In the epilogue of the tragedy, Creon comes onstage with his son's corpse in his arms. In a moment his wife will commit suicide. The arguments of practical reason have alienated him from all ties of blood."

Most scholars grant that behind the confrontation of Creon and Antigone is a Greek belief in what Aristotle called "a universal law of Nature." This law of nature was different from the laws legislated by the *polis*—by society. Antigone championed "unwritten laws," which she insisted represented a judgment more universal than those laws that exist at a specific time and place. "But all your power is nothing against those immortal unwritten laws of heaven," she tells Creon. "They are not simply now. They were and they shall be forever—deeply felt but beyond man's utterance."

As Grant notes, what drives Antigone's decision to challenge Creon is not only her love and loyalty to a brother, but also her revelation that human actions must reflect both passionate belief and objective reason. Creon, on the other hand, speaks for the world, the state, and expediency. His case is reasonable, respectable, and important. But his conception of duty is lower than Antigone's. They use the same words but mean very different things, and ultimately Antigone, the woman of a compassion born of nature, makes the most impressive statement of her case. As for Creon, his flaw is his machismo—his masculine pride. Even among the patriarchal Greeks, pride—or *hubris*—was a severely criticized flaw of character. "Creon has a powerful sense of order, but with that special, classic *hubris* which makes important men do wrong he tries to correct a moral standard over which he has no control . . . what Creon saw as justice, in Sophocles' view, was pride." (Grant)

The tension in *Antigone* between an individual and a community, between reasonable law and passionate belief, between loyalty to the dead or to the living are vivid and valid themes of the tragedy, but there is another impulse that vivifies the drama. In many works of Greek literature, women are not only property and sexual objects but also symbols of otherness, of the unknown. They are active metaphors of the mysteries of nature; so it is not surprising that a powerful dramatic figure like Antigone should speak in behalf of the mysterious, unrecorded laws that arise from nature itself. As such, Antigone emerges as a character from the brooding underworld of matricentric myth, taking form in a drama that flows freely between the *polis* of consciousness and the personification of the unconscious.

Classics professor Charles Segal has written brilliantly about this vision of women in his interpretation of one of the most perplexing and startling tragedies of classical Greece, *The Bacchae* by Euripides. "More closely connected than the male members of the *polis* to the biological processes of natural life, to birth, growth, and change, [women] are most closely associated with Dionysus as a god of vital energies and also more closely associated with the release of repressed emotionality that he embodies. In their direct participation in the creation of life, they not only are closer to nature, but they also challenge the yearning for autonomy, for the timeless, for immortality and transcendence that characterizes male creations in the *polis,* the ageless works of plastic or verbal art, the deathless fame of the great heroes. Embodying the otherness of nature in its closest proximity to human life, women stand between culture and nature. They are part of the city, but they also have a closeness to something beyond the city and potentially destructive of it . . . they are destroyers and devourers of the king."

*The Bacchae* is a deeply religious play, created out of the very essence of primordial Greek experience by a nonreligious playwright who, for a lifetime, was outspoken in his hostility to the Olympian deities. Translator of the play William Arrowsmith notes that "*The Bacchae* is finally a mysterious, almost a haunted, work, stalked by divinity and that daemonic power of necessity which for Euripides is the careless source of man's tragic destiny and moral dignity. Elusive, complex and compelling, the play constantly recedes before one's grasp, advancing, not retreating, steadily into deeper chaos and larger order, coming finally to rest only god knows where—which is to say, where it matters."

The subject of the play is derived from history: the invasion of Hellas by the frenetic rites of Dionysus. The story of King Pentheus of Thebes is Euripides' ritualization of a myth. Behind the events of the play is a series of revolutionary events that cause great social turmoil in all of Greece. Those events are particularized in the city of Thebes and in the confrontation of King Pentheus and the god Dionysus.

At first, the king refuses to receive Dionysus or his religious followers in the city. When they nevertheless make their way into Thebes, King Pentheus imprisons the worshippers of Dionysus. These actions are dramatizations of the century-long resistance to the new religion, which eventually led to a time when Dionysus became the god of all the Thebans. As Cadmus, the former king of Thebes, explains to the confused and fearful people in the Euripides play, "the whole city fell under the Bacchic rage."

This much of the story is a vague reflection of actual events. The invasion of the religion of Dionysus, however, is only the superficial focus of the play. It is not about that revolution. "Dionysiac religion is the field on which the action of the play takes place, *not* what it is deeply about." (Arrowsmith)

What the play is about is religious intoxication. And that "uncivilized" and earthy kind of passionate faith is clearly an echo of the suppressed rites of the Mother Goddess.

Dionysus (or Bacchus) is the son of Zeus and of the mortal Semele. Disguised in human form he returns to his native Thebes from a pilgrimage in Asia, where he established his dances, mysteries, and rites. His return is prompted by his determination to end the slander of his dead mother by her envious sisters, one of whom is Agave, the mother of King Pentheus of Thebes. These women have denied that Zeus is Dionysus' father. Because of this insult Dionysus has enchanted the women, and they have become crazed with his power, and are cavorting and wandering in a stupor on Mount Cithaeron. King Pentheus has also refused to acknowledge the divinity of Dionysus, and the enraged god declares that before he is done the king and every other person of Thebes will be forced to recognize him as a god.

This threat means nothing to the king. He becomes all the more determined to put an end to the wild rites that celebrate Dionysus and to imprison the religious fanatics, the Bacchantes. King Pentheus is enraged to learn that all the women of Thebes have gone mad and left the city for the mountain, where they are drunkenly dancing in honor of the god.

Pentheus decides to arm all the men of the city and to march against the women on their sacred mountain. But the disguised god Dionysus persuades the king that in order to guarantee the success of his invasion he must dress as a woman. "What is this?" he asks. "Will I then pass from man to woman?" And Dionysus replies, "Yes, lest they kill you, if you are seen there as a man."

Dressed in a gown, animal skins, and long blonde curls, Pentheus sets out to conquer the women and put down the revelers of Dionysus. But, as Segal notes, "these women are 'unconquerable by force' . . . because Pentheus' illusion of strength, as of sanity, masks his underlying weakness, much as his authoritarian exterior masks an uncertain and unstable identity that the god can easily sway from warrior to woman, from claims of hypermasculinity to feminization."

On the mountain, the disguised Pentheus climbs a tree in order to observe the rites of the women. His own mother, crazed by the intoxication of the ritual, sees her son and, believing him to be a wild beast, she slaughters him. In wild jubilation and frenzy the women descend upon his corpse and devour it.

This startling plot is a perfect embodiment of what has been aptly called the *irresistible irrational*; those "things utterly non-human and non-moral," in the words of Cambridge classicist Gilbert Murray, "which bring man bliss or tear his life to shreds without a break in their own serenity." King Pentheus, like Creon and Agamemnon, is doomed because he fails to recognize the irresistible nature of the irrational elements of the unconscious; those impulses that Carl Jung called "the shadow side" of human mentality. The Greeks persistently suffered with the contradiction of their Apollonian order and reason, on the one hand, and, on the other hand, their fascination with the disorder and irrationality of Dionysus. Traditionally, as *The Bacchae* demonstrates, they ascribed to women the realm of spontaneity and madness. The Dionysian cult gave women a power and importance that were otherwise denied them in fifth-century Athens. In the masculine Greek mind, Dionysus released the emotional violence associated with women and gave it "a formalized place in ritual, a ritual not of the *polis* but of the wild, particularly in the *oreibasia*, the revel on the mountains where those emotional energies, repressed in the city, could have full play . . . In setting women and Dionysus together against the king and his rigid definition of the city, *The Bacchae* forms a kind of quintessential tragedy, a distillation of the conflict between human power and human impotence and of the contradictory movements between reason and the irrational in our ability to understand ourselves . . . For *The Bacchae* is not only about the god of ecstatic religion, wine, and madness; it is also about the god of tragedy and about the 'Dionysiac' in its relation to artistic illusion and artistic truth." (Segal)

The play explores elements of the feminine which were largely repressed in ancient Greece. In dealing with the roots of art and myth, it also deals with the aesthetic and religious free passage between what the rationalistic Greeks saw as the irreconcilability of the unconscious and the conscious. *The Bacchae* ritualizes that passage in the form of those symbolic powers of women long lost under the social strictures of patriarchal mentality. The play is exceptional in its dealings with a myth of origins that relates equally to the sources of art and imagination as well as the evolution in Greece of the irrational aspects of the Dionysian cult. As such, the dramatic action of Euripides' *The Bacchae* depicts women as having a subversive influence on Greek thought.

The sexual inferences of the play are both subtle and powerful. By the fifth century, the once heroically masculine Dionysus, male child of the supreme male deity Zeus, had been transformed into an effeminate beardless youth in women's clothes. At the climax of the drama, it is Pentheus—and not the female revelers—who is envisioned as a beast. He is hunted and killed by the women whom he set out to destroy. And, finally, his limbs are devoured by those "dangerous female powers" he hoped to tame and to subjugate. As Segal remarks, "Euripides seems to be drawing on a widespread cultural representation of the passage of male adulthood, wherein being hunted, devoured, caught in the wild, trapped by a powerful maternal figure, and resorting to guile [a female disguise] rather than force are all homologous expressions of failed passage."

Euripides uses this intensely vulnerable aspect of Hellenic masculinity as a tragic force, setting patriarchal King Pentheus of the orderly city against the overwhelming Dionysian powers of nature, even to the extent that he makes the king's own mother both a celebrant in the intoxicating cult and the assassin of her own son. Like the Creon of *Antigone,* Pentheus is a rational despot who regards the *polis* and its civil laws as the ultimate good. "He sees himself as the self-appointed champion not only of males against females but of Greeks against barbarians." (Segal)

As for Dionysus, his role in Greek life is even more complex. In his birth from Zeus's "immortal fire" and "male womb," the Greeks used Dionysus to act out, in Segal's view, "a fantasy of the male's independence from the female cycle of menstruation and birth, with their attendant uncleanness, and achieves that independence from the female which recurs wishfully throughout early Greek literature."

These re-readings of some of the major classics of Greek literature make it clear that the domination of masculine values in Hellenic mentality was never able entirely to eradicate the primordial powers of the Mother Goddess. Though the heroic attitudes and actions of these strong women were persistently denigrated by a masculine revision, and though they were usually treated as "aliens" with disordered minds and wild natures, the male fascination with such otherness persisted at the center of Greek mythology and its ritualization as theater.

As I have already pointed out, the authority of women was given over to a feminized male earth spirit, Dionysus, whose impact on Greek mentality was so complex that it remains today a major subject of speculation by psycho-analytic scholars. For the Greeks, the tension between order and chaos, nature and reason, civilization (*polis*) and barbarism, male and female, was a major source of self-examination. The dread of women was built into the foundations of Greek culture. This phobia resulted in a conflict of gender identity so great that it expressed itself in a form of masculine socialization that made the male a subject of adoration by males. The ramification of this idealization of men resulted in the inevitable masculine comradery and homoeroticism that typified Hellenic society. As Foucault (1985) points out, the primary object of sexual interest for a Greek male was another male, specifically an adult free man. "The second included women, of course, but women made up only one element of a much larger group that was sometimes referred to as a way of designating the objects of possible pleasure: 'women, boys, slaves.' "

This so-called bisexuality, however, was not a result of gender ambiguity (as it is in other non-Western cultures). It was built upon the Greek ideal of beauty and pleasure. "We can talk about their 'bisexuality,' thinking of the free choice they allowed themselves between the two sexes, but for them this option was not referred to a dual, ambivalent, and 'bisexual' structure of desire. To their way of thinking, what made it possible to desire a man or a woman was simply the appetite that nature had implanted in man's heart for 'beautiful' human beings, whatever their sex might be." (Foucault, 1985)

What we have here is not the ambiguity of sexuality that we've discussed in relation to non-Western cultures, in which sexual preference is not a major moral issue. In ancient Greece a form of homoeroticism evolved out of quite the opposite condition: an emphasis upon the differences between the sexes, and, specifically, a degradation of the power of women, resulting in the same kind of alienation between the sexes that I have already described as the basis of strongly heterosexual social groups that place high priority on the separateness of men and women and, as such, build a massive barrier between them. Societies that do not value women are strongly sexist, designating females as sexual property and as objects unworthy of love. The fact that such societies are heterosexual or homosexual is beside the point. Either way, they are the result of the fear of the power of women. In a strongly heterosexual society the antagonistic attitude of men toward women is essentially the same as it is in the homoerotic world of the Greeks. As I've already mentioned, the world of the Hadze hunters of Tanzania is divided by a social category so dominating that males and females seem to belong virtually to different species—"a division between two hostile classes, each of which is capable of organizing itself for defence or attack against the other." (Douglas, 1984) This heterosexual antagonism manifests itself in many cultures. I am thinking particularly of twentieth-century Germany and America, nations in which male self-idealization inevitably results in both a preference "to go off with the guys" and in a subtle contempt for and distrust of women as an alien species. Such machismo usually takes the form of a homoeroticism that is carefully disguised through socialization, in forms such as exclusive men's clubs, specialized male involvement in sports, stag parties, and a form of Anglo-Saxon language considered to be unsuited for what was once called "mixed company." What I am saying here is that a masculine mentality born of the fear and contempt of women manifests itself in both the idealized masculinity associated with machismo as well as the male fascination with maleness—with one's own masculinity, in the form of narcissism, and with the maleness of other men, in the form of homoeroticism.

The Greeks were less intolerant of women than they were convinced of the utter perfection of men. Much as Caucasians of America and Europe once conceived of blacks as nonhuman creatures unworthy of humane treatment, the Greeks believed that women, like slaves and non-Greeks (whom they called barbarians), were not truly human and were therefore not in possession of the divine spirit that animated free-born Hellenic males. The Greek ideal of nobility was expressed in the concept of *areté*. The aim of the upbringing and education of a young man was the development of *areté*, a word conveying a common Greek concept of virtue for which we have no precise equivalent in present-day languages. (Vanggaard) Qualities of both mind and bodily skill are the basis of *areté*. Homer spoke of a certain man who had "great *areté* in the swiftness of his feet, in his actions in battle, and in his mind." Pindar wrote of "*areté* of the fist" when celebrating the merits of a boxer. As sociologist Thorkil Vanggaard has observed, "thus we see *areté* as expressing a view of human nature quite different from ours, unaware, as the Greeks were, of the concept of a dualistic division between mind and body."

For the Greeks the supreme good was *areté*, which could be possessed only by free-born Greek men. *Areté* was a physical and temperamental idealization of males which is endlessly recapitulated in the visual arts of the Hellenic world. Nobility and high-mindedness were only one aspect of "the good," for it also included male physicality and sexuality. The gymnasium was therefore not simply a place of military training and "self-improvement." For the Greeks, it was also a center of culture. For them beauty was virtuous. Such beauty, however, was essentially a male attribute. For the Hellenes the phallus symbolized the full force of manliness, not just procreative power. This applied to gods as well as to mortals. The full force of such manliness was *areté*. Vanggaard observes that "the phallus is the symbol of *areté* with all its complexities of meanings. Apollo's power of manliness is concentrated in his phallus, and as Crimon, invoking Apollo, celebrated the pederastic act with the son of Bathycles, he transferred his *areté* to the boy through his phallus with the help of the god . . . it is the semen of the man, administered to the boy *per anum,* which is the carrier of his *areté.*"

Homoeroticism resolved and ritualized the tension of the Greeks' social attitudes about themselves and others. Their political rejection of women as barbarians—aliens without nobility or spirit—required them to submerge the power of women in a thorough revision of history and mythology. They glorified themselves in an effort to denigrate females, much the same way that Western historians once glorified whites while they ignored heroes who were Asian, Black, Hispanic, or female by writing them out of the events in which they were major characters. This kind of ethnocentricity is discovered in most cultures. Few people conceived of themselves as anything other than "a chosen people." The Greeks simply perfected this stance in relationship to all those who threatened them with their otherness. Many peoples were the brunt of their revision of history, but none as much as women. The ancient power of women was mythologically and politically their greatest threat. That paranoia is everywhere visible in Hellenic art. The delicacy of boys was admired, but effeminacy in an adult male was scorned. Passivity was identified with women and that identification carried a negative connotation. The Greeks detested but were fascinated by "the other." They built barriers between men and women, and they degraded the role of women. Therefore they could not tolerate what they conceived as the feminine sex role. As Foucault (1985) tells us: "It appears that the primary dividing line laid down by moral judgment in the area of sexual behavior was not prescribed by the nature of the act, with its possible variations, but by the activity and its quantitative gradations . . . For a man, excess and passivity were the two main forms of immorality in the practice of the *aphrodisia* . . . immoderation derives from a passivity that relates it to femininity. To be immoderate was to be in a state of nonresistance with regard to the force of pleasure, and in a position of weakness and submission; it meant being incapable of that virile stance with respect to oneself that enabled one to be stronger than oneself."

The Greek form of homoeroticism was not based upon a concept of sexuality that ignored the distinctions between men and women. To the contrary, it evolved out of a society that emphasized those distinctions and which detested effeminacy, much as "butch" homosexuals in today's America detest "queens." Ironically, in hyper-masculine societies machismo is of the utmost importance to both homosexual and heterosexual males. In social systems that place less importance on distinctions of sex, like those of many North American Indian tribes, there is a full spectrum of acceptable sexual behavior that makes the dualistic connotation of heterosexuality as opposed to homosexuality meaningless, and which therefore does not place a stigma on women who behave in a masculine manner or on men who behave in a feminine manner.

The tension in the Greek world between the Apollonian masculine ideal and the irrational and "feminine" Dionysian mode can be seen as the metaphor of a battle that persists within males of the West: a contest between feminine/

masculine, order/disorder, civilization/barbarism. That conflict, much publicized in psychiatric literature, is evident in the most disparate cultural evidence, from ancient Babylonian inscriptions to neoclassical French painting of the nineteenth century. Curiously, its most active manifestation is a dreamlike sexual paradox—an abhorrent and fascinating figure in whom the sexes are fused. The androgyne is the symbol of this ambiguity, in which the distinction and therefore the tension between male and female is metaphorically resolved. The androgyne, however, does not represent a resolution of sexual dualism in the West as it does, for instance, in the Asian concept of Yin and Yang, which are not opposites but complements of one another. To the contrary, the Western myth of the androgyne is a corruption of nature, persistently evoking reverence and awe as well as horror and scandal. It is a symbol that is both fascinating and repulsive to the Western mind. The very fact that we consider gender behavior to be absolute and sexuality to be "natural," results in our assumption that to be other than strictly male or female is to be "unnatural." We even wince at the suggestion that all human fetuses look the same and do not develop male characteristics until relatively late in gestation. So great is our obsession with gender distinctiveness that we have devised a complex moral cosmos around our sexuality, making deviation an abomination so great that for centuries it could not even be discussed by decent people, who found the idea of sexual ambiguity utterly disgusting.

Though much of our attitude evolved out of interpretations and distortions of Greek thought, and though there are many apparent similarities between our sexual attitudes and those of the Greeks, in fact, the Greeks had both a different ethic and a different psychology of sex. Perhaps their sexual mystique was haunted by a denial of the power of women (rather than a dismissal of women themselves) because they were less widely removed from the age of the Mother Goddess than we are. While we envision women as powerless, the Greeks grasped their power and recognized its threat to their patriarchal ideals. Their destruction of the power of women was not a moral but a conscious political issue, not unlike the enthusiasm with which the Christian Fathers destroyed the political influence of pre-Christian deities, priests, and priestesses. The Christians vilified their religious competitors, turning a competing people's god into their devil. But for all their moral outrage, their motives were not moral as much as political. To win power for their tribal cause and to keep their Christian deity strong, they had to steal power from another people's mythology and another people's deity. This missionary attitude was as true of the Greeks as it was of the later Christians. For the Greeks the enemy was the mythology of women and not women themselves. And they stole power from the powerful mythology of women because that mythology had worked for thousands of years among hunting and gathering peoples. In all battles of domination, the contestants villainize their enemies. But there is something in a mythology that cannot be negated. And since no militaristic or cultural victory is ever unconditional, the victors are always willing to settle for a compromise and a resulting ambiguity not unlike the symbolic androgyne, who survived as a psychic metaphor of an unwinnable battle between Apollo and Dionysus. Apollo killed Python, winning dominion of the shrine at Delphi and symbolically vanquishing the feminine forces of disorder so patriarchal "enlightenment" could prevail. But, significantly, whenever Apollo was absent, Dionysus remained forever in command at Delphi. Thus the submerged forces of nature could not be denied. Nature always lingers in metaphor, myth, and ritual even when it vanishes from consciousness. This prevalence of interest in "the wild world" helps to explain the immense fascination the French have always had for disenfranchised Spanish gypsies and that Americans have had for disinherited Indians, peoples whom they equate with untamed nature. In such metaphoric forms the chaotic and unconscious continue to have a tremendous subversive power upon us. What is true of us was also true of the Greeks. Even during their golden age, they persisted in writing about primordial goddesses and female characters whom they had utterly vanquished. In much the same way, Christians still celebrate Christmas with Yule logs and decorated sacred trees, and they commemorate Easter with rabbits and egg hunts that have absolutely nothing to do with the birth or death of Jesus Christ in the Near East. They are subversive elements of pagan Europe that survived the defeat of ancient deities and have ultimately become more powerful symbols of Christian holy days than the symbols devised by Christianity.

The homoerotic Greeks wouldn't understand our attitude about sex. For us, sexuality has a complex relationship to evil. We find a denial of sex in almost every word spoken by our God. But the Greek immortals and mortals delighted in sex as an aspect of beauty and pleasure. They did not understand the sex act as a source of evil. As noted by the Hellenic scholar K. J. Dover, "The Greeks neither inherited nor developed a belief that a divine power had revealed to mankind a code of laws for the regulation of sexual behavior; they had no religious institution possessed of the authority to enforce sexual prohibitions." For the Greeks the "problem" was not the morality of the act of sex, but the larger issue of the relationship of sex to civilization, of disorder to order, of passion to *polis*. They admired nobility and expected free men to behave according to an ethical standard that represented not god but the city—that social entity which was the matrix of the Greek ideal of civilization. They idealized men and dismissed women, yet they recognized the feminine (the Dionysian) in men, and were not entirely constricted by the Apollonian view of the world that has come to dominate Western consciousness. "This structure of consciousness," explains Jungian theorist James Hillman, "has never known what to do with the dark, material, and passionate part of itself, except to cast it off and call it Eve." Contrarily, Hellenic culture was flexible enough to institutionalize the Dionysian cult that gave to women a power and an importance that were otherwise denied to them in fifth-century Athens. "Dionysus releases the emotional violence associated with women and gives it a formalized place in ritual, a ritual not in the *polis* but in the wild, particularly in the *oreibasia*, the revel on the mountain slopes where those emotional energies, repressed in the city, can have full play." (Segal)

The ways in which these Hellenic attitudes were manifested in mythology, and the forms in which that mythology was ritualized into socially acceptable actions, represent the matrix of the Greek world. As we have seen, aspects of that mythology provided a celebration of the *arete* of men and the dismissal of the rest of humankind. Other myths provide a more affirmative vision of who we are and why we behave the way we do. In a simple story that Plato attributed to Aristophanes we have a fascinating and revealing glimpse of such a myth.

The first people of the world were entirely different from you and me. They were not tall or short—but round. And they had not one but two faces, each looking in the opposite direction. They also had four arms and four legs. What is more, the genitals of these original people came in pairs, doubly male, doubly female, or one male and one female.

This is the description of the original people of the earth found in Plato's dialogue the *Symposium,* which is set at a banquet. During that famous and fictional dinner party, a distinguished assembly of male literary guests offered recitations on the nature of love and sex. For his contribution, the comedic Greek playwright Aristophanes told a traditional Greek tale about the origin of sexuality. Unfortunately Aristophanes provided little information about the sexual practices of those mythic people. But this much we know: In the beginning there were three sexes, one entirely male, one entirely female, and also a third having the characteristics of both men and women. The unlimited amorous potential of this ancient race made them proud. So great was their arrogance that they took the liberty of insulting the gods. To their misfortune, this unbridled arrogance resulted in their downfall.

As punishment for their impudence, Zeus split each of the offenders in two. What had been whole was now splintered into halves. The once round and symmetrical people were forced to stumble about on two instead of four legs, barely able to keep their balance. They could see ahead but they could no longer see behind themselves. And, worst of all, they now possessed only one set of genitals. What is more, these forlorn creatures had an unpleasant hacked-off appearance. In short, they looked dreadful, and that would never do. After all, the Greek gods had an obsession for beauty. So they agreed that minor adjustments were required to improve the appearance of our splintered ancestors. It became Apollo's task to put things right. As a result of his artful efforts, the unsightly deformity caused by Zeus's clumsy surgery was beautified. The skin of the creatures was pulled over the amputated surface and tied in a knot which we now call the navel. The sexual organs of these transformed people were also transposed. The original position of the genitals had permitted certain sexual practices that were considerably different from those now in vogue among human beings. But after Apollo's handiwork, the genitalia were relocated at the pit of the torso, where they now exist.

Thus, Aristophanes explained, we are who we are today. "Our original body having been cut in two, each half longs for the half from which it was severed." When these yearning halves meet one another, they throw their arms around each other, in hope of growing back together again. Once they re-encounter their other halves, they cannot bear to be separated. Such is the madness of passion. "Each of us then is just the broken tally of a person, the sad result of a severance which deprives us of our wholeness." Those who were once halves of a person who was both male and female must search the world for the man or woman who was once their other half. Such men and women are lovers of people of the opposite sex. But not everyone is so inclined. A woman who was half of a female whole seeks the love of another woman and gives small regard to men. And those males who were halves of a masculine whole long for the love of men. "Originally," concludes Aristophanes, "we were whole beings, before our wickedness caused us to be split by Zeus. But we must praise the god who is the cause of this, because he gave us our chief blessing by bringing us home to our own, and if we revere the god, he will surely restore us to our happy ancient nature and heal us and make us whole again."

That ancient folktale, which Aristophanes artfully recast as a comic recitation, was far more than a source of mirth. It was a significant myth that provided the Greeks with answers to abiding riddles about human sexuality. What is desire? Why are people driven to find a mate? Why are they obsessed with their beloved and cannot endure separation? The explanations offered by the myth were quite satisfactory for the rational Greeks. As far as they were concerned, human beings are actually halves of what they once were, and it is perfectly natural that one half should look for its complementary missing half. The myth justified the compulsion of sexuality at the same time that it explained the existence of homoeroticism in a society for which male homosexuality was a commonplace.

As countless sculptures attest, for the Greeks perfection was symbolized by the male youth, a handsomely androgynous being not quite of this world. Thus Aristophanes' myth recapitulated a fundamental human response to the mysteries of human desire, and with that recapitulation it transcended the Greek world and stated the nearly universal belief that is often associated with matricentric societies: Our sexuality arose from a pristine and undifferentiated perfection—a wholeness to which we persistently wish to return. For the Greeks the androgyne was the materialization of that totality, embodying both eternity and immortality. Even for the highly masculinized Jews and Christians of a later time, the echoes of the primal myth of the Great Mother persisted in the form of her androgynous offspring. As the social historian Gonzales-Crussi points out: "Side by side with Christian orthodoxy there flourished esoteric doctrines that maintained the existence of an androgynous deity responsible for the creation of an equally androgynous first man. Controversy raged for a long time over a cryptic biblical passage: '*Elohim* created man in his image. In the image of *Elohim* he created him. Male and female he created them.' (Gen. 1:27) Gnostics, neo-Platonists, cabalists, alchemists, and assorted propounders of esoteric doctrines took this to mean that a bisexual deity had fashioned man in his image and semblance." In his *Philo-*

*sophical Dictionary* Voltaire suggested: "If god or the secondary gods created man male and female in their likeness, it would seem in that case that the Jews believed god and the gods to be males and females." The fathers of the Catholic church also pondered the meaning of the word *Elohim*. Did it signify God alone or God together with His celestial attendants? Many church scholars came to the conclusion that the reference to more than one divine person was implied, and found biblical support for their views. "Adam is become as one of us." (Gen. 3:22) Gonzales-Crussi reminds us that the church "admitted the synthesis of male and female essences in Adam, and therefore in God, in whose image man was created. To the joint male and female principles man owed, while in Eden, his domination of the world. The joint principles were dispersed and brought asunder as a result of the fall, but redemption will signify a reconstitution of the pristine condition, when in symbolic synthesis the Divine Unity will again be attained."

Most Eastern religions have recognized the bisexual nature of their deities. Hermetic philosophy is partly based on the acceptance of the hermaphrodite and the androgynous inner person, known as the *homo Adamicus*. This view of Adam is explained by sex historian Rom Landau: "Adam must have had the potentialities of both sexes, since a female organism could be derived from him. The implications of this did not elude the Church, and one Pope, at least, Innocent III, tried to fight against its interpretation in terms of bisexuality, by condemning such reading of this passage in Genesis."

Sociologists have often speculated that the male-female character of the human being is a primary aspect of world mythology. The emphasis of research on this subject has usually been the homosexuality of the ancient Greeks and their legendary defeat of those Amazons whose matriarchal rule was displaced by the invading Dorians. But the Greeks were by no means the only ancient people who engaged in a great mythological struggle against the Earth Goddess. As Campbell (1964) observes, "toward the close of the Age of Bronze and, more strongly, with the dawn of the Age of Iron (ca. 1250 B.C. in the Levant), the old cosmology and mythologies of the goddess mother were radically transformed, reinterpreted, and in large measure even suppressed, by those suddenly intrusive patriarchal warrior tribesmen whose traditions have come down to us chiefly in the Old and New Testaments and in the myths of Greece." Historians of the origins of Near Eastern religions, like Judaism, have discovered elements which reflect that revolution. The Hebrews had a patriarchal system that required a patriarchal God. The Jews engaged in a great struggle against both polytheism and the influence of female fertility deities. Apparently a temple in honor of Ishtar was located in Jerusalem as late as the time of Josiah, when it was defiled. In this regard, historian Geoffrey Parrinder notes that "when Jeremiah was carried off to Egypt he was shocked to find Jewish women there worshipping Ishtar, the Queen of Heaven, with cakes and drink offerings . . . that they were not alone in worshipping a goddess has been shown from the papyri of Elephantine, an island in the Nile in Upper Egypt, opposite Aswan. These writings which belonged to a Jewish military colony, founded at an uncertain date, mention the worship of Yahweh but also of other gods of whom one, Anathyahu, bore the name of the female deity Anath combined with Yahu, and this suggests that she was regarded as the spouse of Yahweh."

The Judaic and Greek efforts to subdue female deities were only part of the masculine revolution that changed the Near East and transformed the human body from the image of the Neolithic Venus to that of a kingly male. The disintegration of the powers of the Great Mother had begun when ancient civilizations in Babylon, Assyria, Sumer, and Egypt enforced their concepts of private property, class structure, and patriarchal hierarchy. The egalitarianism usually associated with the Earth Goddess began to erode. Civilization became the antithesis of cultivation—in both its agricultural or artistic sense. Passion became the enemy of reason. At the heart of this antagonism was the image of passionate, wild, sexual, and cultivating women. Today we can comprehend that this negative view of women helped to explain the depths to which men of many different societies have felt threatened by passion, intuition, and feeling. Not only does this stance suggest a masculine sense of the superiority of women, but it also asks questions about the very sources of masculine identity itself. This Western patriarchal heritage helped to institutionalize a connection between masculine identity, domination, and self-control. It made a connection between dominance over one's sexual and emotional life (nature) and all that is meant by civilization. As Foucault (1986) points out, even our concept of sanity arises from this institutionalization.

Pat Caplan elaborates on Foucault's famous observation, when she says that "just as madness was perceived by the eighteenth century as a relapse into animality, so it has been a male identification with reason that has supposedly allowed an escape from a state of servitude in which reason is enslaved to the passions. Male sexuality therefore becomes a sign of an animality that we have not been able to leave behind us. It is women [Pandora and Eve], defined as sexual creatures, who have subsequently been seen as constantly tempting men away from the path of reason and morality. It is as if women are to be blamed for reminding men of their sexuality. But this also becomes part of a history of men forsaking responsibility for male sexuality since, once aroused, sexuality is supposedly beyond the control of reason. For the Greeks and for us, sex threatens the very sense of self-control that defines men's rationality. It is a threat to the existence of civilization. If men could have had a choice, they would have perhaps eradicated sexual desire completely, were it not for the importance of children to survival of male identity and hence a masculine dream of immortality."

Thus the relative egalitarian status of men and women of an earlier matricentric period collapsed, and yet its powerful influences persisted in myth and iconography. As Anna and Robert Francoeur point out, "the ancient psychic theme of the Divine Mother continued to provide the framework through which the male ruler received his power and authority. Thus the great pharaohs of Egypt were enthroned on the lap of Queen Isis, the Divine Mother. This theme also persisted in portraits of the Christ Child reigning from the lap of his mother."

Christianity wanted to assign the goddess to the past, but she would not disappear into mythological forgetfulness. This mythic resonance is emphasized by Joseph Campbell (1964): "Like the Titans of the older faith, Adam and Eve were the children of the mother-goddess Earth. 'The man,' we read in the Bible, 'called his wife's name Eve, because she was the mother of all living.' As the mother of all living, Eve herself, then, must be recognized as the missing anthropomorphic aspect of the mother-goddess. And Adam, therefore, must have been her son as well as spouse: for the legend of the rib is clearly a patriarchal inversion (giving precedence to the male) of the earlier myth of the hero born from the goddess Earth who returns to her to be reborn."

It is this inversion of the story of Adam and Eve that transformed the body into a manifestation of sin.

# FIVE
# The Body as Sin

In the Persian tale of genesis, there were two creators.
They were neither born nor made, for they were eternal.
It was these contrary powers who made the imperfect
world in which we live. One of these creators was called
Ahura Mazda, the great Lord of Light. And there was
also the dreadful Angra Mainyu, the Demon of Darkness. Because they were the fathers of the cosmos, they
put both light and darkness in every part of nature. Their
good and evil are always battling one another in the vast
cosmic battlefield where all things are in a state of perpetual disorder.

Ahura Mazda was omniscient and so he could see
forever before and behind himself. Thus he knew that his
enemy Angra Mainyu existed although Angra Mainyu
did not have the vision to realize the existence of Ahura
Mazda. Creation began when the Lord of Light gave
birth out of his spirit to spiritual beings, who existed in
perfect harmony for 3,000 years, motionless, without
thought, and without tangible bodies. At the close of
those luminous years, the Demon of Darkness arose
from the night and, perceiving the spiritual glory all
around him, he attempted to destroy the creatures of the
light, for he was malicious and wished only to destroy
goodness. But his power was not sufficient to annihilate

the creatures of Ahura Mazda, and in defeat he retreated to his abyss, where he created all the fiends of the world who eventually rose against the light.

The Lord of Light knew that before the power of evil could be broken, there first must be a period of 3,000 years in which Good would rule supreme, after which there would be 3,000 years when good and evil would be intermingled. Knowing these things, the Lord of Light proposed peace between himself and the terrible Angra Mainyu, promising that if Angra Mainyu would withdraw for 3,000 years there would then be a time when the two gods would have equal power. The Lord of Darkness was content with this arrangement, and returned to his abyss.

At once Ahura Mazda created Good Mind and Sky. Not to be outdone during his exile, Angra Mainyu made Evil Mind and the Lie. From Good Mind came the Light of the World, the Good Religion, Righteous Order, Perfect Sovereignty, Divine Piety, Excellence, and Immortality. To protect these virtues, the good lord Mazda made the army of the constellations. He also made the moon, the sun, and then water, earth, plants, animals, and human beings.

Now wicked Angra Mainyu had slept for 3,000 years. A female fiend named Jahi (Menstruation) sprang up from the dark and screamed to her lord, "Arise, father of us all! I shall make evil in the world which will bring misery to Ahura Mazda and his Archangels. I shall poison the righteous man, the laboring ox, the water, plants, fire, and all creation."

Angra Mainyu arose and kissed the fiend on her forehead, which instantly brought to her that pollution called menstruation. Angra Mainyu was pleased. To reward her, the Lord of Darkness asked, "What is your wish that I may give it to you?"

"A man is my wish," she answered.

The lizard body of Angra Mainyu changed into that of a young man of 15 years. Jahi was greatly pleased with this handsome youth, and he became her helpless consort.

Now Angra Mainyu sprang up at the constellations, against which he flung the planets, destroying the fixity of the sky. Next he poured his anger into the water that the Lord of Light had made, bringing terrible drought. Into the earth he sent the serpent, scorpion, frog, and lizard. The earth was repulsed by such noxious things and it shook so hard that the mountains rose. Then Angra Mainyu stabbed the earth to its heart, and this great wound became the passage forever opened to hell. The next attack of the Lord of Darkness was against the first-created man, Gayomart, whom he detested because Gayomart was a pure, spiritual, and nonphysical being, who lived in sublime peace with the Sole-Created Ox in Eran Vej, the central land of the seven lands of the earth. Now the Lord of Light Ahura Mazda brought forth from Gayomart a sweat of the spirit and from that sweat he made the youthful body of a boy of 15 years, tall and radiant and good. But when that fair youth looked upon the world he was filled with fear, for he saw that the world was dark and that the earth was covered with vermin. Everywhere was chaos. The heavens were in rebellion. The sun and moon flew through the sky in confusion. The planets made battle with the stars.

The evil Angra Mainyu released upon first-made man the Demon of Death, but he would not die for his time had not yet come. In frustrated rage the Lord of Darkness attacked the first-made man with avarice, want, pain, hunger, disease, lust, and lethargy. So it was that the first ancestor of humankind suffered all of these woes until, at last, he died. But when he fell to the earth, he gave forth seed and there grew from it a plant of one stem and 15 leaves, which was the first human couple, wrapped in each other's embrace so closely that it could not be seen which was the male and which the female or whether they were two separate living souls. From the plant they came forth as Mashya and Mashyoi and the breath entered them, which is the soul, and the Lord of Light Ahura Mazda said: "You are humankind, the ancestry of the world, created perfect in devotion. Perform the duties of the law, think good thoughts, speak good words, do good deeds, and do not worship demons."

But Angra Mainyu caused the first man and woman to quarrel. Demons shouted at them, "You are human! Worship the demon, so that your demon of malice may be quelled." And so it was that evil entered the lives of men and women. They were born into a corrupt world which is torn by the battle of good and evil. And so it will ever be until the prophet Zoroaster is born and the battle against evil is finally won. For thus speaks the Bundahish.

It is apparent that this Persian tale of genesis is thoroughly pessimistic. It takes for granted the corruption of matter, nature, the world, and the body. Even with its promise of redemption and the eventual defeat of evil, it is, nonetheless, so grim a vision of existence that we may find it difficult to imagine how it could have become the basis of a religious philosophy called Zoroastrianism, which ruled the lives of millions of people for thousands of years. It therefore comes as a shock to realize that our own viewpoint was greatly influenced by the moral cosmology implicit in this Persian myth of Creation, Fall, and World Renovation. In fact, as we shall see, Persian Zoroastrianism greatly influenced the Messianic ideas of Judaism and Christianity as well as the world view of Islam. This dismal, polemical cosmogony of absolute good and evil is very familiar in our own religious mythologies.

It is drawn from the Zoroastrian epics known as the Bundahish, *The Book of Creation*, which was produced in the late Sassanian restoration period, 226–641 A.D., although the Zoroastrian tradition dates from the seventh century B.C.

Like our own genesis, the key to Persian mythology is cosmic dualism, with a persistent battle taking place between the forces of good (or light) and the forces of evil (or darkness). That conflict is reflected in every aspect of our lives, profoundly and superficially. We take for granted the notion that darkness equates with evil and that light is a reference to good. We are completely comfortable with the depiction of dark villains threatening fair heroes in melodramas and science fiction, of cowboys wearing white hats and riding white horses in their battles against the bad guys who wear black hats and ride dark horses. We fear the dark. For us, the forces of darkness are evil. The night has a bad reputation. It is filled with demons, vampires, werewolves, and all the other creatures associated with the feminine moon that cannot tolerate the light of day. Even Mozart's beguiling Queen of the Night in *The Magic Flute* is envisioned as the consummately evil and devouring mother.

We find great comfort in such polemic attitudes. They provide the superstructure upon which we build our value systems of innocence and guilt, good and evil, pain and pleasure, normalcy and abnormalcy. So it taunts us to be told that this comfortable dualism is not an ultimate truth held by all peoples of all times, and that other cultures have drastically different visions of the cosmos. From what we know of the earliest cultures, it seems that myths, rites, and philosophies were comparatively affirmative in their vision of existence. Pleasure was valued over pain. It was assumed that life would bring fulfillment and pleasure, rather than denial and pain. Evil was not a given—an inescapable aspect of cosmic corruption. This affirmative attitude of antiquity would not persist in Western mentality. About 600 B.C., there occurred what Campbell has called "the Great Reversal," when the prevailing world view shifted from an affirmation of life to a negation of life, from the expectation of reward, comfort, and innocence to the acceptance of punishment, discomfort, and guilt. The Great Reversal was an epic moment in history, when a negative conception of destiny arose that would eventually be symbolized by that Original Sin which makes pain and punishment an implacable aspect of Western life.

"Life became known as a fiery vortex of delusion, desire, violence, and death, a burning waste." (Campbell, 1968) The first indications of this reversal can be found not only in the teaching of the Persian prophet Zoroaster, the founder of Zoroastrianism, but also in the sermons of the Buddha: "All things are on fire," and the axioms of the Orphic cult of Greece: "*Soma sema*— the body is a tomb.*"

"In the Buddha's teaching, the image of the turning spoke wheel, which in the earlier period had been symbolic of the world's glory, thus became a sign, on one hand, of the wheeling round of sorrow, and, on the other, release in the sunlike doctrine of illumination. And in the classical world the turning spoked wheel appeared also at this time as an emblem rather of life's defeat and pain than of victory and exhilaration." (Campbell, 1968)

The cosmic order of the Mother Goddess, "ever cycling in a mighty round of ineluctably returning ages from eternity, through eternity," was a holy wheel that made its majestic rounds, like a divine machine, untouched by any act of humankind. "The sun, the moon, the stars in their courses, the various animal species . . .

would remain forever established in their modes; and truth, virtue, rapture, and true being lay in doing whatever had been traditionally done—without protest, without ego, without judgment . . . the orientation of such an order of thought was metaphysical; not ethical or rational, but transethical, transrational. And in the Far East, as well as in India, whether in the mythic fields of Shinto, Taoism, and Confucianism, or in the Mahayana, the world was not to be reformed, but only known, revered, and its laws obeyed." (Campbell, 1968)

As we shall see, the mythologies underlying just such a mechanistic fatalism would eventually overtake first Christian religious dogma and then Western science and industry.

The touch of evil inherent in Campbell's Great Reversal is not a preoccupation of egalitarian peoples. In sharp contrast to the patriarchal systems of Zoroastrian myth and Old Testament stories, divine wrath was not a conspicuous element in the mythic systems of the most ancient Near Eastern religions. For instance, in the traditions of foraging tribes there is no evidence of the theme of guilt connected with nature and sexuality. Physical matter is the body of the Goddess, so it cannot be corrupt. "The boon of the knowledge of life is there . . . and it is yielded willingly to any mortal, male or female, who reaches for it with the proper will and readiness to receive." (Campbell, 1968) As we have already seen, there are a number of deities who represent this access to the mysteries of nature. They are the consorts and sons of the Great Goddess. Returning to her bosom in death, the god is reborn—as spring returns to winter, as the moon is reborn out of its own shadow, and as the serpent leaves its skin and is born into a new body. In the same world where we now see only sorrow and death, another system of mythology saw rapture and an everlasting cycle of becoming.

All this changed with the Great Reversal. Nature, matter, the body, sexuality, and every other aspect of the physical world ceased to be the center of expression and rapture. In Zoroaster's mythic view, for instance, the world was corrupt and required the correct and prescribed human behavior for it to be redeemed. Wisdom, virtue, and truth had to be engendered in the world by human intervention in the corruption of nature. The crucial barrier between ultimate being and nonbeing was no longer discovered in the physical world of nature but in a rationally determined system of ethics. "The primal character of creation had been light, wisdom, and truth, into which, however, darkness, deception, and the lie had entered, which it was now man's duty to eradicate through his own virtue in thought, word, and deed." (Campbell, 1968)

On one level or another, most of us take for granted the axiom that we must redeem ourselves from the inescapable corruption of the flesh through acts of virtue.

That underlying acceptance of the dangerousness of nature came to us in large measure from Persian Zoroastrianism. It is important to recall that in the teaching of Zoroaster, as already noted, two contrary powers made and maintain the world in which we live: first, Ahura Mazda, the Lord of Light, and his antagonist Angra Mainyu, the Demon of Darkness. These two powers are envisioned as explicit aspects of the cosmos, for they have existed eternally. The Demon, however, is not himself eternal, for it is promised in the Zoroastrian system that he will be undone at the end of time, when Light alone will prevail. "This is not the old, ever-revolving cycle of the archaic Bronze Age mythologies, but a sequence, once and for all, of creation, fall, and progressive redemption, to culminate in a final, decisive, irrefutable victory of the One Eternal God of Righteousness and Truth." (Campbell, 1968)

This description of the course of the world is deeply familiar to us, so much so that we often overlook the fact that it is only one of many ways of envisioning the cosmos and its destiny. Like the second chapter of Genesis, the Zoroastrian myth clearly evolved out of the ancient mythologies of planting societies. In the mythologies of such nature-oriented, matricentric primal peoples, however, there is no moral criticism of life and of the world as is discovered in these Levantine doctrines of the Fall; nor any theme, consequently, of moral Redemption. Both the Old Testament of the Jews and the Bundahish of the Persians represent the Fall as the answer to the moral enigma of evil and suffering in the world. Yet their two views of this mythic predicament differed absolutely, as do their views, also, of the Restoration. For in the Persian myth, which had so great an influence upon the creators of the Bible, evil is seen from a cosmic point of view, as antecedent to the Fall of humankind, whereas in the Bible the Fall is the fault of human beings, whose disobedience brought calamity into the natural world. So specific is this metaphor of corrupted and redeemable nature that in the descriptions of the Fall and Expulsion from Eden the calamity in nature is represented iconographically by the decline and death of the Tree of Life from which the forbidden fruit was picked. In Christian iconography, that same metaphor is retained and transformed when Christ is crucified on the dead tree and the drops of his blood bring it back to life.

Christianity thus inherited a Judaic concept: that evil and redemption are functions of human activity. In the Hebrew Messianic ideal, "natural evil was in the eyes of the prophets the result of human evil. God, the creator of nature, cannot be the source of evil: if this were not so, two forces, good and evil, would be used by Him in mixed confusion and His character would not be com-

plete, harmonious, essentially great. The deeds of man
are, therefore, the source of evil both in society and in
nature." (Klausner)

In this Judaic view, nature (meaning the world and the
matter of which it is composed) is not corrupt. Nature is
God-made and God-given, and as such, Judaism is a
life-affirming religion. Pain, evil, death, misfortune, and
suffering are not implicit aspects of nature. To the contrary, the Supreme Being of the Jews created evil because of human evil and for the punishment of human
evil. It did not exist *a priori* in nature, but was wrought
by a perfect God to punish the disobedience of imperfect
humankind. According to this Judeo-Christian premise,
if the evil of evil persons should come to an end, then all
evil would cease, even natural evil such as disaster and
catastrophe.

This is a confounding premise, but it nonetheless exists
at the core of Western mentality and is reflected in many
of our attitudes: the belief that illness is some sort of
cosmic punishment for misconduct and the fear that misfortune is the result of evil behavior. Campbell (1968)
approaches this paradox with characteristic humor. "How
evil can have had its source in God and yet not in God but
in evil persons, I shall not attempt to argue; but the
contrast of this tangle of thought with the Zoroastrian
system warrants a moment of consideration." In the Persian
myth the cause for the corruption of the world *is not a
person but a principle.* This is an important and essential
distinction between the Zoroastrian concept of nature
and the quite different idea of nature inherited by Christians from Jews. Yet the peoples who follow Judaism,
Christianity, and Zoroastrianism are impelled by almost
identical sex-negative attitudes, for despite differences
the dominant idea of all three religious creeds is that
nature is corrupt, regardless of how that corruption origi-

nated. For Zoroastrianism evil is an intrinsic aspect of the world just as it is in the East Indian principle of *maya,* the world-creating force of illusion. The sin of Adam and Eve, however, was disobedience, which, as Campbell points out, is not a matter of ontology but of ethical pedagogy.

In summary, both Zoroastrianism and Old Testament doctrine place a great stress upon traditional codes, attempting to elevate tribal custom to the status of cosmic law. But on another level, these two religious mythologies have profoundly dissimilar visions of the cosmos; so much so that their immense and contradictory influence upon Western religious thinking about good and evil has caused everlasting paradoxes. The biblical view understands the Fall as an element of actual human history; an offense against God which denigrated the character of humankind, and established the need to mortify the wickedness of the flesh and to redeem oneself from damnation. The Persian cosmic view is not historical fact but "symbolized philosophy" which envisions the corruption of the world as a metaphoric explanation for the existence of pain, sorrow, and death. In the end, however, the Persians subscribed to the same negative vision of the world and the body as the Jews did. These differences and similarities between Judaism and Zoroastrianism are significant. Each religion, in its own way, is concerned with a world-denying attitude that later impacted on Christian philosophy. In the Western world view, this "Great Reversal" lent a profound cosmological negativism to our concept of nature, the body, and sexuality. It is a negative mentality hidden behind every action described in the first three chapters of the Book of Genesis.

As we know, in the beginning the God of the Hebrews created the heaven and the earth.

Then, as the story continues, "God said, 'Let us make

man in our image, after our likeness. And let them have dominion over the fish of the sea, and over the fowl of the air, and over the cattle, and over the earth, and over every creeping thing that creeps upon the earth.' So God created man in his own image, male and female he created them. And God blessed them, and God said to them, 'Be fruitful, and multiply, and replenish the earth, and subdue it, and have dominion over every living thing that moves upon the earth.' "

The story of Creation then provides a second and different version of the origin of human beings. Although God had previously created both a male and a female out of His own Being and in His own image, now he creates out of the dust only the male called Adam: "In the day that the Lord God made the earth and the heavens, when no plant of the field was yet on the earth and no herb of the field had yet appeared—for the Lord God had not caused it to rain upon the earth, and there was no man to till the ground, yet a mist went up from the earth and watered the whole face of the ground—then the Lord God formed man of the dust of the ground, and breathed into his nostrils the breath of life, and man became a living soul.

"And the Lord God planted a garden in Eden; and there he put the man whom he had formed. And out of the ground the Lord God made to grow every tree that is pleasant to the sight and good for food; the tree of life also in the midst of the garden, and the tree of knowledge of good and evil.

"Then the Lord God commanded the man, saying, 'Of every tree of the garden you may freely eat, but of the tree of the knowledge of good and evil you shall not eat, for in the day that you eat of it you shall surely die.' "

Then God decided that Adam should not be alone.

"And so the Lord God caused a deep sleep to fall upon Adam, and he slept. And he took one of his ribs, and closed up its place with flesh. And the rib, which the Lord God had taken from man he made a woman and brought her to the man."

Significantly, Genesis then quotes Adam as saying: "This is at last bone of my bones and flesh of my flesh. She shall be called Woman, because she was taken out of Man."

Then into the innocence of the garden of Eden comes the inevitable Judaic metaphor of the corruption of nature and the origin of sin and pain.

Tragedy is introduced by the serpent. This seems to be the same serpent long associated with the Mother Goddess. Now, however, it becomes the source of corruption in Eden. The story of the Fall is so metaphorically loaded with sexual attitudes that I must quote from it in some detail.

The serpent said to the woman, "Did God say that you shall not eat of any tree in the Garden?"

And the woman answered, "We may eat of the fruit of the trees of the garden, but of the fruit of the tree which is in the midst of the garden, God has said, 'You shall not eat of it, neither shall you touch it, lest you die.' "

The serpent seems to understand something about God that comes to us as a considerable surprise. God appears to be jealous of his powers of knowledge.

The serpent said to the woman, "You will not die. For God knows that when you eat of it your eyes will be opened, and you will be like God, knowing good and evil."

For many scholars this dissident dialogue between the serpent and Eve constitutes a metaphysical exchange between a reptile long associated with the Mother Goddess and the newly created Judaic mother of humankind. In the words of the serpent and the response of Eve we may be seeing the re-emergence of attitudes of a repressed matricentric philosophy.

"When the woman saw that the fruit of the tree was good and that it was a delight to the eyes, and that the tree could make one wise, she took its fruit and ate, and she also gave some to her husband, and he ate. Then the eyes of both of them were opened, and they knew that they were naked. And they sewed fig leaves together and made themselves aprons."

God, though presumably omnipotent, cannot find Adam when he searches for him in the garden. "Where are you?" God asked.

To which Adam responded, "I heard the sound of Thee in the garden, and I was afraid, because I was naked, and I hid myself."

God then asks, "Who told you that you are naked? Have you eaten of the tree of which I commanded you not to eat?"

And the man said, "The woman whom Thou gave to be with me, she gave me the fruit of the tree, and I ate it."

The Lord God said to the woman, "What is this that you have done?"

And the woman said, "The serpent beguiled me, and I ate."

So God said to the serpent, "Because you have done this, you are cursed above all cattle and above every wild beast of the field. Upon your belly you shall go, and dust you shall eat all the days of your life. And I will put enmity between you and the woman and between your seed and her seed. He shall bruise your head and you shall bruise his heel."

To the woman God said, "I shall greatly multiply your pains in childbearing. In sorrow you will bring forth children. And your desire shall be for your husband, and he shall rule over you."

And to Adam the Lord God said, "Because you have listened to the voice of your wife, and have eaten of the tree of which I commanded you, saying, 'You shall not eat of it,' cursed is the ground because of you. In toil you shall eat of it all the days of your life. Thorns and thistles it shall bring forth to you. And you shall eat the plants of the field. In sweat of your face you shall eat bread till you return to the ground. For out of it you were taken, for you are dust, and to dust you shall return."

Then the Lord God said, "Behold, the man has become like one of us, knowing good and evil. And now, lest he put forth his hand and take also the tree of life and eat and live forever," . . . the Lord God sent him forth from the garden of Eden, to till the ground from which he was taken. He drove the man out, and he placed at the east of the garden of Eden the cherubim, with a flaming sword to guard the way to the tree of life.

No narrative of the Western world has had the immense influence upon every aspect of our thinking as these stories recounted in the first three chapters of the Book of Genesis. With the possible exception of the Mosaic Ten Commandments, none has been as philosophically insinuative or as consistently subjected to a wide variety of interpretations. Elaine Pagels, a historian of religion, has written an exceptional survey of the relationship between western social values and Judeo-Christian mythologies. Like me, she is interested in the process by which traditional patterns of gender and sexual relationship arose from biblical epics—patterns so obvious and "natural" to those who have accepted them that nature itself seemed to have ordained them. As Pagels observes, "abrupt changes in social attitudes have recently become commonplace, especially with respect to sexuality, including marriage, divorce, homosexuality, abortion, contraception, and gender . . . For Christians, in particular, such changes may seem to challenge not only traditional values but the very structure of human nature."

Not all these viewpoints were invented by Christians in the first four centuries after the birth of Christ, when the Christian movement transformed itself from a minority sect into the state religion of the Roman Empire. Christian doctrine borrowed heavily from Jewish tradition, which is self-evident when we realize that Christianity is in many respects a protestant form of Judaism, substantially built upon Judaic faith and mythos as well as Aristotelian and Stoic philosophies.

In the first century, the Roman historian Tacitus saw the new Christian movement as a "deadly superstition." Its members were subject to arrest, torture, and execution. But then in 313 A.D. the Roman emperor Constantine was converted and Christianity began its global mission. Accompanying this spread of Christian faith was a revolution in sexual attitudes and practices.

Yet, in many ways, that moral revolution was subtle, for when the attitudes of Jews and Christians from the first centuries are examined, we discover that rarely do they specifically mention sexual conduct. What is more, there are few treatises on marriage, divorce, and gender. Apparently, the doctrines governing sexuality did not arise out of theological debate. The revolutionary sexual attitudes surfaced in terms of myth rather than as intellectual doctrine. For the Jews and Christians were greatly preoccupied with one of their seminal myths: the story of Creation. It was in discussions, interpretations, and sermons about Adam, Eve, and the serpent that their attitudes about sexual conduct were revealed. From about 200 B.C., the story of Creation became for many Jews and later for Christians a primary source of God's commandments, and for the revelation and defense of many basic ideals and attitudes.

Despite the primacy of the story of Creation, it is not one tale, told with consistent detail. As I have indicated earlier, in the discussion of Lilith, very early on Jewish scholars noticed narrative inconsistencies in the account of Genesis. Though we usually consider Genesis to represent a solid fact of religious history, it has been, to the contrary, both in its original oral form and in its later written versions, an epic consistently open to different interpretations. Christianity was largely built upon this flux of Judaic theological debate about Genesis. Thus both Jews and Christians at various times and places have given the story of Creation widely different and even contradictory readings. There is contained within the story itself many elements that give rise to contention and radical interpretation. For instance, many centuries ago Jewish scholars noted with some discomfort that Genesis contains not one but two versions of Creation. The first begins with the first chapter and recounts how God created the world in six days, crowning his efforts with the creation in his own image of *adam*—"humanity" (Genesis 1:26). In Genesis 2:4, however, a different story is told: the Lord created man out of dust, and, after creating all the creatures and finding none to be a suitable companion for Adam, God put Adam to sleep and made a woman out of his bone. As Pagels reminds us, today biblical scholars tend to agree that the two creation myths were originally separate (one far older than the other), and were later joined to make up the first three chapters of Genesis.

Among traditional Jews of antiquity, only the worship of pagan gods caused more indignation than pagan sexual conduct. Jewish teachers considered certain sexual practices of non-Jews to be abominable. For centuries Jews taught that the entire purpose of marriage and of sexuality is procreation. And thus Jewish custom banned as "abominations" any sexual act which was not conducive to procreation. Though tolerated by many non-Judaic peoples, prostitution, homosexuality, and abortion were condemned by Jewish custom and law. Polygamy and divorce, however, were often accepted insofar as such practices increased for men the opportunities for reproduction. Jewish law even decreed that a man should be bound for only ten years to a childless marriage before he was permitted either to divorce his wife and marry another, or to retain his barren wife and to take a second mate to produce his children.

Despite such stringent, patriarchal attitudes about reproduction as it related to nonprocreative forms of sexuality, Jewish literature abounds with celebrations of sensual pleasure, though it is expressed only from the masculine viewpoint. The abundance of nature and fecundity in general were greatly valued by Jews, whose mythic values evolved out of their agricultural and herding activities in an ungenerous and arid region. Sexuality was closely associated with the creative values of reproduction. The Jews also echoed the sensual delight of pleasure that had always been an implicit aspect of Asian mentality. *The Song of Songs* is one of the great erotic poems of the Near East. Thus, the Jews were somewhat ambivalent on the subject of worldly pleasure: They praised sensuality at the same time that they insisted upon a great many restrictions in sexual behavior.

By and large, Christians borrowed only the negative elements of Judaic sexual mores, and gradually devised what is arguably the most sex-negative tradition of world history. In fact, men and women who converted to Christianity often adapted attitudes about sexuality that were considered bizarre by their families and friends. It is curious that the attitudes about sexuality arising from so-called Judeo-Christian origins are now considered to be both normal and obvious, despite the fact that in early Christian times attitudes such as the disapproval of divorce and polygamy and the approval of chastity and nonreproductive marriage would have been viewed as quite abnormal.

Jesus himself had very little to say about marriage, divorce, and celibacy, if we can judge his viewpoint from New Testament reports. The rules of sexual conduct were formulated generations before Jesus, when Jews began to interpret their accounts of Creation, specifically in Genesis, to prove that their tribal customs were proper and civilized and not barbaric or peculiar, as non-Jewish religious leaders claimed. Jews saw the confluence of their customs and their interpretations of Genesis as proof that their sexual and moral behavior was a reflection of the very structure of the universe itself.

Most Jews had good reason to deny the propriety of celibacy. After all, they pointed out, a major premise of Judaic custom was built upon the contention that God's first commandment to man and woman was to procreate. It was here, on this matter of celibacy, that early Christians undertook the most revolutionary step in their reconstruction of Jewish sexual values. Though trained in Jewish tradition, Jesus himself was responsible for radically changing traditional attitudes about celibacy. That revolution in sexual viewpoint contributed some of the unique elements of Christianity. That revolution was also the major force behind the Christian assessment of the body as an object of sin. As Pagels observes, "by subordinating the obligation to procreate, rejecting divorce, and implicitly sanctioning monogamous relationships, Jesus reverses traditional [Jewish] priorities, declaring, in effect, that other obligations, including marital ones, are now more important than procreation. Even more startling, Jesus endorses—and exemplifies—a new possibility and one he says is even better: rejecting both marriage and procreation in favor of voluntary celibacy, for the sake of following him into the new age."

Of course, Jesus did not invent celibacy. It existed among Jews, such as the strictly ascetic Essene sect of Palestine as well as the Therapeutae monastic groups in Egypt. But such celibate Jews were considered extremists by the majority of their fellow Jews. Therefore, it was not until the advent of Christianity that celibacy became the basis of a true revolution in Near Eastern sexual attitudes.

The zealot of celibacy was the Christian disciple Paul, who, some 20 years after Jesus' death, acknowledged, in Corinthians, that marriage was not a sin but that there was great virtue in renouncing it. But the majority of Christians rejected this denunciation of marriage and procreation, which was built upon the premise that the sin of Adam and Eve was sexual and that the forbidden fruit of the tree of knowledge was *carnal* knowledge. Early Christians, like Jews before them, insisted that, to the contrary, and according to such early Christian teachers as Clement of Alexandria, the conscious participation in reproduction is "cooperation with God in the world of creation." Adam's sin, Clement insisted, was not sexual indulgence but disobedience, thus agreeing with the majority of his Jewish and Christian contemporaries that the essential theme of the story of Adam and Eve is moral freedom and moral responsibility. Many twentieth-century scholars advance the same argument. Foucault suggests that the Fall is the mythic basis of the idea of sexuality as punishment. According to this Augustinian line of thinking, it was because Adam tried to escape God's will and wanted to acquire a will of his own that "as a punishment of this revolt and as a consequence of this will to will independently from God, Adam lost control of himself."

So, as Augustine argues, it was that "his body, and parts of his body, stopped obeying his commands, revolted against him, and the sexual parts of his body were the first to rise up in this disobedience." As Foucault (1981) concludes, "sex in erection is the image of man revolted against God. The arrogance of sex is the punishment and consequence of the arrogance of man."

The conception of the libido as the stigma of the Fall runs throughout Christian mentality. Phallic symbolism, once so prominent in pre-Christian iconography, became a controversial element in the Church. As art historian Leo Steinberg points out, the symbolism of the male sexual organ usually signifies power. In the West, the male organ had always been seen as a weapon against death, the instrument that perpetuates the race. But from the Christian point of view, the phallus was responsible for compromising that rationality and control that is always identified with masculine nobility. As the dogma of the Church became entrenched, phallic iconography was expelled. But the ancient tradition of associating male sexuality with power was too great a mythic tradition to be dismissed by the Church. So the penis was reconstructed in Christian terms. Whereas the phallus of Dionysus symbolized the generative powers of nature, "Christ's sexual organ—pruned by circumcision in sign of corrupted nature's correction—is offered to immolation . . . What the Christian art of the Renaissance took from pagan antiquity was the license to plumb its own mythic depths . . . The member exposed stands for God's life as man and or man's death, perhaps even for his Resurrection." (Steinberg) The sexuality of Christ was converted into a nonsexual symbol of divinity made corporeal. Yet, at the same time, the naked body of Christ retained its traditional power as a phallic symbol of spiritual victory over death. This remarkable conversion of nature into anti-nature and sexuality into anti-sexuality was made possible by the crucial fact that Jesus was the Son of God born immaculately of a virgin—without sexual intercourse. "By dint of continence, through the willed chastity of the Ever-virgin, it obviates the necessity for procreation since, in the victory over sin, death, the result of sin, is abolished. In such orthodox formulation, the penis of Christ, puissant in abstinence, would surpass in power the phalli of Adam and Dionysus. And it is perhaps in this sense that the old connotation of the phallus as anti-death weapon is both adapted to the Christ context and radically converted." (Steinberg)

This new phallic context is visible in countless works of art, created by medieval and Renaissance artists, in which the nude Jesus is depicted in sexually explicit images. For their original audience, these works of art were highly legible expressions of a mythic iconography. That audience possessed the same visual literacy that allowed people to "read" the religious epics depicted in the stained-glass windows and frescoes of churches and cathedrals. But today we are perplexed, if not embarrassed, by sculptures and paintings in which the Virgin fondles the penis of the infant Jesus or in which the crucified Christ is shown with his hand clutching his groin. As Steinberg has observed, the creators of these symbolically loaded images could not anticipate that "the process of demythologizing Christianity would succeed in profaning our vision of their sacred art."

Curiously, for all of its apparent explicitness, this Renaissance depiction of the sexuality of Christ was profoundly anti-sexual, demonstrating not the regenerative power of the phallus, but the Christian victory over nature. The symbolic attitudes about virgin birth and circumcision are aspects of a persistent denigration of the body and somatic experience in general, which are negative concepts in Western culture.

Such attitudes, it deserves repeating, were revolutionary attacks upon ancient Near Eastern religious ideals. From the Judaic viewpoint, such anti-sexuality was a heresy. In Genesis, the sexual purpose given to men and women was procreation. As such, nature and the world were good, not corrupt, to be used and exploited. Humankind was commanded by God "to replenish the earth, and subdue it; and have dominion" over the creatures of the sea, air, and earth. "There was no world-renunciation here, and Judaism has generally been opposed to both celibacy and asceticism . . . Priests and rabbis married and the High Priest was compelled to marry . . . Body and soul were closely bound together, so that it does not say that man was supplied with a soul, but [to the contrary] that he 'became a living soul' . . . This psychological unity was very different from the Hellenistic dualism, with its contrast of physical and spiritual, which [became entrenched] from the time of Paul and affected later Christian teaching on sex." (Parrinder)

The Apostle Paul was outspoken on the matter of the opposition of flesh and spirit. "The flesh lusts against the spirit, and the spirit against the flesh; and these are contrary the one to the other. Those that are after the flesh mind the things of the flesh, but those that are after the spirit the things of the spirit. For to be carnally-minded is death; but to be spiritually-minded is life and peace." (Gal. 5:17; Rom. 8.5f.) Paul's cosmic dualism had far more allegiance with the opposition of good and evil, of darkness and light found in Zoroastrianism or the dualistic conflict of the Greeks between spirit against matter, than with the holistic approach of the Jews.

But the ascetic Pauline and Zoroastrian mentalities eventually overwhelmed the worldly Judaic influences upon Christianity. By the close of the third century the debate between various antagonistic voices on the subject of the dualism of body and soul, matter and spirit had become the core of major upheaval in Christian philosophy. Out of the welter of theological possibilities there arose several bodies of heretical doctrine which caused endless disputes, power struggles, and persecutions in medieval Europe. These traditions throw much light on our current attitudes about love and sexuality.

One of the most influential of these heretical doctrines is called Manichaeism. The founder of Manichaeism was Manes (Manichaeus in Latin), who lived in Persia in the third century A.D. It is unknown to what extent he was influenced by Persian Zoroastrianism, but there is considerable similarity in his major premise that there are two primary elements in the universe, the goodness of God and the evil of matter. Accordingly, all goodness came from God, while all evil came from matter, which was called the Devil. Evil (matter), however, was not a cosmic force that took the form of a deity, as it did in Zoroastrianism. Contrary to the Zoroastrians, Manichees held that matter was concupiscence, a "disorderly motion in everything that exists." Matter or concupiscence was female, the "mother of all the demons," and the soul was imprisoned in it. The object of Manichaeism was to release the soul from the body. Severe asceticism was used to achieve this goal.

Quite another kind of heretical tradition was Pelagian, founded by an English or Irish monk named Pelagius. When he first visited Rome in the fifth century, he commenced a prolonged debate with Augustine, whose sympathies were clearly with Manichaeism. Pelagius insisted upon the redemptive importance of the human response in love to God, an attitude which was deplorably optimistic from the Manichaean point of view. Though Pelagius did not specifically condone sexual intercourse, he refuted the orthodox concept of original sin and he did not agree that the corruption of Adam's sin is endlessly transmitted through reproduction. Pelagianism was humanistic, tolerant, and gentle. It insisted that each person is capable of virtue and redemption. Though vigorously banned as a heresy, the optimism of Pelagianism survived covertly as one of the most vivid folkloric aspects of Christianity; while the Manichees were persecuted with equal fervor by Zoroastrianism, Islam, and Christianity, and the last vestige of the pessimistic sect vanished in Chinese Turkestan in about 1000 A.D.

Despite the total defeat of Manichaeism as a heretical philosophical force, with rare exception Christians unanimously embraced as truth the Manichaean vision of the world as corrupt, fortifying their sex-negative point of view with a literal reading of the first three chapters of the Book of Genesis.

Such literalism was anathema to several other heretical groups that were not in the least literal-minded about their interpretations of the Old Testament. They are usually grouped together and called Gnostic Christians, and their interpretations of the story of Adam and Eve confounded and outraged orthodox churchmen. As Pagels shows, the Gnostics insisted, for instance, that Genesis made no sense if taken literally, for, in their view, the story was intended to be read symbolically and allegorically. "And whereas the orthodox often blamed Eve for the Fall and pointed to women's submission as appropriate punishment, gnostics often depicted Eve as the source of spiritual awakening." (Pagels) These religious radicals dared to tell the tale of Eden from the point of view of the serpent, and depicted him as a teacher of divine wisdom who desperately tried to get Adam and Eve to open their eyes to their creator's true and despicable nature.

What distressed the Church Fathers "even more than the gnostics' rejection of moral absolutes or their violation of church discipline was that gnostic readings of Genesis threatened the message of freedom that had made Christianity so powerfully compelling to so many converts [who were Roman slaves] . . . Church leaders unanimously denounced the gnostics for denying what the orthodox considered to be humanity's essential, God-given attribute, free will." (Pagels)

The influence of the Gnostics on the Church was more subversive than political, contributing an enduring element of dissent in ecclesiastical matters. Their position on intellectual freedom, however, was largely replaced by an emphasis upon spiritual freedom, a concept which provided moral support during the difficult years when Christians were political subversives in the then-pagan world of Rome. Then gradually, during the third and fourth centuries, the Christian movement gained power throughout Roman society. With this shift in their political situation, the insistence upon freedom of choice was no longer a viable cause for Christians. The emperor had given them that freedom. The world had invaded the church and the church the world. How was Christianity to deal with the worldliness of its Church, in which a bishop now provided many civic rewards, such as tax exemption, increased income, social power, and even influence at court?

To use Foucault's term, the "politics of truth" had drastically changed. The Romans were no longer the instruments of Christian suffering, no longer providing them with the emotional basis for their acceptance of denial, self-sacrifice, and martyrdom. The world of the senses was becoming less corrupting than the world of power, luxury, and wealth. To resolve these contradictions, some of the most ardent Christians decided that the renunciation of the world through elective poverty and celibacy must become essential elements in their search for spiritual freedom. Thus, the vast changes in the political life of the Church had a fundamental impact on Christian ideologies. For nearly four hundred years Christians had regarded the supreme significance of Adam's disobedience and his subsequent suffering as a testament of *freedom*. For many tribes and nations subjugated by Rome, that stance had been a powerful incentive to be converted to Christianity. The embrace of freedom was a great comfort to the politically brutalized subjects of the Roman Empire who were converts to the new faith. It had given Christians motivation to become members of a dissident church and the courage to endure the punishment that resulted from such membership. Then, with the emergence of Augustine as the major force in Christianized Rome, this frame of mind suddenly changed.

In the late fourth century, Augustine, Bishop of Hippo, was living in an entirely different political world from his Church predecessors. Christianity was no longer a dissident sect but the state religion of Rome. Christians were now free to follow their faith and were officially encouraged to do so. Such a drastic transformation of the social circumstance of Christians required yet another revision of the reading of Genesis. It was Augustine who undertook this new interpretation of Adam and Eve, resulting in a viewpoint vastly different from the majority of his Jewish and Christian predecessors. As Pagels notes, what had been read as a tale of the right to quest for human freedom now became an Augustinian story of human bondage. Hitherto, most Jews and Christians had understood from Genesis that God gave humankind the right of moral freedom, and that Adam had misused it and thereby brought death and pain into the world. Augustine, however, was not content with the travails of such an interpretation, and he went a good deal further. He contended that Adam's sin not only caused our mortality but also corrupted our sexuality. If these notions contradicted the notorious sexual conduct of Rome, they indirectly sanctioned the limitations placed on the political freedom of Romanized Christians, a forfeiture that the followers of Jesus paid to Rome for its sanction of religious freedom. It was Augustine who reread Genesis to fit the limitations of Christian freedom within the Roman world. He observed that Adam's sin had not only made sex irreversibly corrupt, but it also cost us our free will, rendering us incapable of genuine political freedom. "Augustine's theory of original sin offered an analysis of human nature that became, for better and worse, the heritage of all subsequent generations of Western Christians and the major influence on their psychological and political thinking." (Pagels)

As Augustine saw it, celibacy was the rejection of the world and the way to gain control over his own life. It represented the paradox of attaining freedom through self-denial. In his confessions, Augustine described his joy when, to attain the "freedom of celibacy and renunciation," he gave up his career, his social position, the woman with whom he had lived and who had borne him a son, as well as his impending marriage to a wealthy heiress. His non-Christian contemporaries thought of this renunciation as both social suicide and gross impiety. It is significant, of course, that for nine years during his youth (from age 19 to 28) Augustine had been a follower of Manichaeism, that most life-denying of early Christian philosophies. Thus it isn't surprising that Augustine insisted that the whole human race inherited from Adam a nature irreversibly damaged by sin. As he proclaimed in *The*

*City of God,* "For we all were in that one man, since all of us were that one man who fell into sin through the woman who was made from him." Aware that there might be objection to the notion that millions of persons not yet born were in some sense "in Adam," Augustine explained that although "we did not yet have individually created and apportioned forms in which to live as individuals," what did exist was the "nature of the semen from which we were to be propagated." The semen itself, Augustine argued, was already "shackled by the bond of death" and transmits from generation to generation the damnation incurred by sin. Thus Augustine concluded that every human being ever conceived through semen is born contaminated with sin. The single exception to this predicament, of course, is Jesus Christ who was immaculately conceived without semen. (Pagels)

As Pagels shows, there is both a political and sexual implication in Augustinian precepts. He claims that in the beginning, when only Adam existed and before the creation of Eve, he discovered within himself the first government—which ruled with rational soul, "the better part of a human being," over the body, "the inferior part." Eve compromised that perfect balance, bringing about Adam's assertion of his own autonomy which, Augustine declared, was tantamount to rebellion against the rule of God. "The punishment for disobedience was nothing other than disobedience. For human misery consists in nothing other than man's disobedience to himself"— consisting of bodily impulses rebelling against the mind. What epitomizes humankind's rebellion against God is the "rebellion of the flesh"—a spontaneous uprising in the *disobedient members.* "The soul, which had taken a perverse delight in its own liberty and disdained to serve God, was now deprived of its original mastery over the body."

The Augustinian body was the manifestation of sin. This legacy of original sin bequeathed to us by Augustine has had terrible psychological and political ramifications. Christian people became the vassals of a worldly religious empire which paradoxically disavowed the world in which it had immense power. For instance, Bishop Ambrose defended slavery, arguing that slaves had no advantage for the exercise of the Christian virtues, and that men cursed with original sin were not fit to govern themselves. Their duty was to procreate without pleasure; insofar as Augustine had taught that "this world must be used, not enjoyed."

"Augustine draws so drastic a picture of the effects of Adam's sin that he embraces human government, even when tyrannical, as the indispensable defense against the forces sin has unleashed in human nature . . . Those who share Augustine's vision of the disastrous results of sin must, he believes, accept as well the rule of one man over another—master over slave, ruler over subjects—as the inescapable necessity of our universal fallen nature." (Pagels) Again, as Foucault has observed, "the politics of truth" had changed, and Augustine had evolved a religious justification for the fact that Christianity was now the state religion of Romans who had once persecuted Christians.

Augustine argued for a view of nature that is scientifically unnatural. He contends that death does not constitute the natural end of our lives but was put upon us because of the sin of Adam and Eve. Pain, labor, suffering, oppression, and death are seen as punishments that we brought upon ourselves. In Augustine's view, human choice brought mortality and sexual desire upon the human race and, in the process, deprived Adam's progeny of the freedom to choose not to sin. "But how did Augustine persuade the majority of Christians that sexual desire and death are essentially 'unnatural' experiences, the result of human sin?" (Pagels) It is an important question, particularly since Augustine's contemporaries and many scholars of the Church ever since have fought valiantly against his assertions. Yet Augustine went further than even those Jews and Christians who agreed with him that Adam's sin brought death upon humankind. "He insisted that Adam's sin also brought upon us universal moral corruption . . . From the fifth century on, Augustine's pessimistic views of sexuality, politics, and human nature would become the dominant influence on Western Christianity, both Catholic and Protestant, and color all Western culture, Christian or not, ever since . . . This cataclysmic transformation in Christian thought from an ideology of moral freedom to one of universal corruption coincided with the evolution of the Christian movement from a persecuted sect to the religion of the emperor himself." (Pagels)

In Christian Europe, more than in any other society, the body and its sexuality became a form of divine retribution. To deal with this irreversible calamity of biblical history, a passionate asceticism was supposed to rule our lives. But at every turn, the great majority of Christians neglected the dogma of Augustine. "At no time in the world's history," concludes medievalist James Bryce, "has theory, professing all the while to control practice, been so utterly divorced from it." The vain efforts of high-minded churchmen to curb excesses point to the most violent paradox of medieval life—its phenomenal license. "In theory, life was regulated by elaborate forms and codes, hedged in by religious rules that had the most awful sanctions. In fact, life ran wild in uncouth freedom, with a reckless defiance of all the rules upon which salvation depended. Social records indicate that vice and crime were far more prevalent than they are in the skeptical, cynical modern age . . . Furthermore, much of this lawlessness was condoned." (Muller) Much of the fanaticism and intolerance which are now thought of as characteristically "medieval" were, in fact, common only to the later Middle Ages. "Almost all historians are agreed that the late eleventh and early twelfth centuries were periods of 'openness' and tolerance in European society, times when experimentation was encouraged, new ideas eagerly sought, expansion favored in both the practical and the intellectual realms of life. And most historians consider that the thirteenth and fourteenth centuries were ages of less tolerance, adventurousness, acceptance—epochs in which European societies seem to have been bent on restraining, contracting, protecting, limiting, and excluding. Few scholars, however, are in exact agreement about why this change took place." (Boswell)

The efforts to restrain a long-established libertine spirit resulted in countless contradictions. Professed morality and actual conduct were entirely at odds. For instance, in the fourteenth century, at the same time that religious miracle plays and parables deplored the body and sexuality, it is estimated that about 40 percent of the children born in Europe were illegitimate. Obviously, Augustine's piety and asceticism could not capture the minds of the folk, though he nonetheless succeeded in forever changing the society in which they lived. Despite the indignation of the Church, there persisted a rich folk tradition of epics, legends, fairy tales, and rhymes which sanctioned the joy of the body. Such social forces are visible in the grand literature of writers of the period such as Chaucer and Boccaccio. The eventual decline of Church dogma and the rise of bourgeois social realism served to reenforce the robust sexuality of folk traditions. Such revivals of rustic values found renewed expression in the nationalism which preoccupied the intellectuals of the Renaissance. But such social movements in the arts could never remove the shadow that Augustine had cast upon the world.

Everywhere in today's Western world is the residue of Augustine's dogma. It influences even those who are not consciously ruled by religious values. It is built into our social metaphors and most fundamental attitudes. We accept as fact the virtue of spirit and the contamination of body; we build our figures of speech upon a goodness embodied in light and an evil that hides in darkness. We are also inclined to look upon illness as a punishment for sin and misfortune as retribution for transgression. The human body still has a terrible reputation, especially the unchaste female body. Even today women are looked upon not so much as the creators but simply as the custodians of the progeny they carry within their bodies. And in some insidious recess of the male mind, women are still regarded as polluters of men. Despite centuries of philosophy and science that have provided innumerable alternatives, we are still driven by the subversive negativism of Augustine.

Augustine pitted the Church against nature. He abolished natural law in order to enthrone spiritual law. His City of God existed outside the world of flesh and passion. It is therefore a curious fact that one of the most startling and innovative achievements of the era dominated by Augustinian philosophy occurred during the Age of Chivalry, when a group of ingenious and subtle poet-musicians in Provence invented the concept of courtly love that was the starting point for all the subsequent European manifestations of romantic love. It is this passionate vision of love that, quite remarkably, sprang without precedence from the lyrics of the troubadours that transformed the human body into a metaphor for the romantic lover.

# SIX
# The Body as Lover

*My lords, if you would hear a high tale of love and of death, here is that of Tristan and Queen Iseult; how to their full joy, but to their sorrow also, they loved each other, and how at last, they died of that love together upon one day; she by him and he by her.*

Tristan is the proud son of King Rivalen of Lyonesse, and Blanchefleur, the sister of King Mark of Cornwall. He is a fine hunter, horseman, fencer, and knight. During his exploits in Ireland he kills King Moraunt and the terrible giant Morholt, who has dared to demand tribute in men and money from King Mark. During these battles Tristan is wounded by the poisoned weapons of his foes. Knowing that he will die without the aid of a healer with great magic, Tristan seeks the assistance of princess Iseult, daughter of the king of Ireland, who is renowned for her powerful medicine. When he recovers and returns to King Mark's court, he speaks so glowingly of Iseult's beauty that Mark decides to make the Irish princess his queen.

Tristan is sent back to Ireland as the ambassador of his king, to solicit Iseult's hand in marriage. She is enthralled by the prospect of being queen of Cornwall and accepts King Mark's proposal. Tristan escorts the fair princess to England, but on the voyage they both unknowingly par-

take of a magic potion and, as a result, Tristan and Iseult
fall passionately in love with one another. So great is
their passion that they cannot escape it, even after Iseult
becomes queen. Their secret meetings are the cause of
malicious rumors. Soon the court is filled with gossip
about their affair. King Mark refuses to believe the stories of adultery. The lovers are as resourceful as the
enemies who hope to entrap them and turn the king
against them. Eventually, however, they are discovered
together. Tristan flees to Brittany in order to escape the
rage of King Mark. Believing that Iseult has forgotten
their love, Tristan marries another Iseult, the daughter of
King Howel of Brittany, who is called Iseult of the White
Hands. But after the marriage Tristan will not come to
his wife's bed, for he is still in love with the first Iseult.
He escapes his duties as a husband by going off on his
adventures, only to be wounded once again. On his death-
bed, he fatefully learns that he can be cured only by his
first love, the fair Iseult. A messenger is dispatched to
Cornwall to fetch her, and is ordered to hoist a white sail
if he succeeds in bringing Iseult to cure the dying Tristan.
When the vessel comes in sight with a white sail dis-
played, Tristan's jealous wife, Iseult of the White Hands,
tells her husband that the sail is black. Believing himself
to have been forsaken by his love, Tristan dies.

*Then the sail fair and full drove the ship to shore, and
Iseult the Fair set foot upon the land. She hearing mourn-
ing in the streets and the tolling of bells in the chapel
towers, she asked the people the meaning of the knell and
of their tears. An old man said to her:*

*"Tristan is dead."*

*Iseult went up to the palace, and crouched at the side of
her beloved's body. And when she had turned to the east
and prayed to God, she lay down by the dead man. She*

*kissed his mouth and his face, and clasped him closely;
and so gave up her soul, and died beside him of grief.*

*When King Mark heard of the death of these lovers, he
crossed the sea and came into Brittany; and he had two
coffins hewn for Tristan and Iseult. He took their bodies
away with him upon his ship to Tintagel, and by a chantry
to the left and right of the apse he had their tombs built.
But in one night there sprang from the tomb of Tristan a
green and leafy briar. It climbed the chantry and fell to
root again by Iseult's tomb. Thrice did the peasants cut it
down, but thrice it grew again as flowered and as strong.
They told the marvel to King Mark, and he forbade them
to cut the briar any more.* (Bedier/Belloc)

There are several versions of the legend of Tristan and
Iseult. But as early as 1160 the archetypal form of the
story was formalized by a poet of whom we know scarcely
anything except that he was called Thomas of Britain,
which could mean that he was born either in Great
Britain or in Brittany. Wherever his homeland, Thomas'
literary style and philosophical stance derived from a
unique form of lyric poetry that had originated in the
south of France and had rapidly spread throughout Europe. In the French-speaking territories of the north,
courtly society had achieved an autonomy in literature
not unlike the poetry that had come into flower at least a
generation before in Queen Eleanor's Provençal land of
Aquitaine. A new mythology was taking shape as the
basis of these literary forms. It was a mythology which
retained little of the elements of improbability with which
we usually associate mythic tales. It is true that this new
mythology retained some elements of the kind of fantastic epic familiar in religious myth, but it uniquely combined them with a less metaphysical and more secular
and romantic form of myth. Behind this new kind of

mythology was a passionate form of love that had come to be regarded "less as a random stroke of fate and more as a positive, even educative and purifying force." (Hatto)

The motifs and manner of the story of Tristan and Iseult betray attitudes about the body, love, and sexuality that were previously unknown in mainstream European sensibility. By some still-unexplained social process the angst of Augustine had been thoroughly sensualized. In all the versions of the Tristan myth there is a mystical language with strong religious overtones, providing a mystic sense of the sexual that is entirely absent from the myths of love and sex with which we have been concerned. The poets of the various versions of the Tristan and Iseult legend were "propagating an esoteric cult of worldly love by means of a story as if predestined for it, and with an intensity which others devoted to the joy or the salvation of their souls." (Hatto) The impulse behind the story is not only a rich and hitherto forbidden *passion*, but it also contains a deep sense of sorrow and noble frustration rather than simplistic joy and fulfillment. Even today we recognize the spirit of romance in the tale, though Tristan and Iseult is a tragic story, not the "happily-ever-after" fairy tale that television audiences often associate with romance. Yet here in a medieval epic are all the characteristics of what we now call romantic love. When it was devised, such a love story was a radical and immensely influential innovation. Its imprint on our mentality is undeniable.

The story of Tristan and Iseult is preoccupied with an ecstasy so overflowing with the love of life and with sexual bliss that it inevitably leads to premonitions of death. Such a myth is needed to express the melancholy fact that passion is often linked with death. And passion is also associated with infidelity. For it is not by accident that the great love affairs of the late Middle Ages were played out between chivalrous knights and other men's wives. Prior to the chivalrous age of passion, which is typified by romantic narratives like Tristan and Iseult, marriage was devoid of romance. As we have seen, sensual or emotional indulgence—marital, premarital, or extramarital—was excluded from life by Christian orthodoxy. Except for the followers of certain heretical cults, marriage was a solemn and emotionless feudal institution, sanctified by the Church principally as a mechanism of procreation. Love, sensuality, and passion were regarded as aberrations. So remote was passion from married life that in a famous judgement delivered by "a court of love" held in the chateau of the Countess of Champagne, love and marriage were deemed to be entirely incompatible.

Today we take it for granted, at least initially, that men and women who marry love one another, and only later in their relationship elevate the power of mutually owned property, the responsibility of parenthood, and the demands of social expectation as the basis for remaining wed. We forget that in most of the world, including Europe, until this century, most marriages were considered to be practical and political matters from the outset. Among aristocrats, as recently as the nineteenth century, marriages were often arranged when the bride and groom were still children. We also take it for granted that the natural purpose of love and marriage is sexual fulfillment, whereas until the twentieth century, far more often the real goal was the production of progeny as heirs and/or as uncompensated labor in home industries and on farms. Therefore, what took place at the end of the eleventh century was a drastic revision of how antiquity and Christianity had once conceived of marriage. The new prevailing accent of love was a state of passion. Despite the sexuality of the Tristan tale, love was associated with a suffering caused by the fact that, at least ideally, the bliss of sexual union for which the lovers yearned was not attained. If this attitude did not reflect reality, at least it became axiomatic that love was most noble when denied and that chastity was the highest evidence of humankind's claim to precedence in nature. "By the thirteenth century, lyric poets no longer sang of the joy or agony of physical love, but accepted without demur the premise that their lady was worthy of their love precisely because she was too pure to reciprocate it. Thus the quarrel between the body and the soul was reestablished. And on that division, Christianity flourished." (Warner)

Nonetheless, this unprecedented view of sexuality was a unique rebuttal of Church doctrine, which accepted the dogma of chastity at the same time that it insisted upon the virtuousness of passionate love. Nothing like this had ever happened before. As C. S. Lewis wrote in *Allegory of Love,* this concept represented a revolution in attitudes about love, the body, and sexuality. "The new thing itself, I do not pretend to explain. Real changes in human sentiment are very rare—there are perhaps three or four on record—but I believe that they occur and that this is one of them."

It was in this way that our fundamental *romantic* assumption that "love is sensual" was born. But, paradoxically, it was a sensuality without sexuality—a Platonic and Augustinian construct of love; an idealized abstraction far removed from our idea that marriages are relationships based upon love, and that the object of lovers is sexual satisfaction. The major psychological motive for this new ideal of love must have been the absence of love in arranged marriages. But there were other social constructs that could have encouraged this new and unique approach to love, such as the feudal law of inheritance, which allowed women to hold rank and property in their own right. This potent social and economic power of aristocratic women was easily translated into the personal ideals of love and marriage. In feudal society and in the Age of Chivalry, the most important concern was the acquisition of land. Owning land, more than having other forms of wealth, was the most significant form of power. And one of the least bloody and most civil methods of dealing with the orderly transmittal of property rights from one family to another and from one person to another was marriage. The fact that women could inherit and own land gave them unprecedented social importance in a European culture which had usually devalued women. However unimportant women may have been in other respects, they possessed enormous power as heiresses.

Ironically, it was probably the wealth of women that provided the milieu in which romantic love was both invented and condoned. The romanticizing of avarice for the land owned by women was both a political and sexual revolution, providing the basis for a new mythology which, in turn, prescribed new conventions for adventures in love and sexual conduct. Behind this unorthodox attitude about women and sex, however, loomed the inflexible sex-negative and sexist heritage of Judaism and Christianity. The Age of Chivalry, therefore, was a time of immense contradiction. It is just such an attitude that is reflected by Tristan's tryst with Iseult. The tension set up by this sexual encounter betrays something fundamental about both the Christian and the courtly visions of love. For Tristan to fall madly in love with Iseult would have been perfectly correct. But according to their own pronouncements ("If she love me, it is by the potion which holds me from leaving her and her from leaving me"), the famous lovers did not really love one another. They saw themselves irresistibly drawn into a sexual encounter by a love potion. As adulterous lovers they would have been celebrated by the courtly morality of the Middle Ages, but as a man and woman who engaged in the fulfillment of passion without truly loving one another, they become a new kind of tragic couple. That tragedy is concerned with the failure of restraint.

In the Middle Ages the term "adultery" eventually attained an extolled interpretation, entirely contrary to the Augustinian ascetic view of the word. This novel connotation of adultery implied a devotion to a higher moral law (that of passionate love) rather than the loyalty associated with the Christian view of marital fidelity. Ultimately, this unprecedented contest between fidelity and infidelity represented a conflict between irreconcilable religions: that of a new chivalrous code of passion and that of the older Christianized feudal morality of asceticism. It is this conflict that provides just the kind of lover's *obstruction* that is always a central motif of courtly romance. Restraint was a necessity not of morality but of passion itself. For this reason, lovers always invented obstructions which frustrated rather than satisfied their desire for one another. As the medieval poets proclaimed: "Whatever turns into a reality is no longer love."

Tristan and Iseult, however, allowed their passion to become real—although most versions of the myth mitigate their blame by attributing their indulgence to the blinding impulse of a love potion. In fully possessing his lady, Tristan ignored the principal obstruction which was central in the morality of chivalry. As Denis de Rougemont, the author of the definitive work on romantic love, has pointed out, Tristan's experience was intended to illustrate a tension between chivalry and feudal society and a conflict between two kinds of religious mythologies. The lovers are therefore a metaphor of this fundamental contradiction. Like all great lovers, they assume that their passion has led them beyond good and evil into a state outside ordinary human experience. What the lovers of the Age of Chivalry loved was love itself. Insinuated into this personal passion is a familiar Christian sentiment: the passion of the crucifixion which is inextricably associated with death and redemption. Death, then, becomes both the obstruction and the object of romantic love. Eventually, in the eighteenth century, this feudal intertwining of passion and death would become one of the primary aspects of Romanticism, a legacy of medieval tales such as Tristan and Iseult.

Death is the ultimate obstruction among many obstructions that stand between the lovers and their sexual fulfillment. The obstruction builds upon the ecstasy of passion. It attains an emotional value greater than that of passion itself. "Death, in being the goal of passion, kills it." (Rougemont) The self-imposed chastity of medieval love was therefore a form of ecstatic death—a crucifixion, a passionate denial, even a symbolic suicide. The chaste passion of lovers became a triumph over desire just as death and redemption was thought to be a triumph over life. Tristan and Iseult's death is a death for love, a deliberate death coming at the end of a series of ordeals which have purified the lovers and prepared them for a death of transfiguration. (Rougemont)

As I have already mentioned, the narrative based on the myth of Tristan and Iseult was deeply influenced by a poetic style that had its obscure origins in the south of France, where the idealization of romantic love was first articulated. Medievalist David Herlihy has observed that such medieval poetry and romance are as much an aspect of mythology as the ancient religious texts, but they differ strikingly from biblical and classical epics in the great importance they concede to love. Here, then, we have a fundamental revision not only in what we mean by *mythology* but also in what we mean by *love*. The origin of this revolution in cultural attitudes occurred in the south of France, where medieval poets from all social classes wrote not in Latin but in Provençal, the language of daily life, thus creating the first cultivated vernacular lyric poetry of Europe. This poetry was meant to be sung. The creators of these lyrical songs were called troubadours, the word *trobador* deriving from the Provençal verb *trobar*, meaning "to discover, to invent, or to devise." By the early thirteenth century, the troubadours had become widely acclaimed artists, singing their poetry in all the courts of the grand lords and ladies. So great was troubadour influence that Provençal became the preeminent language for lyric compositions and was used by countless poets, French, Spanish, Italian, and German. Most of this literature was concerned with a special conception of love, which was called *cortezia,* or courtly love. The fascination with *cortezia* was absorbed and distilled in the major literary works of the period: in *The Romance of the Rose, The Romance of Tristan and Iseult,* and in the great Arthurian romances of northern France.

The derivation of the troubadour literary styles and forms is greatly contested. Each scholarly theory has been toppled by refutation. One scholar attributed the origin of the characteristic troubadour "emotional mysticism" to the love lyrics composed by the Arabs of the Middle Ages. Another scholar tried to convince us that there are resemblances in the rhythms of both Arab and Provençal lyric poetry. In the renowned study by Denis de Rougemont, to which all discussions of romantic love are indebted, he observed that many of the troubadours addressed their poems to male lovers, which could have been a reflection of the strongly homosexual basis of Arabic poetry. Still other authorities suggest that Latin poetry of the eleventh and twelfth centuries may have provided models to the troubadours, although this explanation has been refuted because troubadours (who were both aristocrats and peasants) were insufficiently educated to have been aware of this poetry.

Despite such controversies, there are at least a few uncontestable facts about the poets of courtly love. For one thing, in their works (and presumably in society) women suddenly became idealized persons of great importance. There were reasons for this. One of them had to do with marriage. As I've already indicated, in the Middle Ages marriage was usually the product of an agreement between great families. Such marriages had little to do with love and nothing whatsoever to do with passion. They were Church-sanctified contracts concerned with property, power, and the family lineage by which legacies were passed from generation to generation. Under Church law marriage was indissoluble, extramarital sex was condemned, and thus, at least theoretically, male lineage was protected—always a concern when inheritance passes exclusively in the male line and the adultery of a married woman therefore poses a problem. Patriliny traditionally demands the chastity of a wife, otherwise she can deceive her spouse with heirs that are not his true kin. But when women are also the benefactors of great wealth, as they were in the Middle Ages, a rare matriliny both increases the attractiveness of women as something other than chattel and also greatly lessens the disruptiveness of a wife's adultery. (Warner) Men in the time of the troubadours were anxious to captivate women whose immense inheritances were protected by the continuance of Roman Law. And the fact that many aristocratic women were rich and powerful in their own right was probably another reason that the concept of love during the period gave such glorified focus to women.

From what I have said, it is clear that despite Church codes to the contrary, the Middle Ages were unexpectedly tolerant in matters of sex by comparison to many earlier and later ages. Except for monks, priests, and nuns, no one was required to be chaste. Adulterers were not driven out, as the Fathers of the Church commanded. Infractions of sexual conduct were merely concealed. With sufficient tact and concealment, people could do as they wished. "If it is permissible to characterize a period so long and so changeful with a simple phrase, we may say: the essential was dissimulation. This applied to politics, and also to sex-life. On the surface, everything centered round loyalty." (Lewisohn) The feudal system was built upon various forms of trust and fidelity: the vassal to his liege lord, the wife to the husband, the child to the family. Such fidelity left little place for other kinds of relationships. Perhaps more than at any other time, human associations were implicit parts of social structures. This elaboration of feudal fidelity brought with it the elevation of infidelity into a fine art. "Church and State alike tolerated the adulterous relationship between the young knight and the baronial lady. A cavalier might even bring religion into his affairs of the heart. It was the thing to choose a celestial patroness, and the usual practice, incredible though it sounds, was to invoke the Virgin Mary to patronize the liaison and soften the married lady's heart toward her knightly suppliant." (Lewisohn)

In Germany the troubadours were called *minnesingers* or "singers of love." What these Germanic bards were proclaiming, indirectly but quite plainly, was "Lo! All you are told in Church about the sanctity of marriage applies only to the peasant. The great do not need to trouble with it. For *minne* law is above the law of marriage."

The most vital source of inspiration of troubadour

poetry was an un-Christian mythology and ritual of extra-marital love. Conceiving of love as a redemptive passion, the poets evolved a quasi-religious ceremonial form of romance, dividing it into distinctive ritual stages. The first was "hesitating," during which the lover could not find the courage or the words to make his feelings known to the married woman who was his beloved (or *dompna*). In the second stage, called "pleading," he proclaims his love. In the third stage, "hearing," it is the lady's turn to hesitate, as she considers the lover's request and by the ambiguity of her responses kindles in him feelings of both joy and despair. The last stage is *druerie* (or "service"), when the lady accepts the lover's suit and he becomes her devoted servant. He never divulges the lady's name, but he sings her praises and does great deeds in her honor.

This kind of romantic ritual was entirely unknown in the cultures of the Jews, Greeks, and Romans. In such societies, passionate love was an excess and an embarrassment, something that distinguished families hoped would never occur among their kin. A person who loved with passion was considered to be a lunatic, a moonstruck fool worthy of nothing but laughter and pity. Even in the Middle Ages, before the advent of courtly love, the attitude toward passion, derived from antiquity, was that "the passion of love was a type of disease . . . a symptomology had been developed and forms of therapy (such as coitus) were suggested as treatment. Sexuality was looked upon as normal physical behavior, whereas passion was considered a disease." (Luhmann)

In the age of courtly love all this was abruptly changed. Passion was an expression approaching religious ecstasy. The blending of sensual love, loyalty, and humble servitude to womankind expressed in a highly allegorical, mystical, ambiguous, and sometimes erotically crude language is unique to the troubadours and to medieval courtly love.

The cultural context of this revolutionary notion of love is easier to identify than to pinpoint in terms of cultural origins. The scholar of chivalrous love Charles Albert Cingria remarks: "Between the eleventh and twelfth centuries, poetry—whether Hungarian, or Spanish, Portuguese, German, Sicilian, Tuscan, Genoese, Pisan, Picard, Champagne, Flemish, English, etc.—was at first Languedoc; which is to say, that the poet, who had to be a troubadour, was expected to speak the troubadour language which was never other than Provençal. The whole of the Occitanian, Petrarchian, and Dantesque lyric has but a single theme—love; and not happy, crowned, and satisfied love (the sight of which yields nothing), but on the contrary love perpetually unsatisfied— and but two characters: a poet reiterating his plaint eight hundred, nine hundred, a thousand times; and a fair lady who ever says 'No.' "

The question of the origins of the troubadour's attitudes and lyrics may never be completely resolved nor may we ever know for certain the degree to which the poetry reflected the actual daily behavior of men and women of the Middle Ages. "One of the most remarkable features of the rise of romantic love was that the same period was characterized by extremely barbaric, brutal and disgusting practices by both men and women. Sexuality might very well be the theme of magnificent poetry but at the same time, to judge from contemporary poems and romances, the first thought of every knight on finding a lady unprotected and alone was to do her violence . . . But whatever interpretation is used to explain [it] the fact remains that the concept of courtly love invented by the troubadours in Provence was the starting point for all the subsequent European manifestations of romantic love." (Henriques)

Denis de Rougemont notes with emphasis: *"The cultivation of passionate love began in Europe as a reaction to Christianity (and in particular to its doctrine of marriage) by people whose spirit, whether naturally or by inheritance, was still pagan."* This rebirth of European Eros within the constraints of Judeo-Christian culture is well documented. The earliest passionate lovers whose story has reached us are Abelard and Heloise, who met for the first time in 1118. And it was in the middle of this same century that love was first recognized and encouraged as a passion worth cultivating. But such love clearly collided with every moral stricture of Christianity. Under the converted Constantine and under the Carolingian emperors Church doctrine became the criterion of the ruling class, which forced Christian values upon the entire population of the West. "This, of course, meant the repression of the old pagan beliefs, which became the hope and refuge of natural inclinations frowned upon and not disposed of by the new rule. In the eyes of the ancients, marriage, for example, was a utilitarian institution of limited purpose. If not adultery as understood today, at least concubinage was allowed by custom, for slaves could be both used and abused. But Christian marriage, inasmuch as it is a sacrament, imposed on the natural man a constancy which he found unbearable. Anyone compulsorily converted came under the restraints of the Christian code, but lacked the support of any actual faith. Inevitably the barbarian blood of such people must have rebelled, and they were all disposed to welcome a revival of the pagan mysteries in Catholic guise, since this brought a promise of 'emancipation.' " (Rougemont)

That revival was easily focused upon the traditional power of women, for the "pagan" influence of the Mother

Goddess had persisted in folklore throughout Romanized Europe. Even in the far West, the druidical cult of the Celts turned woman into a prophetic being whose impact was felt throughout Western Europe. It is not surprising, then, that the myth of the passionate love of Tristan and Iseult was born in Ireland and Cornwall, and was recapitulated in literary forms and styles later invented by the troubadours of southern France. The idolization of woman became a ritualization of repressed sexuality and a sublimation of (or perhaps only a complex cultural rationalization for) the incredible brutality of medieval life. Woman reemerged as a symbol of both the repressed inner life and the lost matricentric mentality that had once dominated European tribes. Remarkably, the sinful flesh that Augustine had preached against so persuasively was now transformed into a new conception of the human body: as a reservoir of profound sensuality and feeling, a body that anticipated but indefinitely postponed the physical act of sex because its fulfillment dissipated the greater pleasure of expectation that kept passion alive. This kind of sexual script, with its hesitant rhythms, is not often associated with quickly aroused, quickly satisfied, genital-focused male sexuality. It is far more often envisioned as characterizing the female sexual response. Thus, again, it was the symbol, if not the fact, of woman that was at the core of courtly love.

"How many paths through the history of the medieval West lead to woman!" exclaims the noted French medievalist Jacques Le Goff (1980). "The history of heresies is, in many respects, a history of woman in society and religion. If there is one innovation in the area of sensibility with which the Middle Ages are generally credited, it has to be courtly love. It is built around an image of woman."

Equally significant in terms of its pre-Christian appeal was the rise of the cult of the Virgin Mary during the time of Blanche of Castile, mother of King Louis IX (ca. 1260). In the Virgin's traditional aspect of Queen of Heaven, she easily blended with the aristocratic and powerful ladies who were the passionate beloveds of poets. It is not surprising, therefore, that much of the late poetry of the troubadours makes implausible associations between the Virgin and the ladies for whom they express deeply sensual passion.

Despite the countless contradictions of sexually exploitative knights, who made a cult of their adoration of the feminine, the emergence of courtly love in the Middle Ages stands as an exceptional and unexpected metaphor of the demasculinization of history, climaxed by the "stunning breakthrough in the twelfth century" of the cult of the Virgin Mary. (Le Goff, 1980)

The Virgin's identification with courtly love is both peculiar as well as subtly fitting. This is precisely why in the romantic West, even today, the term love still implies chastity. *"E d'amor mou castitaz,"* sang the Toulouse troubadour Guilhelm Montanghagol—"Out of love comes chastity."

Passionate love also required a ritual in the guise of Christian ceremony—like the ritual of *domnei* or *donnoi,* love's vassalage. As medievalist Frederick Artz has suggested, the code of courtly love represents the feudalization of love—"the devotion of the lover to the lady derives something from the devotion of the feudal vassal to his lord. In other words, the feudal rites of vassalage, the oath of service sworn by a knight to his lord, were transformed in the age of courtly love into a servitude of Amor. It is through the beauty of his songs of praise that a poet wins his lady. On his knee he swears eternal constancy to her, just as knights swore fealty to their suzerain. If accepted, the knight is given a ring by his lady as well as a chaste kiss on the brow."

Denis de Rougement provides some of the ultimate questions in regard to the riddles of courtly love. What is the origin of this notion of a love perpetually unsatisfied, he asks, and what is the motive for singing the praises of a fair lady who always says "No"? And how is it that a literary form was available at precisely the time when poets needed a literary form for their expression of new ideas about love? "Within no more than about twenty years there were established together, on the one hand, a vision of woman entirely at variance with traditional manners—woman was set above man, and became his nostalgic ideal—on the other hand, a new but fully developed poetry of an extremely complex and refined character—a poetry equally unknown in antiquity, and to the few centuries of romantic literary vigor that had followed the Carolingian Renaissance." (Rougemont) Either these elements simply dropped out of the sky or they had a basis in history.

It is generally agreed today that both Provençal poetry and the courtly notion of love seem to have been in contradiction to the social and religious conditions prevailing in their time. They appear not to have reflected the society in which they were born but to have contradicted it. They express the same falsity that we discover in the citizens of modern democracies who deeply believe in their mythology of equality at the same time that they enact and enforce inequality in countless attitudes, deeds, and feelings. In much the same way, the historical context of the invention of passionate love provides more enigmas than explanations. The poetry of the period is essentially all that remains of courtly love, and that romantic poetry clearly did not reflect the unsavory state of affairs in regard to the sexual behavior of the knights of the Middle Ages nor the position they allotted to women in the feudal world of Europe. Passion might very well have been the idealized theme of the magnificent poetry of the troubadours, but at the same time that they were composing it, to judge from contemporary evidence, the exploitation of women was brutal. The *Lai de Graelent,* by Marie de France, recounts how a gentle and perfect knight meets a damsel alone in the forest. He brutally assaults and rapes her. He is excused for his conduct, however, for during his miserable act "he was courteous and honorable." The same contradiction is discovered in the instructions given to the good knight Sir Perceval by his mother: "If thou see a fair lady, pay court to her, whether she will or no; for thus wilt thou render thyself a better and more esteemed man than thou wast before."

Different interpretations have been given to the controversies of this early literature of romantic love. Some scholars insist that the lawlessness and brutality of the period were overlaid by an idealized mythology of the feminine, which was sometimes acted out and at other times totally disregarded. Another interpretation is that the knights and troubadours constituted a realm of culture and gentility in an otherwise barbarous world. As historian Barbara Tuchman has noted, "More than a code of manners in war and love, Chivalry was a moral system, governing the whole of noble life. That it was about four parts in five illusion made it no less governing for all that. It developed at the same time as the great crusades of the twelfth century as a code intended to fuse the religious and martial spirits and somehow bring the fighting man into accord with Christian theory. Since a knight's usual activities were as much at odds with Christian theory as a merchant's, a moral gloss was needed that would allow the Church to tolerate the warriors in good conscience and the warriors to pursue their own values in spiritual comfort."

The knight's sword was visualized as being the arm of

the Church, dispensing justice to widows, orphans, and the oppressed. Thus Ramon Lull, the champion of chivalry, could state that "God and chivalry are in concord."

Chivalry was looked upon as a universal brotherhood of all Christian knights. "If tournaments were an acting out of chivalry, courtly love was its dreamland . . . Courtly love was a greater tangle of irreconcilables even than usury. It remained artificial, a literary convention, a fantasy (like modern pornography) more for purposes of discussion than for everyday practice . . . these tales exalted adulterous love as the only true kind, while in the real life of the same society adultery was a crime, not to mention a sin . . . Yet, if the code was but a veneer over violence, greed, and sensuality, it was nevertheless an ideal, as Christianity was an ideal, toward which man's reach, as usual, exceeded his grasp." (Tuchman)

The explanations for the invention of passionate courtly love constantly change with a society's perceptions of itself. Thus sexual politicians such as Marina Warner convincingly envision the social ascent of women in the late Middle Ages as a romanticization of the power plays of males who sought to be awarded through marriage or escapade the very substantial inheritances of titled women in an epoch of many politically powerful females.

An inescapable aspect of the poetry of courtly love is the fact that many of its authors actively denigrated the object of their prize: women. For social critics of our day, there is nothing very surprising about that behavior, since it is consistent with generations of masculine attitudes about women.

In the Age of Chivalry, for instance, the so-called *goliard* lyrics often presented women in a brutal and unsympathetic way, "an expression of the sour antifeminism so frequently found in the Middle Ages, and fostered by orthodox Church teachings in which woman, the

cause of man's Fall from Eden, was denounced as a
'Gateway to Hell.' " (Marks) At the very same time,
other troubadours described women with fantastic respect. Even in the crudest poems of the troubadour
Guilheim VII women are viewed as a source of delight
and righteousness, and not as objects of scorn.

"Courtly love came into existence in the twelfth century during a complete revolution of the Western psyche.
It sprang up out of the same movement which forced
upwards into the half light of our human consciousness,
and into lyrical expression by the human spirit, the Feminine Principle of *Shakti,* the worship of Woman, of the
Mother, and of the Virgin." (Rougemont)

Medievalist Johan Huizinga has provided an important
summary of the social role of courtly love, describing an
ideal which provided the impetus for the self-image of
the aristocrats of the Middle Ages, an image built upon a
remarkable idealization rather than a reality. "Love became the field where all moral and cultural perfection
flowered. Because of his love, the courtly lover is pure
and virtuous. The spiritual elements dominate more and
more, till toward the end of the thirteenth century, the
*dolce stil nuovo* ["sweet new style"] of Dante and his
friends ends by attributing to love the gift of bringing
about a state of piety and holy intuition . . . The aristoc-
racy could feel less dependent on religious admonition,
because they had a piece of culture of their own from
which to draw their standards of conduct, namely, cour-
tesy . . . and if they did not altogether succeed, they at
least created the appearance of an honorable life of courtly
love."

The legacy of the troubadours is perhaps richer than
we will ever fully realize. To knights and women and
artists of the Middle Ages the cult of courtly love provided an exceptional freedom of expression. As an ideal,

if not as a social reality, that new concept of love became the vehicle for a hitherto unknown individuality—an individuality that, without the reconciliation of idealized passion, would surely have been regarded as outright heresy during those stringent times when the Church was midwife at the birth of Europe. Thus the troubadours were the instruments of a unique exploration of the mythology of *individuals*—the invention of self and psyche as made visible by passion—unrestrained by the inflexible, collective dogma of the feudal state and church. Freedom was achieved not as a right to become a social individual but as the right to feel one's own feelings. In its way, that achievement was perhaps more revolutionary than the creed of the *Declaration of Independence.* Given the fact that the institutional world of feudal Europe gave no voice either to individuals or their sexuality, it is significant that troubadours chose to correct that neglect by inventing one of the first truly private, rather than collective, forms of "populist" art, one that did not rely upon the recapitulation of the events, images, and icons of Judeo-Christian mythology, but dared to discover its themes and artistic forms in the secret life of our highly personal sexualities. This unprecedented artistic heresy, at least in the sex-negative West, would not be given a name until the advent of Romanticism, when, appropriately, the troubadour's passionate vision of love and death triumphed as both the spirit and the voice of an age.

# SEVEN
# The Body as Machine

"They administered beatings to dogs with perfect indifference and made fun of those of us who believed the creatures felt pain and therefore pitied them. They insisted that the animals were clocks; that the cries they emitted when struck were only the noises of some little spring that had been triggered by the blow, but that the animal itself had absolutely no feeling. They nailed the animals to boards by their four paws and, while they were still living, they vivisected them in order to see the circulation of blood which was a subject of great interest and conversation."

These are the words of Jean de la Fontaine, the seventeenth-century author renowned for his skill as a storyteller. His narration sounds very much like a Kafka-esque revision of one of La Fontaine's famous animal tales. But the excerpt is not drawn from the *Fables*. It is La Fontaine's eyewitness account of animal experiments that took place again and again in France during his lifetime.

The harrowing scene, in which experimenters systematically manipulated a living creature as if it were a senseless machine, exemplified an attitude toward life that had surfaced during La Fontaine's time. For our purposes, that attitude may be said to constitute a radical and new kind of mythology.

Because La Fontaine's account appears to be journalism rather than the kind of religious mythology with which I have opened many of the chapters of this book, perhaps I should restate more precisely my remarks in the introductory chapter, where I suggest that it is possible to decipher the La Fontaine scene as the seventeenth-century equivalent of just the kind of value-loaded myths with which we have been concerned. A particular set of socially constructed values not only shaped the experiment La Fontaine witnessed, but it also continues to shape our comprehension of that scene today. What puzzles us is that La Fontaine appears to be dealing journalistically with a set of observed *facts*. But we must remember that the Old Testament and all other religious epics were, and in many cases still are, understood as depictions of factual events. In this way, it is possible and it is also productive to view La Fontaine's journalism as a reality built upon a particular canon of belief and as a secular aspect of mythology in its modern aspect.

This revised definition of "mythology" brings into question the whole concept of "objectivity." What, after all, are *observed events*? Is observed reality influenced by the observer? Such questions have greatly preoccupied us since the Age of Enlightenment, when philosophers began in earnest to question the basis of how we are able to know things about ourselves and the world around us. Though common sense resists such questions, it has been widely agreed that in our day, as in the past, "objective facts" are reflections of arbitrary belief systems. In short, we see what we believe. As such, *mythology,* as we will be discussing it now, becomes a broad enough term to encompass not only the fabled cosmogonies of the past but also the cosmogony which is the basis of our constructs in science. Such a mythology is what Joseph Campbell often called "the myths we live by."

Campbell's premise was corroborated by one of the leading and most influential historians of science, Thomas Kuhn: "The more carefully [historians] study, say, Aristotelian dynamics, phlogistic chemistry, or caloric thermodynamics, the more certain they feel that those once-current views of nature were, as a whole, neither less scientific nor more the product of human idiosyncrasy than those current today. If these out-of-date beliefs are to be called myths, then myths can be produced by the same sorts of methods and held for the same sorts of reasons that now lead to scientific knowledge."

The notion that mythology can have a relationship to science, the one source of twentieth-century information in which we have almost unlimited confidence, may seem unlikely. Yet philosophers, like Kuhn and Paul K. Feyerabend, have suggested that objective, impersonal science is indeed just that—a form of mythology, a belief system or paradigm which is true without being an expression of absolute truth. "There is, I think, no theory-independent way to reconstruct phrases like 'really there'; the notion of a match between the ontology of a theory and its 'real' counterpart in nature now seems to me illusive in principle." (Kuhn)

Kuhn's premise is not easy for us to accept, since "mythology" is often looked upon as the superstitions of some other people, and not the "reality" of our own culture.

We must rethink some of our basic ideas. If even "objectified" science is a construction based upon a belief system, then it too must be understood as an aspect of mythology. As such, the term "mythology" attains a factual meaning and can no longer be used to describe a shibboleth or an extravagant religious fiction.

What interests us here is how our mythology of science impacts upon our vision of the world, the body, and our sexuality. Crucial to that vision is the mechanistic para-digm that has dominated the mentality of scientists ever since the days of La Fontaine, when the French philoso-pher Descartes proposed the revolutionary idea that ani-mals are pure, soulless *automata*.

No one knows exactly how or when this theory of Mechanism originated in the mind of Descartes. A story-teller, like La Fontaine, might suggest that the philo-sophical revolution that has dominated scientific thinking for at least two centuries began quite innocently one fine day in the 1630s, when Descartes visited the royal gar-dens at Versailles, famous for their intricate automata—those ingenious water-powered mechanisms that take the shape of sea nymphs and an immense figure of Neptune, complete with trident, advancing menacingly upon the spectator. Descartes was intrigued by the self-moving ma-chines whose power was contained within their own mech-anisms. Such mechanical devices were not new. Descartes was fully aware that clocks are automata, but what fasci-nated him at Versailles was the notion that an automaton could simulate the movement of animal life. And, in-deed, Descartes himself constructed an automaton, al-though little is known about it.

The mechanistic view of the world had probably preoc-cupied Descartes long before his visit to Versailles. Car-tesian philosophy, supported by elaborate mathematics, deduced that the universe and all the things in it are automata. Science writer Gary Zukav puts it this way: "From Descartes' time to the beginning of this century, and perhaps because of him, our ancestors began to see the universe as a Great Machine. Over the next three hundred years they developed science specifically to dis-cover how the Great Machine worked."

Cartesian Mechanism inevitably shaped the conception of the human body. Descartes laid the philosophical foundation for physiology by advancing the notion that the bodies of humans and animals can be regarded as machines. But since moral principles obviously do not apply to machines but do apply to Christian human beings, Descartes assumed that humans must therefore be more than automata in human shape. The element that makes people more than automata is the soul, "a spiritual agency that is not itself part of the body."

To experiment with dogs, from this Cartesian view, was perfectly proper because soulless machines (*bêtes-machines*) do not feel discomfort or pain; they simply respond to mechanistic stimulation. Human beings, insisted Descartes, are quite another matter. As far as he was concerned, it is from their incorporeal soul ("residing in the pineal glands") that humans derive their freedom of action. Without belief in such a freedom of choice there could be no basis for Christian ethics. "For the purpose of dealing with the intersection of morals and human biology, nothing has thus far replaced the Cartesian body-soul dualism." (Stent)

"When a man in falling thrusts out his hand to save his head," Descartes observed, "he does that without his reason counseling him so to act, but merely because the sight of the impending fall penetrating to his brain drives the animal spirits into the nerves in the manner necessary for this motion, and for producing it without the mind's desiring it, and as though it were the working of a machine." This kind of behavior, he continues, "will not seem strange to those who know how many different automata or moving machines can be made by the industry of man, without more than a very few parts in comparison with the great multitude of bones, muscles, nerves, arteries, veins or other parts that are found in the body of each animal. From this aspect the body is regarded as a machine which having been made by the hands of God, is incomparably better arranged, and possesses in itself movements which are much more admirable, than any of those which can be invented by man."

As far as Descartes was concerned, the most remarkable of God's mechanistic achievements in creating animal machines was the circulation of blood. In discussing circulation Descartes acknowledged his debt to William Harvey, whose *De Motu Cordis* had been published nearly ten years before Descartes' *Discourse on Method*. In one significant way, however, Descartes took exception with the circulatory theories of Harvey. Descartes preferred a mechanistic explanation of the action of the heart, whereas the English doctor's account involved the view of ventricles as muscular sacs and not mechanisms. From Descartes' viewpoint (which proved to be erroneous), for the heart to function required nothing but heat, rarefaction, and expansion, properties found in inanimate things. This mechanistic vision of physiology was a landmark in the seventeenth-century triumph of Mechanism—the theory that all natural phenomena can be explained by the motion of geometrical matter.

Such Cartesian ideas have had enormous impact. Descartes inaugurated a major shift to a paradigm with which, to a very great extent, we are still living today. Despite its scientific tone, his dualism and his depreciation of the physical world as "dead matter" was profoundly Christian. It resonated with Augustinian morality, and therefore made Christian dogma the premise upon which a supposedly nonreligious and objectified science was built. Though seemingly incongruous, this marriage of scientific technology and western Christian dogma was inevitable. "Unlike the deities of paganism, the Christian god was a creator God, architect of the cosmos, the divine potter who shaped men from clay in his own image. In the Christian conception, all history moves toward a spiritual goal and there is no time to lose; thus work of all sorts is essential, and becomes, in a way, a form of worship. Such ideas created a mental climate highly favorable for the growth of technology." (Casson) There was, however, a basic difference in spiritual direction between the churches of the East and the West: the Eastern Church in Constantinople held that sin is ignorance and that salvation comes by illumination; the Western Church in Rome believed that sin is vice and that rebirth comes by disciplining the will to do good works. Consequently, the Greek Orthodox saints are normally depicted as contemplative figures, while the saints of Roman Catholicism are activists. "The Western attitude toward work and toward technology, as an expression of Christian faith, thus stands in contrast equally to the ancient Greco-Roman attitudes and that of the medieval Eastern Church. It is dramatically symbolized in a manuscript of the Gospels produced at Winchester shortly after the year 1000. Here, God is portrayed as He would never be in the Eastern Church, as a master craftsman holding scales, a carpenter's square, and a pair of compasses." (Casson) Whereas the Eastern Church forbade music, in the West, as early as the tenth century, the Winchester Cathedral installed an organ with 400 pipes fed by 28 bellows that required 70 men to pump them. The East never permitted clocks in or on its churches, while in the West, as soon as mechanical clocks were invented they appeared both on towers outside and on walls within churches. Thus in the West technology was hailed as a Christian virtue. And due to this technological predisposition, how simple it was for Descartes' Mechanism to merge with Church doctrine and for Cartesian mentality, as we shall see, to provide the ethical incentive for the Industrial Revolution in the West.

Beneath the Christian and Cartesian celebration of

Mechanism was a polemic concerning the immaterial spirit. In much the way that the Church was focused upon the disembodied soul, Descartes was concerned with rationality as a disembodied process. Thus, Cartesian Rationalism stressed the reality of thought and its independence from the material world. "I think, therefore I am." He insisted that the proof of his existence depended upon his thinking, but did not depend upon the existence of his body or of the world. (Kenny) What "existed" of the material world was a God-made mechanism powered by the dynamics of mathematics. This consuming mechanistic viewpoint was suggested to him not only by the physiological research of William Harvey, but also by the planetary astronomy of Johannes Kepler, who pointed the way from an organic view of the cosmos to one that was mechanical. Kepler insisted that the *Machina Coelestis,* the celestial machine, is not a divine organism, but rather "something like a clockwork in which a single weight drives all the gears." Thus the universe was no longer envisioned as tribal people had imagined it: a living, changing, and growing organism. It assumed the shape dictated by Cartesian mentality: a great, abstract, and eternal machine. (Boorstin)

From Descartes' reworking of the circulatory theories of Harvey he bequeathed to two centuries of scientists the notion that the human body is nothing more or less than a walking machine that pumps blood. From his revision of Kepler's cosmology he gave to us a beguiling picture of the universe as a gigantic mechanism. From Augustine and from the Neoplatonists, who were among the strongest voices of the medieval Church, Descartes formulated his mystical conception of the human soul and his strict dualism of body and spirit. Taken together, these Cartesian principles became the foundation of the scientific mythology of the seventeenth and eighteenth centuries and the basis of the industrial boom of the nineteenth century.

Beyond the immense influence upon the way we conceive of our world and our bodies, what Kepler, Harvey, and Descartes have in common is the fact that they did their landmark work during a time of philosophical upheaval—a period when the conception of nature was totally revised. As I have already pointed out, the human body is a metaphor for nature, and our vision of nature indicates how we think about our bodies. Thus a fundamental revision of our attitudes about nature drastically changes the way we see ourselves. We cannot talk about revolutions in philosophy and industry without also speaking about revolutions in the sciences that provide our visions of ourselves.

Thomas S. Kuhn has written persuasively about these inevitable and periodic shifts in reality. Major changes in political ideals are brought about by a sense that laws and institutions are inadequate in dealing with the problems of a world that they have helped to create. "In much the same way, scientific revolutions are inaugurated by a growing sense . . . that an existing paradigm has ceased to function adequately in the exploration of an aspect of nature to which that paradigm itself had previously led the way."

Is it possible to describe the differences between Galileo and Aristotle, or Lavoisier and Priestley, as a transformation of their visions of the world? Kuhn asks: "Did these men really *see* different things when *looking at* the same sorts of objects?" And then he answers: "Today research suggests that though the world itself does not change with a change of paradigm, the scientist afterward works in a significantly different world."

British physicist L. L. Whyte insisted that most of us have failed to recognize the revolutions in science that have overtaken Cartesian mentality. "The procedure developed by Descartes is the analytical method which assumes that thought must pass from simple, clear, and local facts to the general and complex. This method would be adequate in a world of changeless entities possessing motion but no history, and contemplated by a static mind endowed once and for all with the necessary clear ideas. In Descartes' thought there is no duration, no history, and no approach to an understanding either of the development of form in nature or of the origin of ideas in the mind. Analytical clarity is a comforting illusion, but a dangerous one because it obscures the profound limitations of static dualistic thought . . . Descartes reduced form to quantity, and opened the way to the anarchy of mechanism and the decay of culture . . . Whatever lip service we pay to other ideas, and however certain we are of its falsity, after three centuries we still behave as if we lived in a Cartesian world."

That anachronistic attitude has had a profound impact upon our conception of both the human body and sexuality. "Cartesian dualism is very much alive today and remains the unstated metaphysical premise of medical ethics." (Stent) In fact, most historians of science agree that the whole field of sexology is built upon the Cartesian premise.

By the end of the seventeeth century overt religious influences over sex mores began to decline. In his study of sexual variance in society, Vern L. Bullough notes: "Just as it seemed that a new sexuality would undermine the Western hostility to sex, science came up with new justifications for sexual repression. These ideas appeared first in the medical literature at the beginning of the eighteenth century but gradually became elaborated and more formalized, until by the end of the century they began percolating into the general consciousness. Eventually, they were seized upon by the conservative moralists and became the dominant theme of the nineteenth century, providing the intellectual basis for what we regard as Victorian morality."

Science, or more specifically, *sexology* replaced religion as the arbitrator of behavior. The Judeo-Christian criteria of good and evil were largely replaced by a complex calibration of normal and abnormal. By the time of Queen Victoria, passion had been totally imprisoned in the analytic treatment of emotion, a tradition that had commenced two centuries earlier with Descartes, who converted passion "to clearly distinct psychological categories and to rational hierarchies of qualities, worthiness, and faculties." (Rougemont) What Descartes and the sexologists, who followed his example, did was simply to carry out the Christian precepts invented by Augustine.

Since the time of the triumph of Augustinian philosophy we have experienced our sexuality primarily in our heads, as a moral concept rather than a physical experience. (Foucault) After Augustine, Descartes reasserted in scientific terms the strict division between mind and body, a concept that completely severed our *idea* of sexuality from our bodily *experience* of sex. Sexology became a secularized religion aimed at what gay historian Jonathan Katz has aptly called the "medical colonization" of humankind. Since the late nineteenth century, when sexology was defined as "the science of desire," sexologists such as Krafft-Ebing, Havelock Ellis, August Forel, Magnus Hirschfeld, Sigmund Freud, and many others, have attempted to discover the true meaning of sex by exploring its various expressions and guises. In sexology's search "for the 'true' meaning of sex, in its intense interrogation of sexual difference, and in its obsessive categorization of sexual perversities it has contributed to the codification of a 'sexual tradition,' a more or less coherent body of assumptions, beliefs, prejudices, rules, methods of investigation and forms of moral regulation, which still shape the way we live our sexualities." (Weeks) Inevitably the enforcers of this new code for the judgment of sexual behavior were strongly patriarchal. The materiality of sex coincided with the mechanistic conception of nature as "dead matter" to be molded by males. Sociologist Victor Seidler elaborates on this theme: "The body, in Western culture, is radically separated from a sense of personal identity; the latter is defined in purely mental terms as a matter of consciousness. This reiterates a Christian tradition which had often denigrated the body as a source of spiritual knowledge. The male body in the Cartesian tradition was to be used as an instrument, rather than as something through which individuality could be expressed. Men were to be estranged from their bodies as they were from a natural world they had learned to fear and distrust. Men could only assert their humanity by mastery over the physical world, and by learning to dominate their passions and desires. It is this inherited notion of self-control as *dominance* that has been so closely identified with modern forms of masculinity."

Beyond this masculinization of the human body, sexologists also attempted to unify sexual behavior in order to limit and codify norms. They determined that the best method for defining normalcy was the cataloguing of "abnormal behavior."

At the core of their research was the belief that beneath all the diversity of human experiences and social actions was a natural process. It seemed to sexologists that it was imperative to discover this "universal" basis of human normalcy. Given the mechanistic mood of the times, they believed that their research required a thorough classification and definition of every twist and turn of sexual pathology. This obsessive research resulted in "the exotic array of minute descriptions and taxonomic labelling so characteristic of the late nineteenth century." (Weeks)

Krafft-Ebing gained great prominence with his *Psychopathia Sexualis,* which proclaimed itself as a "medico-forensic study of the abnormal," and introduced a flood of terms concerned with perversities: sexual inversion, zoophilia, urolagnia, coprolagnias, fetishism, kleptomania, exhibitionism, sado-masochism, frottage, chronic satyriasis, and nymphomania. Ivan Block took it upon himself to outline "the strange sexual practices of all races in all ages." Charles Fere explored sexual degeneration in animals and humankind. Magnus Hirschfeld wrote extensively about homosexuality and transvestism; while Havelock Ellis attempted a compendium of all the variations of sexual behavior.

"This concentration on the 'perverse,' the 'abnormal' cast new light on the 'normal,' discreetly shrouded in respectable ideology but scientifically reaffirmed in clinical textbooks . . . The concept of heterosexuality was invented to describe 'normality,' a normality circumscribed by a founding belief in the sharp distinctions between the sexes and the assumption that gender identity (to be a man or a woman) and sexual identity were necessarily linked through the naturalness of heterosexual object choice. All else fell into the vaguely written but powerful catalogue of perversity." (Weeks)

Beneath this incessant inclination of sexologists for categorization and codification were the mythologies of Cartesian dualism. By the nineteenth century the mechanical concept of stored or kinetic energy had become part of popular folklore, inducing wide acceptance of the notion of the male body as a highly refined machine with a limited amount of fuel. "It was then that the possibility of regarding man as a machine became a normal part of people's minds, and in certain respects the new mechanical blueprint of man fitted very neatly over the former theological one. It was also a mercantile age, and this caused man to be felt to be something like a bank . . . It is easy to see the analogy. The more energy you draw from a machine, the less there is left; you must not overload it. The more money you draw from a bank, the less there is left; so it must not be overspent." (Young) From this analogy a curious sexual notion arose in the nineteenth-century West: the conviction that the more a man ejaculates, the weaker he becomes. Thus, it was widely believed that men should refrain from sexual activity before events that called upon their best efforts: business transactions, sporting activities, military confrontations, and political decisions. In this way, an unusual attitude found its way into society: an occult notion, not unlike vampirism, that envisioned women as depleting, stealing, and confiscating the life force of men.

William Acton, perhaps more than any other author of the period, typifies this mechanistic mythology about the relationship between virility and the conservation of semen. He was a specialist in urinary diseases who practiced first in Paris and then in London, where his book *The Function and Disorders of the Reproductive Organs* went through six editions between 1857 and 1875. In the first chapter, Acton urged that working-class young men should be lectured on the merits of fatigue as a means of reducing desire. He insisted that parents should prevent their children from reading the classics, "for desire and an inflamed imagination lead to one thing: the loss of semen, and that dreadful loss represents the loss of vigor, health and, ultimately, sanity itself." As the social critic Wayland Young has pointed out, Acton's sexual inventions are pure mechanism: "If the loss of semen in intercourse is a danger, loss of semen any other way is even worse. The self-sufficient machine and its reservoir of energy, which is a man, may be permitted to part with his vital substance now and then for the procreation of more men, but if he loses any for no return, then he is in the position of an idling machine." Wet dreams were considered so great a source of diminished power in males that Acton himself experimented with an instrument that was inserted up the rectum to press on the vesiculae, thus mechanically inhibiting emission, but he discovered that this method caused considerable local irritation. Instead, he suggested broken sleep and cold water enemas before sleep.

If nocturnal emission was considered dangerous, then masturbation was thought to be intolerable. As far as Acton was concerned, it was willful self-destruction to be avoided at all cost. To make his point, Acton quoted his French colleague Claude-François Lallemand: "However young the children may be, they become thin, pale, and irritable, and their features assume a haggard appearance. We notice the sunken eye, the long, cadaverous-looking countenance, the downcast look which seems to arise from a consciousness in the boy that his habits are suspected, and, at a later period, from the ascertained fact that his virility is lost . . . Habitual masturbators have a dank, moist, cold hand, very characteristic of vital exhaustion; their sleep is short, and most complete marasmus comes on; they may gradually waste away if the evil passion is not got the better of, nervous exhaustion sets in, such as spasmodic contraction, or partial or entire convulsive movements, together with epilepsy, eclampsy, and a species of paralysis accompanied with contraction of the limbs."

The notion that the loss of semen was injurious to the health of males was also the subject of several essays written in 1834 by Sylvester Graham, who imagined a fantastic connection between food and sex. Graham insisted that a diet of "mild snacks" decreased erotic impulses in young men. To demonstrate his point he created a product called Graham Crackers. In 1884 another layman devised a breakfast cereal that was supposed to curtail the inclination of boys to masturbate. His name was John Harvey Kellogg. Few people today realize that Mr. Graham's crackers and Mr. Kellogg's flakes were originally produced as weapons in the nineteenth-century war against masturbation.

Even the official medical view of masturbation has been extraordinary. Edward Wallerstein has noted that "circumcision was conceived as a deterrent to masturbation, which was at the time considered a harmful practice . . . Both Drs. [Alan F.] Guttmacher and [Benjamin] Spock were addressing the topic of childhood circumcision as a therapeutic measure to treat masturbation." Only in the 1940s did medical opinion finally change, so Dr. Spock revised his famous book on the care of children by insisting that circumcision should never be performed to treat masturbation.

As might be expected, Acton had scarcely anything to say about women: "I should say that the majority of women (happily for society) are not very much troubled with sexual feeling of any kind . . . As a general rule, a modest woman seldom requires any sexual gratification for herself. She submits to her husband's embraces, but principally to gratify him: and were it not for the desire of maternity, would far rather be relieved from his attentions."

The most persistent slander of female biology, however, is the view of menstruation as a "sickness" and as a process that relieves the female body of its "poison." As early as the time of Hippocrates, the founder of medical ethics, it was assumed that menstrual blood was toxic because of the essential evil of women. Though men were not regarded as evil, they did become ill on occasion; so the Greeks invented the "therapeutic" practice of bleeding as an imitation of female menstruation.

As much as sexologists of the nineteenth and early twentieth centuries liked to depict their research as objective *science,* there is little doubt that their efforts and achievements were part of the social mentality of the times. The sexual mythologies that they produced were significant and real to them and their world, and, to a very great extent, they remain curiously viable today, even after persistent rebuttal.

"Sexologists were something more than agents of anonymous social forces or even of male imperatives of sexual control . . . They were also something less than neutral observers of the passing sexual scene." (Weeks) A major role of the sexologists was to serve as the new arbitrators of nineteenth-century social normalcy. Many critics of sexology, and particularly feminists of the day, were distressed by the aggrandizement of the medical profession as a new "priestly caste."

Sexology is an outgrowth of the mechanistic mentality which was the basis of seventeenth-century science, concerned with statistics, categories, and moral psychology. As such, the influences of sexology were highly charged with value judgments. Rather than being simply descriptive, sexology at times was "profoundly prescriptive, telling us what we ought to be like, what makes us truly ourselves and 'normal.' It is in this sense that the sexological account of sexual identity can be seen as an imposition, a crude tactic of power designed to obscure a real sexual diversity with the [scientific] myth of a sexual destiny." (Weeks)

But, as most of today's sexual historians insist, sexual identity is not a destiny but a choice made within the complex social context of one's life. Sexual identity, as Jeffrey Weeks points out, is a creation built through choices laid out by history. Foucault (1985) argued that "sex is not a fatality, it's a possibility for creative life." It is not, as we are inclined to believe, a *mechanism* that requires an owner's technical manual to guarantee its proper use. Sexuality also is not a destiny ground out by a seventeenth-century cosmic machine, implacably pressing buttons within us that impel us into automated choices that are preordained by mathematics. Yet the whole of modern sexuality is influenced by an outdated Cartesian Mechanism. As such, it may be an elaborate but necessary fiction, a controlling mythology not unlike every other historical fiction that has motivated and justified the choices and behavior of humankind.

In the twentieth century, a shift in that Cartesian conception of the human automata has steadily overtaken the Western world. Nowhere has its influences been felt more than in the field of sexual history. The social critic Michael Ignatief has made an observation that underlies the sexual pluralism that has reshaped our thinking during the last half of the twentieth century: "If human nature is historical, individuals have different histories and therefore different needs." Foucault (1985) also spoke eloquently of this new standard. He suggested that what we lack is not a transcendent truth, but workable methods of coping with a multiplicity of truths. Foucault believed that we do not need a morality based on absolute values, but an "organic" and malleable ethics that allows us to cope with a variety of choices.

Clearly, such pluralism represents a major shift away from the paradigm of Cartesian Mechanism. It abandons the labyrinth of springs and cogs eternally preset by a clockwork deity. Instead it reinvents the body as a form of social organism that opens the way to the acceptance of diversity as a workable norm of culture. Yet this new liberalism rapidly gave rise to its own contradiction. Although liberalism was supposed to permit us to have free choice, libertarians nonetheless insisted upon forcefully implementing their belief in the truth and merit of unfettered sex, portraying such freewheeling behavior as a new normalcy to which we were supposed to adhere. The problem with moral absolutists and libertarians is that they both take for granted that there is something fundamental and transcendent about sexuality. "Libertarianism and absolutism are mirror images of one another: both are committed to a view of sexuality which transcends the bounds of mere history." (Weeks)

Marxist tradition insisted that the key to our sex lies somewhere hidden in "nature." Therefore Marxists tend to draw lines of limitation in the free exercise of bodily activities in terms of a mythology of normalcy "found" in the biological sciences.

Capitalism, meanwhile, embarked upon a very different agenda. The most persistent and inexorable force in Europe, and particularly in America, has been a sexual liberalization born of capitalism itself.

Since the seventeenth century we have seen many subtle implementations of technology as the major basis of our attitude about the human body. That precept of the "body as machine" was easily translated into the capitalist mentality that impelled the Industrial Revolution. The factory worker became a bodily machine, and workers became collectively known by a strongly mechanistic term: the "work force." The marriage of labor and machine, machine and industry had been anticipated for three hundred years. What the Catholic Church began, with its celebration of labor and technology as necessities in achieving God's good work, Descartes built into a philosophy of Mechanism that celebrated life as a visible aspect of

God's "machinery." It was only a matter of time before technology gave rise to the upheaval of the Industrial Revolution, which literally turned the human body into the cog of a mercenary machine, a work force, an industrial energy in the service of production. At the same time that people were quite literally becoming the tools of industry, the political life of the period was transformed, placing an unprecedented emphasis upon "body count." Just such numerical considerations were the basis of the obsessive statistical research of nineteenth-century sexology. This statistical/mechanistic view of the body emerged in a direct relationship with the rise of industrialization, ruralization, and a form of commerce based upon production for profit.

The Industrial Revolution was truly a *revolution*. It entirely changed the life patterns, demographics, economy, morality, political life, and medical paradigm of the Western world. Commencing with the steam engine and the mechanization of the textile industry in England, the Industrial Revolution produced a new kind of "body"— the urban factory worker who was utterly distinct from the peasant who tilled the land and the aristocrats who lived off their rank and legacies or the small merchant class that lived by its wits. The worker was a new phenomenon whose influence grew dramatically as urban populations rapidly increased. In 1800 there were about 193 million workers in Europe; by 1900 that number had increased to 423 million. With the social ascension of the new working class came new attitudes. Working people were exceptionally eager to take part in life-styles that had long been regarded as privileges of the upper classes. No matter how we politically view the events of the Industrial Revolution, it remains that the advent of industry brought about fundamentally new attitudes: an unprecedented emphasis upon calculation, measurement, and standardization. The great mathematical discoveries of the seventeenth century were widely popularized in the eighteenth century, the period when modern quantification in medicine took place. During the so-called Age of Enlightenment, there had already been a subtle transition from the Renaissance concept of "measure"—in the sense of moderation and balance—to the modern concept of measurement—in terms of statistical bookkeeping—and a new standardization of sexual normalcy. By the 1920s, the economy in America was becoming increasingly dependent on the manufacture and sale of consumer goods. And an ethic that encourages the purchase of consumer products also fosters a mentality built on the ultimate value of pleasure, self-gratification, and personal satisfaction. That American perspective quickly became the basis of one of the most mordant mythologies of history—the vision of the body as commodity.

# EIGHT
# The Body as Commodity

An unmarried woman stares expectantly at her reflection.

*Night after night she would peer questioningly into her mirror . . . She was a beautiful girl and talented, too. She had the advantages of education and better clothes than most girls in her set . . . Yet in one pursuit that stands foremost in the mind of every girl and woman—marriage— she was a failure. Many men came and went in her life. She was often a bridesmaid but never a bride.*

The terrible secret that her mirror holds back and that even her closest friend will not reveal is—*bad breath!*

At the end of this familiar advertisement it is made clear that Listerine, alone of all the inventions of humankind, is capable of solving this woman's tragic problem.

Here, then, is a drastic revision of the mythology of the human body. This powerful new type of myth has assumed an unexpected form: advertising and consumerism, forms of proselytizing far more pervasive in our society than Christian doctrine was during the Middle Ages. And, like all the mythologies of past ages, it provides a framework which determines many of the rules and fashions governing human sexual behavior.

As sociologist Fernando Henriques has noted, "contemporary romanticism can be interpreted in terms of money." The phenomenal amount, running into billions of dollars, spent by men and women in Britain and America in an effort to achieve a popular notion of romantic good looks is "remarkable testimony to the hidden finances of romance." Countless forms of diversion—cinema, theater, television, radio, magazines, novels, and celebrity journalism—have constructed a generally unachievable ideal of beauty, sexiness, and social power. This commercialization of desire "both tries to satisfy an insatiable demand and is extremely profitable. The process is circular. The romantic tradition is already established and these forms serve to satisfy an existing appetite. At the same time the perpetual depicting of romance stimulates the appetite for more." (Henriques)

America is the acknowledged leader in this process of sexualized commodity, built upon a mythology which equates money, power, and desire. Denis de Rougement notes that no other civilization in history has bestowed on the love known as *romance* the amount of daily publicity we casually encounter in television programs, films, songs, essays, novels, and advertisements. "No other civilization has embarked with anything like the same ingenuous assurance upon the perilous enterprise of making marriage coincide with love thus understood, and of making the first depend upon the second . . . [Thus] the cult of passionate love has been *democratized* so far as to have lost its aesthetic virtues together with its spiritual and tragic values." (Rougement)

The origins of this mythology of money and sexuality can be discovered in the nineteenth century, when a social dichotomy emerged in the middle classes. By reputation, if not in fact, it was an era of strong family values that gave substance to an extended bourgeois home life. The morality of the day insisted that love belonged exclusively in the marital bedroom as a ritual of familial perpetuation. In reality, males devised an elaborate and discreet system of social forms that allowed them to pursue erotic pastimes outside the home. The ancient tradition of prostitution was newly outfitted to suit bourgeois needs and sensibilities.

John D'Emilio and Estelle B. Freedman have written insightfully about prostitution as well as many other forms of sexual commodification in America. As they point out, prostitutes were available to serve the sexual needs of men of every class and ethnic background. These men were participating in sexual conduct unknown to women, who usually entered marriage without sexual experience. "Fifty-cent 'crib houses' catered to casual laborers who sat on wooden benches waiting for a turn so quick that they barely took down their pants. One- and two-dollar joints might attract young clerks and other white-collar workers. Fancy parlor houses with ornate decor, racy music, and expensive liquor won the loyalty of the more economically privileged men. In these, the sexual transaction with a prostitute might be but one element in a long evening of ribaldry."

These indiscretions with "low" women gave middle-class men several exclusively masculine benefits: the high cost of their sexual entertainments announced to their male peers their elevated social status; the exclusive masculinity of brothel pastimes provided a fraternity of shared secrets as well as machismo comradery and male bonding. Prostitution allowed men to exercise their sexual fantasies with women of no social standing whom they regarded as subhuman, and thus it permitted them to preserve the illusion of the sanctity of their homes and the asexual virtue of their wives.

Most married women responded to this double standard in ways that were self-defeating: accepting rather than contesting the stereotype of decent, sexually aloof, loyal homebodies who had little power in society and yet were given the responsibility of instilling moral values in their children, particularly in the late nineteenth century, an era of extensive economic and geographic change, when the role of both the church and the state in sexual regulation diminished and that responsibility was increasingly delegated to women.

Many assertive women, perhaps out of a sense of frustration and betrayal, were fierce leaders of movements for moral reform and social purity, principally aimed at the mistresses and prostitutes who consorted with their husbands. Beyond this moral indignation which justified the attack upon "loose women," part of the activism of these cloistered wives was also undertaken in the hope of imposing a single standard of morality—universal chastity before marriage and fidelity within marriage for both men and women. The statistics and literature of the late nineteenth century, however, make it clear that the majority of wives dutifully accepted the sexual carousing of their husbands as "natural male behavior." Thus, instead of widely proclaiming their own sexual independence in the manner of one of their exceptional contemporaries, such as Isadora Duncan, most women were inclined to act out their male-given roles as mothers, as asexual arbitrators of sexual mannerisms, and as guardians of wholesome family life. Unfortunately, this behavior corroborated their husbands' stereotypical view of their wives as "good women of unquestionable moral fiber."

Particularly in the new specialization of gynecology, women were seen as merely reproductive organisms, confined to the home and to lives of continuous childbearing. As Dr. Horatio Storer wrote in 1871, woman was "what she is in health, in character, in her charms, alike of body, mind, and soul because of her womb alone." (D'Emilio/Freedman) This lingering Cartesian mythology of the female body as a reproductive machine allowed men to perpetuate the morality that restrained the sexual freedom of their wives at the same time that they themselves were unrestrained, crying out against "sin" in public while they partook of it in private.

The life of the middle class was secure, respectable, and entirely stultified. Illegitimacy and divorce were socially unacceptable. Any departure from gender norms was unthinkable. Comradery between the sexes was considered inappropriate even after marriage. And before a man and woman entered wedlock, the chaperon was an essential fixture of courtship.

Decent women were not supposed to be sexual creatures, and even young men celebrated their own ability to limit sexual behavior as "manly self-control." Everywhere there were stereotypes that now seem amusing. In 1913, T. W. Shannon published his book *Self Knowledge,* which offered stolid advice to parents. "Boys are, by nature, inclined to be rough, rude, coarse and untidy. They need to associate with girls who naturally have just the opposite tendencies. A girl's ambition is to be beautiful; a boy's ambition is to be strong. These preferences are natural and should be encouraged in them."

According to the norms of the period, women brought stability to the home. Men brought power and prestige. The traditional mentality of Victorian society was highly conservative. But on the eve of the twentieth century economic and social upheaval was creating massive conflict between old and new values. An underground world of nonconformist social behavior was steadily coming into existence. Without knowing it, the middle class was on the brink of a major transformation of sexual values. However, the societal elements at the heart of this decisive change in behavior did not rise out of the powerful, trend-setting world of the middle class. The impetus for change came, instead, from beyond the outskirts of "proper" society, from the mundane world where the working class spent its life.

While the daughters of the middle class busied themselves with needlepoint and lessons in Miss Emily Post's *Etiquette,* many less fortunate women found new forms of sexual experience in the offices, shops, and factories where they worked. Expanding opportunities for female employment outside the home changed the stature of women and fundamentally altered their relationship with men. John D'Emilio and Estelle Freedman, to whom I am much indebted for their excellent study of sexuality in America, have noted: "The novelty of young women working outside the home threw men and women together in a variety of ways. On downtown sidewalks and streetcars, in offices, department stores, restaurants, and factories, and in parks at lunch hour, young men and women mingled easily, flirted with one another, made dates, and stole time together. Freed from the protection, or restraints, of their elders' supervision, young women encountered the sexual and romantic suggestions of male admirers . . . Women exchanged information with each other at work, learning from those older, and passing on to their peers advice and hints about how to comport themselves in this unsupervised heterosocial environment . . . Those working in the new department stores became acquainted with a world of goods designed to arouse desire and attract the attention of admirers."

This new consumerism was not originally created in order to capitalize on the considerable buying power of the middle class, which, except for occasional capricious spending, was highly frugal. The originators of consumer products were after the pay checks of the growing numbers of working people, who were easily induced to spend what little money they had on luxuries that provided a sense of worth and specialness to otherwise drab lives.

After work these young men and women were released into the freedom of urban areas where a variety of amusements sprang up to meet their needs. In every town and city entrepreneurs quickly recognized the commercial potential of catering to this massive new population of young people who, with their pay checks in their pockets, were looking for diversion. Though enterprises of amusement were considered vulgar by the cloistered bourgeoisie, who often organized leagues in an effort to be rid of them, public amusements had existed to the delight of common people ever since the Middle Ages. But only with the nineteenth century did such commercialized diversions become big business. In every industrial area businessmen opened dance halls and amusement parks which offered their patrons welcome relief from the drab and dreary world of wage labor. For all their humbleness and crudity, these new places of amusement seemed like the epitome of glamour to laboring young men and women, who usually spent their evenings in dingy tenements after dutifully putting in 50 hours a week at dull, dehumanizing jobs. The tinsel of the dance halls, in particular, had an immense appeal. There, in a contrived atmosphere of romance and glitter, young, unmarried men and women consorted without the restrictions of the families they had left behind when they came to the cities to find work. This kind of diversion for independent, family-free youth was unknown both to the middle class as well as to the earlier generations of farmers and working people, who watched with dismay as their children were transformed by the new consumer culture.

The modern dance hall, as a variation on the western saloon, was invented by blacks and black musicians who came north from Memphis and New Orleans and originally found work in bawdy Harlem honkytonks where couples performed frenetic and "suggestive" dances with an emphasis upon bodily contact. Once regarded as places hardly better than brothels, dance halls soon found a new white working-class clientele, which eagerly took up the insinuative movements and music for which blacks had been castigated. If the dancing was sexy, the songs were downright vulgar. From descriptions of the turn of the century, it's clear that dance halls for whites and for blacks were charged with an air of physical energy and sexual opportunity.

D'Emilio and Freedman have provided an amusing picture of youthful diversions of the period. Dance halls were just one of many urban pleasures that became fashionable among working-class youth. All such social institutions had one thing in common: They encouraged a new sexual ethic. By the first decade of the twentieth century, vast amusement parks were being constructed beyond the edges of cities. The structure of these parks and the kind of behavior they encouraged contradicted the gentility of middle-class America. Men and women were thrown together by an unprecedented social situation. The rides of the amusement parks encouraged ribald behavior. A journalist of the day described a day at New York's Coney Island as "a delirium of raw pleasure." The barker for the Cannon Coaster called out, "Will she throw her arms around your neck and yell? Well, I guess, yes!" The pitch for the Barrel of Love announced, "Talk about love in a cottage! This has it beat a mile!" The posters for exotic dancer Little Egypt promised "one hundred and fifty Oriental beauties! See her dance the Hootchy-Kootchy! Anywhere else but in the ocean breezes of Coney Island she would be consumed by her own fire!" Concealed air vents sent young women's skirts flying over their heads. Favorite rides such as the Human Roulette Wheel tossed young people into each other's arms. "Strangers conversed with one another. Groups of men and women made their acquaintance. Flirtations occurred, dates were made, and romances begun and ended. Meanwhile, in cities along the ocean and near lakes, steamers and excursion boats with private rooms allowed youthful lovers to escape the city for a day and indulge their romantic attachment for one another." (D'Emilio and Freedman)

With technological advances in the entertainment industry, the dance hall was largely replaced by the movie palace. The early nickelodeons, where astonished people experienced the new art of the motion picture, fascinated the working class. The cinema provided an unprecedented intimacy through its bigger-than-life emotions and images, not to mention the unprecedented proximity of the people sitting together in the dark. The darkness itself was a considerable attraction for young working-class couples who did not have access to an intimate space of their own. The films' preoccupation with romance, depicted in great close-ups, was a revolutionary emotional experience bordering on voyeurism, and this added to the sexually charged atmosphere of the movie house, where the back rows quickly became associated with petting and lovemaking.

The intermingling of the sexes at working-class amusements also brought the practice of dating to full flower. Young men made points with the women they hoped to attract by having enough money to be able to treat the objects of their affections to rides at the amusement park, gifts, refreshments, a night on the town, or perhaps a trip on one of the romantic lake steamers. If a young man could not afford such favors, he might have to do without the pleasure of a woman's company. His financial power as a wage earner began to have an unprecedented impact on his sex life.

Such social changes were strongly resisted by parents, especially among immigrants whose traditional values were strong. The centralizing influences of family life began to dissipate. And with them went the moral traditions that had been a major focus of home life. "Mothers watched as their daughters left home to go to work, where they learned all sorts of newfangled ideas . . . Sons, too, were different. Although male youth traditionally had more freedom, the new generation of working-class men was departing from the patterns of their fathers. No longer satisfied with the sex-segregated environment of the neighborhood tavern, youth now spent their wages in the heterosocial world of commercialized leisure." (D'Emilio and Freedman)

The Worcester *Sunday Telegram* noted one important shift in turn-of-the-century society: "Where a man was in the habit of passing much of his time in a saloon . . . now he passes a portion, if not all of it, in the motion picture houses." In fact, by 1918, the saloon was abandoned by the young and became the haunt of older men.

Again, it is important to repeat that the new consumer culture was made possible by young working-class people who willingly spent most of their wages on entertainment and pleasure. In this profoundly transformed culture the individual had replaced the family as the primary economic unit. The ideal of getting married and raising a family had lost much of its power, and, instead, young people began to understand relationships in terms of sexual pleasure. Reproduction was no longer the prime justification of sex. The popular influence of psychology and the persistent insinuation of sex in advertising brought about many changes in young men and women, who placed great importance upon independence, upon attractiveness as power, and upon personal pleasure and satisfaction as the essential goal of sexual relations.

Eventually this hedonistic consumerism spread from the working class and began to undermine traditional middle-class values of "hard work and self-denial." Advertisers quickly understood the usefulness of sex as a sales device for absolutely every product: mouthwashes, automobiles, beer, toothpaste, diet drinks, investment firms, and movies.

As D'Emilio and Freedman have observed, the shift in white middle-class social values was highly visible in the patterns of nightlife that were becoming ever more popular among affluent young men and women. "The heterosocial world of commercialized amusement that working-class youth enjoyed was spreading to the middle class, though in tamer, more respectable forms." For instance, by the 1910s the cabaret had become the most popular place for middle-class entertainment, an amusement emphatically marked by its many elite distinctions from lower-class places of diversion. A whole new terminology sprang up: getting "dressed up" became an essential aspect of "going out." The pulse of the music drastically dropped and the physicality of the dancing quickly faded.

With the invention and popularization of the automobile, a new sexual commodity became available, with all of its celebrated phallic associations of privilege, power, and masculinity. The automobile became a substitute for the sitting room, which had until recently been the acceptable middle-class meeting place of chaperoned lovers. The automobile provided glamour, economic exhibitionism, and escape from watchful families, as well as sexual facilitation. Parking in lovers' lanes became an implicit part of the youth culture of the automobile that rapidly evolved during the 1920s.

By 1920, the social forms that had sustained nineteenth-century sexual values were in a state of flux. Americans, in particular, were entering a new sexual era. "The new positive value attributed to the erotic, the growing autonomy of youth, the association of sex with commercialized leisure and self-expression, the pursuit of love, the visibility of the erotic in popular culture, the social interaction of men and women in public, the legitimization of female interest in the sexual: all of these were to be seen in America in the twenties . . . This emphasis on personal gratification coincided with the loss of control over most other aspects of public life. Politics seemed distant and outside the influence of most individuals; huge corporations exercised power over the business of making a living; the sprawling metropolis appeared beyond the control of its inhabitants. The body, seemingly, remains one's own. It, at least, could be a source of fulfillment. It, at least, might remain a realm of autonomy." (D'Emilio and Freedman)

In the 1930s and 1940s, a major shift in sexual conduct was ushered in by the motion-picture industry, which rapidly became the single most influential medium for the transmission of social expectations. And as the movie theaters moved uptown, out of the working-class neighborhoods where they had originated, entrepreneurs transformed the once homely structures into vast, exotic dreamworlds. These opulent new movie palaces, a conspicuous show of wealth and splendor, were calculated to appeal to the middle class, and brought a whole new audience to films. The parlor was replaced by these splendid theaters, with their darkness, intimacy, and gigantic, flashing images of romance.

Along with the sexualization of commerce came an increasing commercialization of sex, best represented by the modern pornography industry which gained momentum in America after World War II, in the 1940s and 1950s, and which has openly flourished since the 1960s. But the pornographic mentality was never limited to just explicit portrayals of sex. An undercurrent of sexuality pervaded every aspect of American society. The culture itself became subtly pornographic. Sex became main-

stream, legitimate business. And ultimately sex became
an intrinsic aspect of American mass culture. The promise
of sexual success was literally built into even the most
mundane products. Stoves and refrigerators were identified
with handsome young women in advertisements. A soap
that made dishes sparkle promised the devotion of every
housewife's husband. American "know-how" invented a
bewildering array of do-it-yourself, self-improvement tech-
niques guaranteed to turn every ugly duckling into a
swan. Journalistic gossip, which had always had immense
salacious appeal, became the commodity of an immense
industry. The private lives of celebrities were turned into
nonstop sexual marathons upon which the public was
eager to peep. The mere juxtaposition of males and
females insinuated something thrillingly sexual. To make
a film, even a war film or a prison film, without a major
female character was for years unthinkable. The challenge
of the prepornography period was to see how far you
could go without breaking the law. The much touted
decency of those days had little to do with the law. It was
ultimately an advertisement for repressed but widely available smut. Often the nonpornographic insinuations were
far cruder than the grim reality that eventually overtook
the entertainment industry. Innocence had already died
at the hands of innuendo. By the time hardcore pornography made its open entry into middle-class society, all
that remained of innocence was the pretense of indignation.

For many social critics, the transformation of the human body into sexual commodity is the essential mythological force of our day. Every aspect of the world is
imprinted in one way or another by the ramifications of
this complex mentality. Among the many results of the
commodification of sex, there are two modes of behavior
that observers believe will have a significant impact on
the future. One of these forces is an egalitarian mental-

ity, represented by an array of movements, all of which have at least one thing in common: They hope to redefine bodily experiences in terms of sensual immediacy. They wish to reinvent the body as body.

The other force, the antithesis of this egalitarian attitude about the body, is the inclination to exacerbate the commodification of sex in a manner which results in the sexualization of violence, transforming desire into "fatal attraction." In such a scheme the body, particularly the male body, becomes a lethal weapon.

These two attitudes mediate sexuality in different mythic terms. One approach epitomizes a Darwinian interpretation of social and sexual aggression, while the other operates in terms of the nonaggressive mentality that I have associated with the ancient Mother Goddess.

It is with these opposing myths about the body that I envision two drastically different possibilities for the future of human sexuality. In order to explore these ideas we need to know more about the sexualization of violence. As we shall see, such a process was essentially carried out by males, especially American males, whose sexual modes of behavior have been indistinguishable from the greatly glorified aggression associated with moral evangelism, sports, war, politics, and business. For such people, the allure of sex increases in direct proportion to the degree to which it is profaned.

As we shall see, the transformation of the human body into commodity was only one of many results of the commercialization of sex. The idealistic freedom of expression that opened the door to the depiction of explicit sex in entertainment had its shadow side: scenes of child molestation, rape, sexual dismemberment, and violence. Psychologists have long debated the basis of this sexualization of violence, which has attained immense appeal in our day. It is difficult to determine whether repression controls antisocial behavior or if sexual violence is actually the result of decades of such repression. The liberalization of laws governing the depiction of explicit sex was supposed to decrease the incidents of sexual crime, and worldwide surveys over three decades indicate the correctness of that supposition. At the same time, for many people sexual aggression has been rationalized as "self-expression," "political activism," and "civil rights."

Whatever its rationale, we have come face to face in our era with a highly problematic reality: Do we have the right to use our bodies as weapons against one another? As feminist activist Susan Brownmiller has asked, "Does homosexual sadomasochism have its own, peculiarly male, dynamic, or is it an aberration masquerading as the newest issue?" Must we accept as a political fact of life what Brownmiller calls "the spectacle of white radicals and intellectuals falling all over each other in their rush to accept the [Eldridge] Cleaver rationale for rape"?

"Somehow," activist Cleaver wrote in *Soul on Ice,* "I arrived at the conclusion that, as a matter of principle, it was of paramount importance for me to have an antagonistic, ruthless attitude toward white women . . . I became a rapist."

Here we are faced with a staggeringly difficult event, whose unsavory message is inescapable. A new mythology has been born of the brutality of those who have been methodically brutalized. Out of that myth come all of the most contradictory and perplexing circumstances of our sex lives at the end of the twentieth century. Violence has been sexualized at the same time that sex has been politicized. And into the ongoing, cruel and mindless wars of classes, races, outsiders, misfits, and just plain psychopaths has been introduced an updated model of an ancient tool in the human arsenal: the male body as weapon.

Clearly there are many nagging questions about the

limits of sexual freedom, about the politicization of sex, and about the sexualization of power among men in general, and among sadistic minority males in particular. This association between masculinity and dominance has a history as long as the life of our species. Darwin withstanding, both men and women are equally capable of using sex as a weapon, but sadomasochism is always defined from the male viewpoint. If a woman is aggressive, she is said to be "masculine." Sadism is understood as a masculine misunderstanding of manhood; while masochism is almost always identified with the willing acceptance of abuse by women. In pornography, aggression and sadomasochism are inseparable elements of the commercialization of sex as entertainment. For reasons that are still debated, the market is clearly and predominantly male. And the mentality of pornography is also male. These facts mandate that we consider an uncomfortable but apt observation made by Susan Brownmiller: "Man's discovery that his genitalia could serve as a weapon to generate fear must rank as one of the most important discoveries of prehistoric times, along with the use of fire and the first crude stone ax . . . Indeed, one of the earliest forms of male bonding must have been the gang rape of one woman by a band of marauding men. This accomplished, rape became not only a male prerogative, but man's basic weapon of force against woman, the principal agent of his will and her fear. His forcible entry into her body, despite her physical protestations and struggle, became the vehicle of his victorious conquest over her being, the ultimate test of his superior strength, the triumph of his manhood."

# NINE
# The Body as Weapon

Tralala was drunk. She eyed the men in the bar, who gazed back at her with vacant eyes. At first Tralala tried to hustle a customer away from a couple of the other hookers, but the women drove her away with their angry glances. In a reckless spirit of competition she announced that she would take on the entire bar. Set up in the back of a wrecked car on a vacant lot, Tralala swilled beer as the men in line fought over who was to have her first. As word of the gang bang quickly spread, the Greeks from the luncheonette came over, and then someone put in a call to the Navy base and soon the sailors joined the line of men waiting to have Tralala. Someone shoved a can of beer against Tralala's mouth, and it struck so hard that she spit blood and a piece of tooth. Everybody laughed. Men who had had their turn joined the end of the line for seconds. Then Tralala passed out.

They slapped her a few times and she mumbled and turned her head but they couldn't revive her so they continued to fuck her as she lay unconscious on the seat in the lot and soon they tired of the dead piece and the daisychain broke up and they went back

to Willies the Greeks and the base and the kids
who were watching and waiting to take a turn
took out their disappointment on Tralala and
tore her clothes to small scraps put out a few
cigarettes on her nipples pissed on her jerkedoff
on her jammed a broomstick up her snatch then
bored they left her lying amongst the broken
bottles rusty cans and rubble of the lot and Jack
and Freddy and Ruthy and Annie stumbled
into a cab still laughing and they leaned toward
the window as they passed the lot and got a
good look at Tralala lying naked covered
with blood urine and semen and a small blot
forming on the seat between her legs as blood
seeped from her crotch . . .

The mythology of masculinity which is the basis of this
calmly horrendous scene from a brilliant Hubert Selby
novel, *Last Exit to Brooklyn,* is built upon a mentality
which is an implicit aspect of the disillusionment of America's consumer society at the close of the twentieth century. In the competitive decades since the Industrial
Revolution, when the human body became a machine,
many men have been transformed into lethal weapons by
unrealized expectation, frustration, and economic brutalization. For them sex is no longer erotic. It has become a
pornography, a sexual commodity, a mechanism that,
failing the obtainment of quick pleasure, takes out its
frustration and rage by inducing humiliation. Given the
long history of male contempt and disgust for women and
sex, it is not surprising that economic and racial emasculation impels many men to work out their rage in their
sexual relationship to women. Just such a mind set is
recreated by many artists, like Mr. Selby, in their efforts
to envision the world as candidly as possible. On the

other hand, the same mentality is also used by pornographic entertainers in order to produce an elaborate male masturbation fantasy. Even when sexual humiliation is not the central issue of television, films, and popular novels, something strongly sexual is persistently implied by the undercurrent of sexualized violence, by the brutality aimed at women and culture, and by the arrogant emotional illiteracy of highly celebrated characters like Dirty Harry, Rambo, and the countless other two-dimensional macho heroes who are often held up as examples of idealized males. This is not to say that women are incapable of aggression and violence, but statistics (such as the relatively small number of assaults and murders committed by women in comparison to men) suggest that women are not primary candidates for violent behavior, although the reasons for this are widely debated.

Selby's depiction of masculine sexual humiliation is motivated by literary rather than pornographic motives. The grim flatness of his description of the scene provides a case study. In discussing the sex scene, Susan Brownmiller notes the absence of erotic behavior among the participants. Here is sexuality devoid of sex. The purpose of sexual humiliation, she concludes, is never to satisfy the victim. There is also no *sexual* gratification for the male aggressors. Their behavior suggests the impatience of people waiting their turn to use a vending machine, which breaks downs and elicits their rage. At best, the activities of the men are undertaken like "clinical experiments performed by initiates who are convinced that all sex is dirty and demeaning."

The familiar question, Brownmiller points out, is whether or not Tralala asked for trouble. After all, she is a prostitute. That fact, however, is a justification of Tralala's abuse "that could only be raised by someone who regards all sex as demeaning." Prostitutes do not deserve to be brutalized. And there is something peculiar and ironic about our indignant response to women and men who sell their bodies in a society in which sex has been thoroughly commercialized. Whether or not Tralala invited the sexual event that overtook her is not at issue. What interests us here is the fact that she was gang raped in ways that have very little relationship to the kind of sensual behavior and eroticism usually associated with the pleasures of sex. As Brownmiller makes clear, "what these rapists were looking for was another avenue or orifice by which to invade and thus to humiliate their victim's physical integrity, her private inner space." Tralala was not defiled; she was *invaded*—her body became an object in a territorial battle.

What is the source of this sexuality built upon the aggression of war?

Warfare is an ideal setting for the mythology of masculinity, whether it is a war fought on battlefields, in the saloons of the old West, on the football field, or in the streets of the inner cities. "War provides men with the perfect psychological backdrop to give vent to their contempt for women. The very maleness of the military—the brute power of weaponry exclusive to their hands, the spiritual bonding of men at arms, the manly discipline of orders given and orders obeyed, the simple logic of the hierarchical command—confirms for men what they long suspect, that women are peripheral, irrelevant to the world that counts, passive spectators to the action in the center ring." (Brownmiller)

Rape is also a political act because rape is an expression of power. The film *Fortune and Men's Eyes* depicts the prison life of a good-looking young heterosexual named Smitty. Because of his youth and attractiveness Smitty is raped by King Rocco-Rocky, who turns the young man into his prison "girlfriend." Smitty is determined to end his sexual bondage. One day, while in the showers, when Rocky tells him to fetch the Vaseline that is used in anal sex, Smitty turns on his "husband" and beats him into submission. When the inmates discover what has happened, Rocky is discredited and Smitty becomes the new despot of the cellblock.

At another time which had another mythology, Smitty's "victory over evil" would have resulted in the "happily-ever-after" ending expected in old American melodramas. Smitty would become a good samaritan. That used to be our sentimental expectation of characters who have been brutalized. From the pain of their own experience they gain compassion for the pain of others. But that isn't the way brutality functions in the real world. As we now know, parents who were beaten and sexually abused as children often beat and abuse their own children. So Smitty's first act as victor is to command his gentle friend and cellmate, Jan-Mona, to get the Vaseline. In an effort to save himself from his own friend, Jan-Mona exclaims, "You have power now, Smitty—do you need sex, too?" But Smitty does "need sex." In what other way could he live out the myth of his masculinity within the confines of prison?

Today the relationship of power and sexual humiliation seems to be endemic in America. We have long fantasized about this kind of brutality in the worlds of "savage warriors"—American Indians, Africans, Huns, and Turks—without recognizing how obsessed our own society is with competition, aggression, power, and the kind of physical and economic subjugation that is the basis of humiliation. As we have seen in this survey of the mythologies that inform our sexual attitudes, women have often been the targets of male aggression. They have even been blamed as causing that aggression by their mere presence in the world as sexual beings. But women are not the only victims of the masculine determination to dominate. When a woman is not available to play the role of victim, a young and unaggressive male or a child will do. "Prison rape is generally seen today for what it is: an acting out of power roles within an all-male, authoritarian environment in which the younger, weaker inmate, usually a first offender, is forced to play the role that in the outside world is assigned to women." (Brownmiller)

Is brutality a psychotic response of the racial, economic, sexual, and political outcasts of our world or does it play a more central role in all our lives? Why is it that our fragile bodies are so often used as walls of defense against people who threaten us with their strength? Given the compassion and physical empathy we feel when confronted by someone who is dreadfully wounded, how is it possible that we have entertainments that turn us into spectators of physical violence? Why do people take so great an interest in assault and agony? Aggression and seduction are supposed to be antithetical, and yet how very seductive certain rituals of violence can be!

Until recently no one questioned the impact that negative arousal has upon us. Aristotle posed a theory of catharsis which suggested that witnessing violence purges the spectator of aggression. Today researchers have discovered that Aristotle was wrong. Witnessing or participating in violent activity—real or fictional—tends to heighten violent behavior and to create an association between sex and aggression in both children and adults. A study by Stanley Milgram at Yale in the early 1960s suggests that there is markedly increased hostility in spectators after witnessing aggressive behavior. Milgram and his clinical associates conducted a study in which volunteers were alternately shown two kinds of motion pictures: a violent boxing match and a travelogue. The subjects were then tested for their willingness to release their aggression by administering a measurable amount of electric shock to another person in what they were led to believe was a test of the other person's ability to respond to questions under duress. In reality, the other person received no shock, but the subject was not aware of the trick and was also not aware that he or she was the one being tested. "Subjects who observed films about violent sports are more willing to administer a high level of electrical shock than subjects who see another sort of film." It is undeniable that such aggressivity has a strong connection with a sadism that finds power and pleasure in inflicting pain. The underlying sexual implications of such a response are clear. There is a marked interaction between violent behavior, the administration of pain, and sexual gratification. Professor L. Rowell Huesmann has summarized a great deal of data in his studies of the impact of television on violent behavior. He concludes that the experience of theatrical violence teaches adults and children to behave more aggressively—sexually and otherwise. At the same time people who are highly aggressive are prompted to return to watch more and more media violence because, at least to some extent, the experience of violence tends to desensitize people to violence at the same time that it appears to increase their desire to experience aggressive behavior. This circular situation has been frequently noted among rapists and other persons convicted of violent sexual crimes. Like an addiction, it seems to take a greater and greater severity of violence to "satisfy" the desire to experience aggression. Tests of audience response to television and film indicate that the attractiveness of violence is particularly strong when a story depicts a "heroic male" getting his desired results through acts of brutality. In most cases, the hero's sexuality is inseparable from his brutality.

Aggressive sex has become America's right-wing theater. It is built upon our disgust with sex as animalistic, base, demeaning, and evil. Violence affirms itself by making the acts that emasculate human beings palatable as *sexual play*. It is, however, the sexuality of a machine that manufactures sex as a commodity. As critic John Lahr has said, "The body aspires to become the machine which has replaced it in the real world."

We know that in a consumer society aggression is generated by a sense of uselessness—whether it comes from boredom, emasculation, poverty, ignorance, or brutalization. Yet we are constantly bombarded by messages of opulence, sexual triumphs, wealth, and power. William Faulkner wanted us to prevail rather than merely to survive, but the truth of the matter is that survival is all that most of us can expect. That fate may be the ultimate and tragic condition of our lives, and it may account for the mythology that now informs our sexuality: the tension between melancholy passivity and violent aggression.

Neal Thornberry, a management professor at Babson College at Wellesley, tells us that the message of our society is to excel. "Stand out in the crowd! Do more than the other person so that the boss, your peers, or the attractive man or woman at the health spa will notice you!" But, unfortunately, Thornberry notes, "most of us are average and mediocre." When he stands before a seminar, Professor Thornberry knows "that 68 percent of the class is average. They will remain average, no matter what I do to make them excel."

To fail to excel in our society is a form of death. Success is so greatly prized that anything short of it is believed to constitute total failure. The mythology of consumerism has created a vivid male analogy between economic success and sexual prowess, between social failure and the failure to achieve an erection and to consummate intercourse.

We are all goaded by the need to succeed, although our conception of success is often impersonal and has little to do with either our real needs or our real abilities. Our dreams are filled with things we want and cannot have, making whatever we actually attain seem paltry by comparison to what we expect. We are addicted to the illusion of "the good life" and to a belief that we not only can but must attain it. In fact, we have come to consider such an attainment an inalienable right. It has become an illusion central to our political ideals. We are addicted to that illusion to such an extent that we are willing to do absolutely anything to achieve it. It is a notion of competition that is virtually psychopathic.

In Oklahoma one fine day, a disgruntled postal employee walked into a post office carrying three weapons and proceeded to create a bloodbath, killing 14 people he had never seen before in his life. The melee was prompted by the fact that the postal employee had been reprimanded by his boss. He was angry. He was a failure in a system that worships winners. So he shot 14 strangers and then blew his brains out.

The Oklahoma tragedy is a grotesque microcosm of an ongoing crisis in the dominant male population of all nations, but particularly of America. It is that crisis that is reflected in our nation's mythology and sexuality. The persistent constellation of exaggerated expectation and the consequent failure to achieve one's unrealistic goals results in a profound sense of abashed masculinity and the fear of not being able to uphold the much-glorified role as "breadwinner." It is a fear of impotence that encourages the antics of "boys"—toting weapons, drinking heavily with friends, watching male-dominated sports on television, and talking about women in the exclusive sexual language of males. Such activities and stances give support to fragile egos. But no amount of male comradery placates the sense of worthlessness experienced by many men. The suffocating sense of failure arouses rage and, finally, unfocused sexual violence. The rage is often worked out in vicarious aggressivity: vicious films, gloating over other people's defeats, hunting, baiting females, raising hell in bars, and indulging in domestic violence.

Sex has become the great equalizer. Sexual attractiveness has no basis in economic, educational, or familial status. Singles bars and gay bars have become arenas where those who feel like failures in every other aspect of their lives aggressively compete as sexual gladiators in hopes of attaining social power through the attention they arouse.

Modern sex is built upon a particular type of tension—a tension very familiar to us in the business world. It allows for nothing short of absolute success or total failure. The sex act has become a trophy: part of the competition and part of the violence. Manly or unmanly. Attractive or unattractive. Powerful or weak. Rich or poor. Winner or loser. Conquering hero or wimp. The unrelenting tension between these choices engenders the mythology of the male body as a weapon—a weapon used to fight an internalized and hopeless war against emasculation. Ironically, given the masculine accent placed upon sexual potency, that inner battle and its tensions have rendered many males impotent.

It seems that men have succeeded in becoming the machines that have replaced them. The frankly avowed aim of corporations "to destroy the competition" has become as endemic in business as it has in sex. Likewise, in the field of sports men talk about winning in the most graphically violent metaphors. The star linebacker of the Calgary Stampeders, John McMurty, had these thoughts about football? "It is arguable that body shattering is the very *point* of football, as killing and maiming are of war . . . Watch for the plays that are most enthusiastically applauded by the fans, where someone is 'smeared,' 'creamed,' 'nailed,' 'broken in two,' or even 'crucified.' In football the mouth waters most of all for the really crippling block or tackle. For the kill. Competitive, organized injuring is integral to our way of life, and football is one of the more intelligible mirrors of the whole process."

Many anthropologists agree. Football's symbolic significance has been as a ritualized assertion of male dominance. If macho-obsessed men realized the transparency of the sexuality implicit in sports, they could be overwhelmed with self-doubt and embarrassment. In the opinion of anthropologist William Arens, "this is evidenced in the uniforms worn by the all-male cast. The macho-appearing uniforms accentuate maleness, especially the cod-piece motif that fronts the knickers. Moreover, the myth of feminine evil is seen in the purifying rites imposed on players before the games. No sex the night before is the law and coaches apparently believe in the debilitating powers of sex despite scientific evidence to the contrary."

It is little wonder that men covet their obsession for sports: the exclusive language, the complex statistics, and the elaborate hierarchy of heroes. In the late twentieth century the athlete has been transformed into a masculine sex totem signifying the attainment of the utterly rarified powers that many males fantasize as their principal ideal—a barbaric position of incontestable authority and potency that commands unlimited sex, utter domination, great wealth, deep admiration, unthinkable luxury, as well as respect and love and the kind of fear that keeps other males in a position of submission. Surely this is the description of a type of imaginary social rank reminiscent of the illusive caveman who was supposedly the ancestor of the he-man.

There is good reason to understand such hierarchies of male dominance as part of the Darwinian revolution that has typified the twentieth century's biological frame of reference. As social historians often point out, the cultural application of Darwin's theories of survival provided a biological basis for the class struggles of industrial society and for the so-called battle of the sexes which became a major issue with the rise of feminism in the nineteeth century. People were convinced that Darwin had penetrated into the very heart of gender identification. As such, masculinity and femininity were supposed to be inescapable aspects of the natural laws governing evolution. Males were *supposed* to be aggressive: to hunt and to fend off enemies and to survive. They did all of these things, supposedly, so females could attend to matters of passive motherhood.

This application of Darwinian theory became intensified in the 1920s, when scientist Raymond Dart unearthed evidence of ancient ape-men he called *Australopithecines*. Here, Dart told us, was the ancestor of humankind: a highly successful carnivore and killer of game. Dart envisioned these primordial human creatures as club-swinging brutes who randomly raped any female without male protection, and who were the absolute terror of everything within their reach. It is evident from our discussion of the Mother Goddess that this view of the relationship of men and women in the formative periods of human history is fatuous. Researchers have shown that the role of women in the development of culture and even in the physiological evolution of humankind was both highly influential and pertinent. Yet Dart's image of a masculinized primordial humanity set the pervasive stereotype for many generations of scientists and lay people. It was fashionable to consider these ape-men to be highly aggressive primates of very low mentality, capable of killing their own offspring, and carrying within their very genes an implacable cruelty, sadism, and bloodthirstiness that came to be the quintessential opposite of the Victorian concept of what it meant to be female and feminine.

In the nineteenth century some scientists suggested that "to give women the vote was, evolutionarily speaking, retrogressive . . . Physicians and educators alike warned that young women who engaged in long, hard hours of study would badly damage their reproductive systems." (Fausto-Sterling)

We know that such notions are absurd. Yet we still do not understand completely the fundamental physiology of gender identification. We also cannot speak with certainty about the role of evolution in the formation of sexual conduct. Opinion is greatly divided about the contrasting roles of culture and nature in the formation of sexuality. Even the anatomy and physiology of sex do not explain the statistical fact that men are more violent than women and that men are more inclined than women to sexualize violence. Nor, as we have seen, does cross-cultural evidence support the notion of a geographically or historically transcendent sexuality. Despite the claims of sociobiologists to the contrary, there is no definitive evidence that women are fundamentally different from men or that "love" is fundamentally different from sex. We cannot justify a male disposition for sexual violence with biological and evolutionary excuses. Nor can we accept the inclination during this era of sociobiology, with its materialistic and Darwinian interpretations of sexuality, to consider it any more inappropriate to speak of *love,* rather than of sex, than it is to speak of *mind,* rather than of brain. Metaphor plays little part in sociobiology. As Joseph Campbell once said, "Without a sense of metaphor, we are inclined to confuse the meal with the menu. And so we end up munching on cardboard."

Love is such a metaphor. And it is this metaphor of love that is the antithesis of the sexualization of violence that is so prominent in our day. Despite widespread disillusionment about the positive aspects of human behavior, we must not confuse the menu for the meal and thereby neglect the persistence in relationships of compassion, loyalty, generosity, and love. The Mexican essayist and poet Octavio Paz has observed that "in the history of the West, love has been the secret subversive power: the great medieval heresy, the solvent of bourgeois morality . . . In the first centuries of our era the Gnostics set out to eroticize Christianity, and failed. Today we are witness to a contrary effort: the politicization of eroticism . . . Thus, through a curious process, our era turns sexuality into ideology. It makes pleasure a duty. A Puritanism in reverse. Industry turns eroticism into business; politics turns it into an opinion . . . Sexuality is animal; it is a natural function, whereas eroticism develops within society. The former belongs to the realm of biology, the latter to that of culture. Its essence is the imaginary: eroticism is a metaphor of sexuality . . . We humans see ourselves in animals; animals do not see themselves in humans. By contemplating itself, humanity changes itself and changes sexuality. Eroticism is not brute sex but sex transfigured by the imagination . . . The ultimate consequence of the erotic rebellion would be the disappearance of eroticism and of what has been its loftiest and most revolutionary invention: the idea of love."

# TEN
# Conclusion: The Body as Body

"Plato's image of the cave on whose wall are cast the shadows we mistake for reality is a popular one today. There is a heady promise in various intellectual fields of escape from the conditions of knowledge. With this promise an impossible kind of freedom is being proposed, freedom from necessity of any kind. [But] the cave is the body social mediated by the image of the other body . . . Indeed the illusion of escape may well be a new kind of confinement." (Douglas, 1982)

At every turn, our religious and secular mythologies imprison us.

As physicist Werner Heisenberg has observed, "Natural science does not simply describe and explain nature; it is a part of the interplay between nature and ourselves; it describes nature as exposed to our method of questioning. This was a possibility Descartes could not have thought, but it makes the sharp separation between the world and I impossible."

It is equally impossible to set society and sex against one another, as if they were separate abstractions. We must recognize that sex is highly socialized and that each culture designates various practices as appropriate or inappropriate, moral or immoral, normal or abnormal. Without this recognition we continue to construct boundaries that have no basis in *nature*. "Yet all the time we like to indulge in the fantasy that our sexuality is the most basic, the most natural thing about us, and that the relations between men and women are laid down for all eternity . . . by the dictates of our inborn 'nature.' " (Weeks)

It bears repeating Michel Foucault's renowned observation that sexuality is no more or less than a historical construct. Its meaning and expression are no wider or more extensive than its specific social and historical manifestations, and explaining its forms and variations cannot be accomplished without examining and explaining the context in which they were formed. As we have seen, that context includes the value structure implicit in the mythology that underlies and informs the structures of societies.

Our bodies are the cosmos, for our mythologies about our place in the cosmos are inevitably transformed into anatomical metaphors. The study of the human body and how it is perceived at different times and places reveals an important element of cultural symbolism which has strong implications in relation to sexuality. "Any culture is a series of related structures which comprise social forms, values, cosmology, the whole of knowledge and through which all experience is mediated," Mary Douglas writes (1966). This series of related social structures manifests itself as actions called rituals. "The rituals enact the form of social relations and in giving these relations visible expression they enable people to know their own society. The rituals work upon the body politic through the symbolic medium of the physical body." Rituals are the *embodiment* of the whole of a society's knowledge—constructive or destructive. Ritual is mind transformed into body.

The act of sex is not "natural," for it has been socialized into a variety of cultural rituals. Many creatures take part in mating rites, but in human societies such rituals have become elaborate choreography. Animal sex may be a biological act, but the human invention called eroticism is an act of the imagination. Therefore, the way the body has been envisioned and evaluated by various cultures and eras is a history of the sexual messages transmitted by social myths and the rituals based upon such myths.

The body is the cave on whose wall are cast the shadows we mistake for reality. We are Plato's creatures, forever bound in a cave so that even our heads cannot move. Behind us is a fire, and the shadows of a world we cannot see are cast upon the wall before us. We cannot escape our bonds. We can never look back at the *reality* that we imagine exists beyond our view. We must believe in the shadows for we have no access to the reality they reflect. We can neither imagine nor speak of that reality because it is beyond our experience and outside our communicative capacities. The poet William Blake believed that the body is Plato's cave and, therefore, he insisted rather sadly, "the body is the grave of the soul." But for dancers, like the legendary American Ruth St. Denis, the body is indistinct from the soul.

That assertion leads to a myth of my own which has greatly shaped my thinking.

I have been watching dancers ever since my childhood, when I often visited the studio of Ruth St. Denis in the San Fernando Valley of Los Angeles. At 80, Miss Ruth was no longer teaching or performing in public and had delegated the administration of her school to a young assistant. But now and again, I was fortunate enough to be present on those rare evenings when Miss Ruth came down the stairs from her apartment over the studio. What a spectacular experience that was! Her tall, lithe figure crowned by a great mass of white hair defied her advanced age. Her physical presence was so overwhelming at close quarters that she seemed more specter than person. Her body was more than body, and her smallest gesture was unexplainably expressive, magnetic, magical. I had no idea what her movement meant, but I had absolutely no doubt that it was meaningful. It seemed to me, as a youth, that through Ruth St. Denis I experienced the ritual heart of all that is implied by both eroticism and spirituality.

What is it about a great dancer that transforms the body into spirit, that changes ordinary gesture into powerful ritual? How can something as illusive and nonliteral as dancing contain a potential for expression that verges on religiosity?

Since my youthful encounters with Ruth St. Denis, I have never ceased to be intrigued by those questions. This perplexity about the body is not unique to me. As we have seen, our whole society is mystified by the human body. And of all the arts, none confuses us as much as dancing, for it emerges directly and wholly from the core of our greatly discredited physical selves. Undoubtedly, part of our discomfort and perplexity with dancing comes from the fact that we live in a culture in which the body has a terrible reputation. The abhorrence of the flesh and its association with paganism and evil have resulted in the castigation of the body, even in these libertine times when the attainment of sexual pleasure has become a political obligation.

The dominant religions of the West officially banned the ritual use of dance as early as the eighth century. For all other peoples of the world, such a situation would be unthinkable. For them, dance is an implicit part of religion. The body is a spiritual messenger, and dancing is indistinct from praying.

The Navajo Indian song-dance for rain is the prayer of

a whole people for the regeneration of their spiritual bodies, which permits them to be transformed into the rain for which they pray. Wind is the precursor of the rain, and before the ceremonial dancers can become the rain they must first become the wind. The great prayer which accomplishes this mythic transformation is a complex fusion of dance, song, and music. It recreates the world through a process of ritual which is built upon physical actions that take the shape of a mythology made visible. Such rituals are products of hundreds of generations, a slow, selective process by which certain actions are retained through careful repetition. These rites are indistinct from the world view of the people who perform them. It is the body as an expressive organism which provides the impulse and force of ritual.

It is little wonder that tribal people have retained a strong conviction about the power of their bodies, while we of the West gradually have become so out of touch with our physical selves that in the 1960s and 1970s it was necessary to rediscover our bodies through "consciousness raising" therapies and courses in body language and sexual communication. The recovery of the dignity of our bodies has also seen the reinvention of ecclesiastical dancing, and thus dancers have once again become, in the words of Martha Graham, "the acrobats of God"—a spiritual role they have persistently held in almost every civilization.

For many of us the reemergence of the body as an organ of expression is confounding. Why does something as apparently useless and primitive as body language possess such power? It took many journeys into the heartland of remote nations before I could begin to answer that question. While body movement is unquestionably pleasant to the eye, its real power is more profound than its visual niceties. The body communicates. Yawning is an obvious example of its contagion; so is the desire to stretch when we see someone else stretching. Because of this inherent "infectiousness" of movement, which makes onlookers feel in their own bodies the exertion they see in others, the body is able kinesthetically to convey the most intangible and metaphysical experiences, impressions, feelings, and ideas.

What I discovered among the ritual dancers of Asia, Africa, South America, and Indian America is that the body is capable of communicating in its own secret language. *The most important mythology of our time proclaims that the body is the body.* And dancers like Ruth St. Denis understand something that escapes the rest of us. The body is an organ of expression. It is not simply an embarrassing and utilitarian network of limbs. It is neither male nor female. It is not a weapon nor a mechanism of sin. It is not simply the machinery of procreation, digestion, and other functional activities. It is an organ of expression—perhaps the most vivid facility for the expression of strongly and immediately felt ideas, needs, and feelings.

For ritual dancers, *the body is the spiritual body*—an organism in which motion makes visible the sacred forms of life itself. Our bodies live through motion. And thus motion is one of the most important and pervasive means by which we can celebrate living. Our sexuality is part of the life we celebrate. The human distinction between sensuality, eroticism and the pornographic obsession of genital-focused sex is the same distinction found between commonplace movement and rarified dance. Sex is the shadow on the wall of the cave. Eroticism is the fire itself—that unseen fire that creates the shadows we mistake for reality.

The idea that spirituality can be associated with the body is extremely remote from our belief in the Augustinian and Cartesian dichotomy of mind and body, spirit and flesh. But, as Denis de Rougemont has said, "we who dwell in the Western world are destined to become more and more aware of the illusions on which we subsist." Until recently it was inconceivable that there could be any relationship between spiritual and physical realities. To most of us, bodily behavior, whether play, dance, or nonreproductive sex, was profoundly misunderstood as an activity that was both pointless and profane. Even today, there are many people who look upon these activities as passionate but pointless wastes of energy. This is especially true of the attitude toward dancing of people who are out of touch with their own bodies. I recall my foster father's comment at the close of a dance performance: "If those people would just apply all that sweat and effort to hard work, they could really accomplish something." After all, he asked, what does a dance accomplish? What does play accomplish? And, from the view of those who understand sexuality as inseparable from procreation, what does nonreproductive sex accomplish?

The questions themselves offer almost insurmountable problems. But, as we have seen, there are as many answers to these questions as there are mythologies that guide the diverse lives of peoples and cultures. What dance achieves, what play and sex achieve are the same things that poetry achieves. They transform the ordinary into the extraordinary. Through the sensual and metaphoric transformation of a reality composed of shadows they are able, at least momentarily, to allude to the fire. The sensuality that we identify with eroticism is the kinesthetic expression of the spiritual body as opposed to the genital assertion of the body which we understand as "natural." Again, as Denis de Rougemont insists, the spiritual body exists "wherever passion is dreamed of as an ideal instead of being feared like a malignant fever;

wherever its fatal character is welcomed, invoked, or imagined as a magnificent and desirable disaster instead of as simply a disaster. It lives upon the lives of people who think that love is their fate . . . that it is stronger and more real than happiness, society, or morality."

Love changes biology into a metaphor of the spiritual body in much the way that poetry changes ordinary words into forms that allow meanings that words normally cannot mean. The most curious thing about any human gesture is its power of insinuation, born of the ability of the body to overcome its inherent materiality.

That is precisely what Ruth St. Denis did for me many years ago when she turned the descent of a stairway into a memorable experience. She was in such control of her body, she lived so deeply within her body that she was capable of investing a simple action with the kind of magic that is seen in ritual, with the kind of eroticism that is discovered at the core of romantic love, with the force of metaphor that finds its voice in poetry.

Perhaps the endless transformation of our bodies into visions of the cosmos will find its current resolution in that most ancient mythology of all: the one that was doubtlessly among the first cultural possessions of human beings when they were newly evolved upon the earth. Perhaps we will be done at long last with our obsession with the "wickedness of the body" and the endless ritualization of transgression. For centuries we have comfortably lived with the brain's insolent recreation of itself as mind. Perhaps we can finally begin to live with the more ancient mythology that envisions the fragile, vulnerable, and utterly perishable body as indistinct from soul.

The physicist Niels Bohr has told us: "The opposite of a correct statement is a false statement. But the opposite of a profound truth may well be another profound truth."

Dr. Carl A. Hammerschlag came face-to-face with

Bohr's concept in a hospital in the American Southwest where he has worked for many years as a physician and psychiatrist. One day, while making his morning rounds, he encountered an old man. "I didn't know that he was a Pueblo priest and clan chief," Dr. Hammerschlag explains. "I only saw an old man. He asked me, 'Where did you learn to heal?' "

Dr. Hammerschlag rattled off the details of his medical education, internship, and certification. The old Indian smiled. "Yes," he said, "but do you know how to dance? You must be able to dance if you are to heal people."

At first Hammerschlag was confounded. But over the years he gradually came to understand the great value of what that old Indian taught him. The poet W. B. Yeats also understood that mordant metaphor of dance, for it was Yeats who asked that most simplistic of all questions about the human body: "Who can tell the dancer from the dance?"

For Yeats, as for the Pueblo priest, the body is indistinct from the spirit.

# Selected Bibliography

Arens, William. Quoted by Ray B. Browne (see entry)

Aries, Philippe, and Bejin, Andre. *Western Sexuality*. Oxford: Basil Blackwell Ltd., 1985.

Arrowsmith, William. In *The Complete Greek Tragedies,* edited by David Grene and Richmond Lattimore. Vol. IV: Euripides. Chicago: The University of Chicago Press, 1958.

Artz, Frederick B. *The Mind of the Middle Ages*. Chicago: The University of Chicago Press, 1953.

Bachofen, J. J. *Myth, Religion, and Mother Right*. London: Routledge and Kegan Paul, 1967.

Bedier, Joseph. *The Romance of Tristan and Iseult*. Translated by Hilaire Belloc. New York: Pantheon Books, 1945.

Boorstin, Daniel J. *The Discoverers*. New York: Random House, 1983.

Boswell, John. *Christianity, Social Tolerance, and Homosexuality*. Chicago: University of Chicago Press, 1980.

Briffault, Robert. *The Mothers*. New York: Atheneum, 1977.

Brooke, Rosalind, and Christopher. *Popular Religion in the Middle Ages*. London: Thames and Hudson, 1984.

Browne, Ray B., ed. *Rituals and Ceremonies in Popular Culture.* Bowling Green, 1980.

Brownmiller, Susan. *Against Our Will: Men, Women, and Rape.* New York: Simon and Schuster, 1975.

Bullough, Vern L. *Sexual Variance in Society and History.* Chicago: University of Chicago Press, 1976.

Campbell, Joseph. *The Masks of God.* Vol. 2: *Occidental Myth* (1962); Vol. 4: *Creative Mythology* (1968). New York: The Viking Press.

———— *The Flight of the Wild Gander.* New York: Viking Press, 1969.

Caplan, Pat, ed. *The Cultural Construction of Sexuality.* London: Tavistock Publications, 1987.

Casson, Lionel. *Mysteries of the Past.* New York: American Heritage Publishing Co., 1977.

Cingria, Charles Albert. See Denis de Rougemont.

D'Emilio, John, and Freedman, Estelle B. *Intimate Matters: A History of Sexuality in America.* New York: Harper & Row, 1988.

Douglas, Mary. *Natural Symbols: Explorations in Cosmology.* New York: Pantheon Books, 1982.

———— *Purity and Danger: An Analysis of the Concepts of Pollution and Taboo.* London: Ark Paperbacks, 1984.

Dover, K. J. *Greek Homosexuality.* New York: Vintage Books, 1980.

Eardley, Tony. "Violence and Sexuality." In *The Sexuality of Men,* edited by Metcalf and Humphrey. London: Pluto Press, 1985.

Selected Bibliography

Eisler, Riane. *The Chalice and the Blade*. New York: Harper & Row, 1987.

Fausto-Sterling, Anne. *Myths of Gender*. New York: Basic Books, 1985.

Fischer, David H. *Historical Fallacies*. A Harper Torch Book. New York: Harper & Row, 1970.

Foucault, Michel. *The History of Sexuality:* Vol. I: *Introduction* (1978); Vol. II: *The Use of Pleasure* (1985); Vol. III: *The Care of the Self* (1986). New York: Pantheon Books.

———— *Power/Knowledge*. Edited by Colin Gordon. Brighton: Harvester Press, 1980.

Francoeur, Anna K., and Robert T. *Hot and Cool Sex: Cultures in Conflict*. New York: Harcourt Brace Jovanovich, 1974.

Freud, Sigmund. "Three Essays on Sexuality." *Complete Psychological Works,* Vol. 7. London: Hogarth Press, 1953.

Fromm, Erick. *The Anatomy of Human Destructiveness*. New York: Fawcett Crest, 1973.

Gagnon, John H., and Simon, William. *Sexual Conduct*. London: Hutchinson of London, 1974.

Gassner, John. *Masters of the Drama*. New York: Dover Publications, 1945.

Gay, Peter. *The Bourgeois Experience*. Vol. 1: *Education of the Senses*. New York: Oxford University Press, 1984.

Gilligan, Carol. *In a Different Voice*. Cambridge: Harvard University Press, 1982.

Gimbutas, Marija. *The Goddesses and Gods of Old Europe*. Berkeley: University of California Press, 1974.

Gonzalez-Crussi, F. *On the Nature of Things Erotic*. New York: Harcourt Brace Jovanovich, 1988.

Grant, Michael. *Myths of the Greeks and Romans*. New York: New American Library, 1962.

Green, William Chase. *Moira: Fate, Good, and Evil in Greek Thought*. New York: Harper & Row, 1963.

Guerra, F. *The Pre-Columbian Mind*. London: Seminar Press, 1971.

Guthrie, W. K. C. *The Greeks and their Gods*. Boston: Beacon Press, 1950.

Hammerschlag, Carl A. *The Dancing Healers*. New York: Harper & Row, 1970.

Harding, Esther M. *The Way of All Women*. New York: Harper & Row, 1970.

———— *Woman's Mysteries: Ancient and Modern*. New York: G. P. Putnam's Sons, 1971.

Harrison, Jane Ellen. *Epilegomena to the Study of Greek Religion* and *Themis*. New Hyde Park, N.Y.: University Books, 1962.

Hatto, A. T. Introduction to *Tristan,* by Gottfried von Strassburg and *Tristran* of Thomas. New York: Penguin Books, 1960.

Hegel, Georg Wilhelm Friedrich. *Hegel on Tragedy*. Edited by Anne and Henry Paolucci. New York: Doubleday, 1962.

Henriques, Fernando. *Love in Action: The Sociology of Sex*. New York: E. P. Dutton, 1960.

Herlihy, David. *Medieval Culture and Society*. New York: Harper & Row, 1968.

Hesiod. *Works and Days and Theogony.* Translated by Richmond Lattimore. Detroit: University of Michigan Press, 1950.

—— *Theogony and Works and Days.* Translated by Dorothea Wender. New York: Penguin Books, Ltd., 1973.

Hillman, James. "The Great Mother, her Son, her Hero, and the Puer." In *Fathers and Mothers.* Zurich: Spring Publications, 1973.

Huizinga, J. *The Waning of the Middle Ages.* New York: Doubleday, 1954.

Ignatieff, Michael. *The Needs of Strangers.* London: Chatto & Windus, 1984.

Innes, Christopher. *Holy Theatre: Ritual and the Avant Garde.* Cambridge: Cambridge University Press, 1981.

Jobes, Gertrude. *Dictionary of Mythology, Folklore and Symbols.* New York: Scarecrow Press, 1962.

Katz, Jonathan. *Gay American History.* New York: Thomas Y. Crowell, 1976.

Kenny, Anthony. *Descartes: A Study in His Philosophy.* New York: Random House, 1968.

Kerenyi, Carl. *The Gods of the Greeks.* London: Thames and Hudson, 1951.

Kirk, G. S. *Myth: Its Meaning in Ancient and Other Cultures.* Cambridge: Cambridge University Press, 1970.

Klausner, Joseph. *The Messianic Idea in Israel.* London: George Allen and Unwin, Ltd., 1956.

Kott, Jan. *The Eating of the Gods: An Interpretation of Greek Tragedy.* New York: Random House, 1973.

Kuhn, Thomas. *The Structure of Scientific Revolutions*. Chicago: University of Chicago Press, 1962.

Landau, Rom. *Sex, Life, and Faith*. London: Faber and Faber, Ltd., 1932.

Le Goff, Jacques. *Time, Work, and Culture in the Middle Ages*. Chicago: University of Chicago Press, 1980.

────── *The Birth of Purgatory*. Chicago: University of Chicago Press, 1981.

Lewisohn, Richard. *A History of Sexual Customs*. Translated by Alexander Mayce. New York: Harper & Brothers, 1958.

Luhmann, Nilas. *Love As Passion*. Cambridge: Harvard University Press, 1986.

Maclagan, David. *Creation Myths*. London: Thames and Hudson, 1977.

Marks, Claude. *Pilgrims, Heretics, and Lovers*. New York: Macmillan, 1975.

Mitchell, Juliet. *Psychoanalysis and Feminism*. Middlesex: Penguin Books, Ltd., 1975.

Monaghan, Patricia. *The Book of Goddesses and Heroines*. New York: E. P. Dutton, 1981.

Muller, Herbert. *The Uses of the Past*. New York: Oxford University Press, 1957.

Murray, Gilbert. "Excursus on the Ritual Forms preserved in Greek tragedy." Published as a contribution in Jane Ellen Harrison's *Epilegomena to the Study of Greek Religion* and *Themis*. New Hyde Park, N.Y.: University Books, 1962.

Neumann, Erich. *Amor and Psyche*. New York: Harper & Row, 1956.

———— *The Great Mother*. Princeton: Princeton University Press, 1955.

Nygren, Anders. *Agape and Eros: A Study of the Christian Idea of Love*. New York: Harper & Row, 1969.

Olsen, Carl, ed. *The Book of the Goddess: Past and Present*. New York: Crossroad, 1983.

Pagels, Elaine. *Adam, Eve, and the Serpent*. New York: Random House, 1988.

Parrinder, Geoffrey. *Sex in the World's Religions*. New York: Oxford University Press, 1980.

Paz, Octavio. "At Table and in Bed." In *Convergences*. New York: Harcourt Brace Jovanovich, 1987.

De Rougemont, Denis. *Love in the Western World*. New York: Pantheon Books, 1940.

Schwab, Gustav. *Gods and Heroes: Myths and Epics of Ancient Greece*. New York: Pantheon Books, 1946.

Segal, Charles. *Dionysiac Poetics and Euripides' Bacchae*. Princeton: Princeton University Press, 1982.

Seidler, Victor J. "Reason, desire, and male sexuality." In *The Cultural Construction of Sexuality,* edited by Pat Caplan. London: Tavistock Publications, 1987.

Selby, Jr., Hubert. *Last Exit to Brooklyn*. New York: Grove Press, 1957.

Sjoo, Monica, and Mor, Barbara. *The Great Cosmic Mother*. New York: Harper & Row, 1987.

Snitow, A.; Stansell, C.; and Thompson, S. eds. *Desire: The Politics of Sexuality*. London: Virago Publications, 1984.

Spretnak, Charlene. *Lost Goddesses of Early Greece*. Boston: Beacon Press, 1984.

Sproul, Barbara C. *Primal Myths: Creating the World*. San Francisco: Harper & Row, 1979.

Steinberg, Leo. *The Sexuality of Christ in Renaissance Art and in Modern Oblivion*. New York: Pantheon, 1983.

Stent, Gunther S. *Paradoxes of Progress*. San Francisco: W. H. Freeman and Company, 1978.

Stone, Merlin. *When God Was a Woman*. New York: Dial Press, 1976.

Tennant, F. R. *The Sources of the Doctrines of the Fall and Original Sin*. New York: Schocken Books, 1903.

Thompson, William Irwin. *The Time Falling Bodies Take to Light*. New York: St. Martin's Press, 1981.

Thornberry, Neal. "In Search of Mediocrity." *The Christian Science Monitor*. 1 February 1989, p. 19.

Topsfield, L. T. *Troubadours and Love*. Cambridge: Cambridge University Press, 1975.

Tuchman, Barbara W. *A Distant Mirror: The Calamitous 14th Century*. New York: Alfred A. Knopf, 1978.

Ulanov, Ann Belford. *The Feminine in Jungian Psychology and Christian Theology*. Evanston: Northwestern University Press, 1971.

Vanggaard, Thorkil. *Phallos: A Symbol and Its History in the Male World*. New York: International Universities Press, 1974.

Wallerstein, Edward. *Circumcision: An American Health Fallacy*. New York: Springer Publishing Company, 1980.

Selected Bibliography

Warner, Marina. *Alone of All Her Sex: The Myth and the Cult of the Virgin Mary*. London: Weidenfeld and Nicolson, Ltd., 1976.

Weeks, Jeffrey. "Questions of Identity" in *The Cultural Construction of Sexuality,* edited by Pat Caplan. London: Tavistock Publications, 1987.

Whyte, L. L. *The Next Development in Man*. New York: Henry Holt and Company, 1948.

Williams, Walter L. *The Spirit and the Flesh*. Boston: Beacon Press, 1986.

Young, Wayland. *Eros Denied*. New York: Grove Press, 1964.

Zolla, Elemire. *The Androgyne: Reconciliation of Male and Female*. London: Thames and Hudson, Ltd., 1981.

Zukav, Gary. *The Dancing Wu Li Masters*. New York: William Morrow, 1979.

Zuntz, Gunther. *Persephone: Three Essays on Religion and Thought in Magna Graecia*. Oxford: Oxford University Press, 1971.

# Index

# Index

# Index

# Index